ALSO PUBLISHED BY INNSMOUTH GOLD

REMNANTS - FENLAND TALES OF
HORRORS & HAUNTINGS

INNSMOUTH ECHOES

THE DUNWICH TRILOGY

ANCESTORS & DESCENDANTS

WEIRD TAILS

CORRIDORS

THE WOLF WHO WOULD BE KING SERIES
WOLF IN SHADOWS
WOLF IN CHAINS
WOLF IN THE NORTH
WOLF IN THE UNDERWORLD
WOLF UNDER SIEGE
WOLF IN THE WILDS

ASSAULT TEAM 5 SERIES
NAYLOR'S WAR
HUNTED!

MUSIC RELEASES
RITUAL & DREAM
ILLUSTRATIONS OF MADNESS
CIMMERIA

www.innsmouthgold.com

TARGET!

By Robert Poyton

THIS IS AN INNSMOUTH GOLD BOOK

ISBN: 978-1-7399855-5-4   Paperback

Published by Cutting Edge on behalf of Innsmouth Gold.

www.innsmouthgold.com

Cover art by Shelley De Cruz
Copyright@2022 Graveheart Designs

www.facebook.com/graveheartdesigns

Dedicated to
Harry Cane and Walter Poyton

Prologue

The killer awoke before dawn. He was not naturally an early riser but on the day of a job he liked having time to prepare. Besides, today there was only a narrow window of opportunity. He rose and stretched, easing out kinks caused by sleeping on the thin, worn mattress. After a lukewarm shower he dried, dressed and packed his gear. The park was a short walk from the bed and breakfast. He would not be returning.

Twenty minutes after waking, he dropped the key in the box at reception and was out the door. He had paid cash on arrival, there were no staff to see him leave. This was one of several low key B&Bs in the area, used mainly by lorry drivers, judging from the single men filing into the cramped dining room for breakfast. Still, it served a purpose. Anonymous, no questions asked, close to the target area. Valentines Park was a short walk away. It was the largest park in the area, surrounded by long streets of terraced 1930s houses. The town of Ilford acted as a gateway between Essex and London's East End. Many East-enders moved to Ilford on their way east, from there spreading out all the way to Southend on the coast. It was also home to second generation Asian and West Indian families and a had a large Jewish population. In the couple of days he had been here, the killer had walked around the area, always keen to get a feel for a place - its escape routes, its transport services, its people. He'd noticed a lot of youths in the area, groups of them congregated on street corners or outside fast food places. So far, none had given him any trouble.

At this time of morning, the streets were quiet, rush hour was just beginning. The intel was that the target walked her dog at around seven every morning. Presumably, after that she went to work. Not today.

No-one gave the killer a second look as they walked to bus stops and station, intent only on the journey to office or factory. Why would they? A white man in his late twenties, average height, average build, average length brown hair covered with a baseball cap. He wore a black Harrington jacket, stonewashed jeans and Puma trainers, carried a red Adidas holdall in his left hand and kept his gaze down. Over the last couple of days he'd memorised access and exit routes and the park layout. It was a large park but he'd been told the target always used a particular field, presumably the one closest to her home. He moved aside as a pair of joggers trotted past, faces beet red, tinny music bleeding from their Walkmans. Then he was at the park gate. Glancing again at the photo in his right palm, he folded it and dropped it in the bin by the entrance. *Red hair. Small dog.* After a sharp exhale, he took the path across the open space and there she was, right on time.

Placing a hand on the pistol butt in its shoulder holster, the killer set an interception spot and headed for it. It was a clear April morning, there were a few other people about, heading for work or jogging. The target was jogging too, dressed in a navy blue track suit, the dog padding along behind her. He had calculated to reach the path a matter of metres ahead of the target, and turned to face her, being careful not to make eye contact. As she approached, he moved slightly aside, drawing the Beretta in a smooth, easy motion. There were three flat cracks as he put two bullets into the body, then one into the head as the target fell. The dog began furiously barking but the man was already gone. He could have shot the dog but he was a hit-man, not a psychopath.

A few minutes brisk walk and he was at another park gate. As was usually the case, no-one tried to stop or challenge him. In his experience, the sight and sound of a person being shot caused most people to freeze in disbelief. That was one reason so much of his training back home had been in acclimatising to extreme events. Where others froze, he moved. Where others reacted with fear, he responded with focused intent.

The exit took him onto Cranbrook Road, a busy main route serviced by numerous buses. He jumped on one at the nearby stop, slipped off at Ilford Station and ten minutes later, was sat on a Southend bound train.

Chapter 1

Detective Sergeant 'Cab' Calloway checked his mirror, indicated, and swung the Rover into a U-turn. On a normal Wednesday morning he would be heading straight to his office at Ilford nick - not that many mornings were normal in CID. However, just before he reached the station, a shout came through, a reported shooting in a local park. He flicked off the car stereo. The news was full of the situation in the Falklands, and the fact that a British Task Force had been mobilised in response to the Argentinean invasion. Calloway was already fed up of people asking him, presumably because he was Scottish, if the Falklands were anywhere near the Shetlands. Still, that was all happening thousands of miles away. This shooting was in Valentines Park and that was on his patch.

It was a short walk from the side gate to the crime scene. Despite the early hour, the press had already gathered, local uniform keeping them back from the area at the edge of the field. Witnesses were being interviewed over on a park bench, where a young WPC held the lead of a confused looking Yorkshire Terrier. Calloway thanked the PC who lifted the tape and walked across to where his boss, the ever dapper DI Denham, stood chatting to Dr Feld. Just behind them, a woman in white overalls knelt beside a covered body.

"Morning, guv," he nodded. "Doc."

"Morning Cab," Denham responded, then gestured to the kneeling figure. "This is Gemma Bellotti , our new SOCO."

The auburn haired woman peered up over her glasses and nodded with a terse smile.

Calloway returned the nod. "So what have we got then, guv?"

Denham scowled. "Shooting. Professional from the look of it. Two in the body, one in the head.

Calloway bent forward as the SOCO pulled back the white sheet. "Christ, she's just a young girl. Do we have a name?"

"According to what she is carrying, her name is Patricia Clark." Denham let out a breath. Cropped iron grey hair, a military bearing, he was not far off retirement. Calloway had always found him a decent boss. You always knew where you stood with Denham. The DI continued. "We're checking out her address. Anything to add, Doc?"

Dr Feld shook his head. He was a touch older than Denham, a kindly faced man who'd been part of the furniture for as long as anyone could remember.

"Not at this stage. Cause of death obviously appears to be the gunshots, but we'll do a thorough check back at the morgue. Such a shame. So young. I have a grand-daughter her age." He clamped his lips tight as he turned away. Calloway sympathised. You saw the worst of things in this line of work.

Calloway had been a copper for almost twelve years. A native of Dundee, he'd signed up at 19, and moved to Glasgow a few years later after getting married. Things hadn't panned out. Following the divorce, he'd focused more on his work, making DS in 1979 and moving to the Met in 1980. For the past two years he'd established a reputation as a solid grafter. It had been a busy time. Turf wars between the old firms still fighting over the Kray empire; the influx of new, foreign gangs; the A13 bullion robbery and other heists. Not to mention the general political tensions, football hooligans and Saturday night punch ups. It was no wonder he looked older than his 31 years. Not that his dress sense helped. A cheap off-the-peg grey C&A suit, scuffed, brown brogues, receding sandy hair, stubble and an ever-present Marlboro hanging from his lip.

"Anything from the witnesses?" he asked the young WPC as she brought the now whimpering dog over towards the group.

"Nothing much, sarge. A couple of them report seeing a youngish man walking away from the scene, off in that direction." She pointed to the west.

Calloway swore under his breath. "There's how many entrances to the park? A dozen?"

"At least," replied the WPC. "If he popped out onto Cranbrook Road he could have jumped on a bus to anywhere."

"Her dog?"

"We believe so, sir. Poor little thing was stood next to her."

"Alright. Let's get whatever descriptions we have out. It's rush hour, someone must have seen him, wherever he went. Family?"

"Just waiting to hear back from the station." As if in response, her radio squawked and she turned away to answer it. Calloway took out his fag packet and offered one to his boss.

"No thanks, I'm trying to give up," he replied, reaching into his jacket, pulled out a pack of Polo mints and popped one into his mouth. "Photographer's here."

They both nodded at the man ducking under the tape. Denham tapped Calloway's arm.

"Can you finish up here, Cab? I've got a meeting with the Chief Super in twenty minutes. We'll set up an incident room at Ilford. Keep me posted."

Calloway nodded and turned back to the WPC.

"Her parents live in Barkingside. I've got the address."

"Thanks." He rubbed his chin. "Will you come with me, WPC… er, sorry , I don't know your name."

"Yes, of course, sarge. And it's Smith. Debbie Smith. I just transferred in from Lewisham."

"Alright. We'll wrap up here and then go see them. Best bring the dog, eh?"

Calloway took a deep drag on the cigarette and blew the smoke out between his teeth. This was one part of the job you never got used to. He was stood in the porch of the Clarks' suburban semi, having just informed them of their daughter's death. He heard Smith call "goodbye" before she joined him outside.

"All done?"

"Yes. I've arranged for the father to ID our vic. The Family Liaison Officer will be here shortly." She sighed heavily. "That was tough."

"First time?"

"No, I had to do it once before at my old place. Suicide. Gone into the Thames. Awful. He was married with three kids."

"That's rough. Aye, well, it doesn't get easier, that's for sure."

"And they had no possible idea for motive. She had no enemies as far as they knew."

"Jealous ex, stalker, anything like that?"

Smith glanced at her notes. "They've given me her work details, some names of friends, but there's nothing obvious."

"Right. Well we'll start sifting back at the ranch. There must be something, people don't get shot like that for no reason, especially not by a pro."

"Could be a random psycho, sir?"

"I suppose. But have you ever heard of that?"

Smith shook her head. "Can't say I have. Back in Lewisham a shooting was usually gang related. Or someone having an affair with someone else's wife."

Calloway laughed. "Aye. Same back home, too. So what brought you over to Ilford? Lewisham too quiet for you?"

She returned the smile. "Not really. More a case of everyone knowing me. You know, people from school, family. Not everyone was keen on my career choice. I mean Dad was proud as punch, he was a police officer back in the day in Jamaica. Back home, he was respected. But here, in London… you know."

"I can understand that. It wasn't the most popular choice in my old neighbourhood, too. But you're settling in okay?"

Smith shrugged. "For the most part people have been fine. The younger ones, at least. I think it confuses some people though, dealing with a police *woman* and a black one at that. It's not something they're used to."

Calloway nodded. "I thought I had it rough when I first moved down here. I mean what with the Scottish accent, people taking the piss and all that. I know, it's not quite the same, but you'll be fine." He dropped the cigarette and stamped out the butt. "Alright. Let's get back to the station. Get the ball rolling."

"This is Southend, Victoria. This train terminates here."

The killer alighted the train and made his way directly to the row of phone boxes just outside the station. He wrinkled his nose at the faint smell of urine, dropped a coin in the slot and dialled the memorised number. A gruff voice answered and he muttered only a few words. "Finished. I'm staying at Westcliff Lodge, Southend," before replacing and wiping the receiver. The baseball cap went into a nearby litter bin, and he donned a pair of shades. Next, he made his way through the 1960s concrete shopping centre to the previously booked bed and breakfast. He'd chosen this place as it was smart without being too upmarket and had a nice location on Clifftown Parade, overlooking the promenade. The landlady greeted him, all set hair and pearls. His lack of luggage brought an enquiry that he fended off with an explanation of the rest of his sales team arriving later on. That seemed to mollify Mrs King, and he was left in peace to settle in.

As was his habit, he first action was to take the rubber wedge from his holdall and nudge it under the door. Following that, he swept the room for bugs. Highly unlikely, but it was that single lapse in procedure that got you killed. He had not dozed on the train journey down. Easy enough to do, with the gentle rocking of the train and the early start that morning, but he remained vigilant - anyone could be watching. There was more to it than vigilance, though. He recalled the words of his instructors back at the Institute…

"Following any kill, you will likely be brimming with nervous energy. This is quite normal - unless you are a psychopath, in which case, you would not be here. Nervous energy will burn up your reserves. You will feel energised for atime, then tired. Resist that tiredness unless you are one hundred percent certain of your surroundings! Also, your kills should be carried out without emotion. Even then, some part of you will feel remorse, or wonder about your targets. You must find a way to quieten that inner voice, to become truly detached. Now, let us begin with breathing…"

They had been shown how to control their breathing, how to use it to reduce stress. That had been the easy part. Further training saw those skills tested in more and more extreme situations. Attending autopsies. Accompanying paramedics to traffic accidents. Being forced to crawl through trenches filled with offal. There were dark rumours of recruits being pitted against lifers, long-term convicts from nearby jails. If a convict beat you, the rumours went, they would be released. The fights had no rules, two went in, one came out.

He had not undergone that experience, though other training methods had been extreme enough. Everything was designed to prepare you for the kill. Not just the approach and execution, but the escape and aftermath. As the instructor had so often reminded them, *"You are assets of the State. Your training is costly. We are not looking for suicide troops, at least not for your kind of mission. We want you back whole and functioning, not broken."*

Satisfied that the room was clean, he slipped off his jacket. After taking a last look out of the window, appreciating the sparkling sea view, he stretched out on the bed. All he had to do now was wait. Once the call had gone in to his employees, one of their couriers would deliver the remainder of his fee directly to him, in cash, within a few days, as had been arranged. This was the first job he'd carried out for these people, and the only direct contact he had was with that voice on the phone. This was the preferred method, often the less you knew, the better. There was no concern about not being paid - the killer came with a reputation, and a recommendation from a major concern, breaking a deal would be a serious matter.

He'd deliberately chosen Southend as place to wait. Close enough to London, yet also out of the way. A seaside town, used to short-term visitors, its own airport offering flights to Europe. *Yes, this would do.* He kicked off his trainers and reached into his holdall for the Walkman - the sole luxury bought with the deposit payment for the job. Slipping the foam headphones over his ears, he laid back, closed his eyes and drifted away to the soothing sounds of Albinoni.

Chapter 2

Squinting against the bright sunlight filtering through the thin curtains, Calloway rolled over and stretched out a hand towards the radio alarm. He'd been awoken by someone singing "I can make you feel good" to a disco beat. He hit the button, muttering "I feel better already," before sliding out of bed to walk, stretching, into the kitchen. The one bedroom maisonette was small but it suited him. Swearing on finding the coffee jar empty, Calloway popped two slices in the toaster then shuffled into the living room to hit play on the tape deck. The smooth tones of Ella Fitzgerald filled the room. That was more like it. If you had to get up this early, you needed something soothing, not that disco rubbish.

It was his love of jazz that had got him the nickname Cab back in the day. Even when he'd signed up to the job, jazz had been old hat. Most of his colleagues were into The Stones, The Who, or the local pub groups. No-one had shared his enthusiasm for crackly old records save his old Inspector, and that had done nothing to improve Cab's street cred. When he'd transferred from Dundee to Glasgow, the nickname had followed. To be honest, Calloway didn't mind. Police officers in Glasgow often attracted far worse names than Cab…

In London too, as he'd found out after moving down a couple of years back - especially this part of London. Disregard, even hostility for the Old Bill felt even more ingrained here than in the Glasgow tenements and that was saying something. Having said that, most of his team were locals, bar one or two new transfers. They'd all be at the briefing, set for 0730 this morning.

Cab glanced at the clock, wolfed down his toast, and had a quick wash and shave. Grabbing his jacket, he touched the photo of Maisie on the phone table in the hall, and slammed the door behind him. One advantage of the early start was beating the rush hour. The Thursday morning traffic was already building but, just a touch over thirty minutes after leaving Hainault, he was parking his Rover at the rear of Ilford nick.

It was an old, Victorian station, constructed of typical orange brick, one of the last of a dying breed. Barkingside, Stratford, most other areas had new, purpose-built stations, put up in the last ten years or so. Even Forest Gate, one of the oldest stations in the area, was scheduled to move into the new, bunker-like building going up on the Romford Road. Ilford nick dated back almost a hundred years. They still had the old stable block out back, now converted. A grand old wrought iron stairway clung to the rear of the building, though it was never used. "Health and safety" had been the Desk Sergeant's only comment when Cab had asked him about it on first coming here. The same Sergeant nodded to him now as he checked in at the front desk.

"Morning, Cab. Early start?"

"Morning Kit Kat. Aye, that it is. Anything for me?" No-one quite knew where the nickname Kit Kat originated. Some said it was down to the boxes of chocolate bars tucked away below the counter. Darker rumours mentioned something about fingers being broken. Either way, the bulky figure shook his head. "Nope. All quiet on the western front."

Calloway jogged up the stairs towards the canteen, grabbing a coffee before heading into the small office he shared with DC Turner. He just had time to hang up his coat, check the Post-it notes on his phone and glug down half the coffee before heading to the briefing room.

"Morning all." Calloway followed WPC Smith into the room, balancing the sytrofoam cup on his files. Despite the early hour, the core of the team were already there, quietly chatting or reading through files. There was a murmur of replies.

"Alright, let's get started, shall we?" Placing cup and folders on the table, he loosened the knot in his tie. "In case any of you don't know me, I'm DS Calloway. Some call me Cab, you can call me sarge or skipper." He smiled. "DI Denham is the guv on this job, no doubt he'll be popping in at some point. So. We have a shooting in a local park, looks like a professional job."

He turned and indicated the photo pinned to the top of the board. "This is our victim. Patricia Clarke, age 19. Lives… lived at 20 Brisbane Road, just by the murder scene in Valentines Park. Worked at GH Wilson, a solicitor's office in Gants Hill."

"Does she have a boyfriend?" It was DC Turner. Young, beanpole tall, bright and keen, but always looked like he'd been dragged backwards through a hedge.

The equally youthful DC Pavitt answered. Where Turner was scruffy, Pavitt was pin sharp. "Doesn't seem to, sarge. At least not serious. Jonesy and I spoke to her flatmate last night." He referred to DC Jones, at forty the oldest member of the team. He had the hangdog expression of a copper who'd been there, seen everything, and was known for being thorough, if plodding in his approach.

"We did." Jones glanced at his notes. "One Amanda Hsu. They've been flat-mates for about eighteen months. She told us Patricia, Trish, had been seeing a guy for a year or so but that finished before Christmas. Name of James Hurst."

"Let's speak to him anyway." Calloway took another sip of coffee. "Friends? Enemies?"

DC Houlihan spoke next. He was a big, ruddy-faced man, the rugby type. Enjoyed his booze and a punch up. Not Calloway's first choice but manpower was limited and Houlihan was generally steady. "No-one unusual. She was a mod, apparently, hung out with the local scooter gang."

"A mod?" Calloway arched an eyebrow. "Bit young for that wasn't she? Didn't all that finish in the sixties?"

"There's been a revival, skip." It was Pavitt again. "You know, The Jam, Secret Affair, the Purple Hearts. It's big all over East London. My brother plays in a mod band. It mostly started at the Bridgehouse a couple of years back. See, what happened was - "

"Alright, alright, we don't need the full history. Let's find out where these mods hang out and go question them. What else? Any previous?"

"No previous. There is one thing though." Jones checked his notes again. "There was a drugs raid on a house in Seven Kings last summer. Our vic was present at the party going on there. Her name was taken, that was all."

"What drugs were turned up?"

"Pills. Amphetamines, a few bags. Nothing major. One arrest, an Anthony Webb."

"Okay, let's check him out, too. We need to find a motive. Why would a professional hit man target this girl? I'm open to any suggestions at this stage, so examine everything. And I mean everything, let's look at parents, friends, workmates, the lot. The press is already kicking up a storm, local and national. I want this cracked quick. Turner, chase up this Webb laddie. Jonesy and Houlihan, you're on door-to-door at Brisbane Road, let's see if any neighbours know anything. Smith, I want you here as Office Manager, checking and collating statements and any other intel that comes in. Okay? Good, let's get on with it."

Calloway spent the rest of the day in his office, reading through the SOCO report and witness statements and making phone calls following up various leads. None lead to anything. He was stood at the open window having a smoke break when Jones and Houlihan returned from their door to door enquiries. Neither looked particularly cheerful, though Cab couldn't remember any occasion when Jones had. He motioned them to sit, flicking his half-smoked Marlboro out of the window.

"Anything?"

"No, skip, not really," Jones responded.

Houlihan referred to his notebook. "No-one saw anyone or anything unusual. Everyone who knew her told us she was a normal kid, no problems at the house, nothing."

"No loud parties, no gentlemen callers?"

Houlihan shook his head. "None of that. Sounds like she was a nun."

"Alright, alright, less of that. Let's keep it professional, shall we?"

"I checked with uniform, too, skip." Jones continued. "No call outs to the street apart from three to one house. Number 17, there's been complaints about noise from a neighbour a bit further down. Nothing came of it."

"Anything from SOCO, sarge?" Houlihan put his notebook away.

"Zero, apart from the bullets. No footprints, the ground was dry. We have some witness statements of a man matching the description seen walking through Valentines, but nothing from outside the park yet."

"It was rush hour! For Christ's sake someone must have seen him."

"You said it yourself, skip. Rush hour. No-one's looking around, most of 'em would be half asleep or have their boat race stuck in a newspaper."

Calloway sighed. "Aye, I suppose. Smith is still interviewing some potential witnesses, let's hope she turns something up. Gunmen do not just disappear into thin air."

Turner came in, nodding to his fellow DCs.

"Give me some good news, will you?"

Turner laughed. "Well there's good news and bad news, sarge."

"Go on…"

"We've not been able to track where this Anthony Webb lives. Seems he frequents various bedsits and squats around the area. And most people clammed up when we mentioned his name. Think he might be more than a guy who shifts a few pills here and there."

"I hope that's the bad news."

"Oh, it is. I followed up a couple of other leads and found out where he works. The Plessey factory on Ley Street, just down the road."

"Good!" Calloway glanced at his watch. "They'll be shutting in ten minutes, no point going now. Leave it for tonight. I want you to give Smith a hand first thing tomorrow, then take Pavitt with you and bring this Webb character in for a chat. And let's hope he can tell us something. We could do with a break."

Chapter 3

"Here, Spider, can you sort me out some gear?"

Tony Webb placed his pint glass on the bar and turned. It was Kenny, one of the Ilford mod crowd, a regular customer.

"Sorry, mate, I'm all out at the moment." It was true, he'd sold his last bag of pills ten minutes earlier. Kenny's face fell.

Spider hated turning away customers. "Tell you what, you going to the Secret Affair gig Saturday night?"

"Yeah, we're all going." Kenny perked up.

"Alright, I'll be outside, at the usual place. Come and see me there, I'll make sure your sorted."

"Nice one. Cheers, Spider."

Kenny left and Spider finished his drink. The Bell pub was reasonably busy with the lunchtime trade, though Bev the barmaid had spotted the empty glass and moved over.

"Another one, love?" she asked.

Spider thought about it but only had ten minutes before being due back at work. Besides which, he had to make a phone call to his supplier. He was about to respond when Bev nodded her head towards the door. Two men had just walked in. They were plain clothes but had cop written all over them. The first had short hair, a sharp suit, button down shirt and narrow tie. The second, maybe a little older, was tall and gawky, his hair like straw, not only in colour but the way it was sticking out all over the place. The pair glanced around and made their way towards him. The tall one flashed a card.

"Anthony Webb? I'm DC Turner, this is DC Pavitt. We'd like to have a word."

Spider was suddenly grateful he'd sold all his gear. He shrugged. "Why's that, then?"

"It concerns the investigation of a murder. We'd rather talk down at the station."

"We can chat here, can't we? Besides I've got to be back at work in ten minutes."

"Don't worry about that," Turner told him. "We spoke to your boss. It was him who told us where to find you. Said you come in here most lunchtimes."

The smartly dressed one stepped in. "If you prefer, we can nick you and drag you down there. How would your boss like that?"

Spider slid off the bar stool and stared the young copper in the face. He didn't look much older than his own 20 years. There was something familiar about him. Recognition dawned.

"Your Gary's brother, aint'cha? Gary from The Reaction?"

Pavitt flushed and mumbled. Turner took over again. "Come on, Anthony, it's just a chat. It's about a murder. It won't take long."

Spider brushed invisible fluff off the chest of his Ben Sherman shirt and checked his hair in the mirror behind the bar. "Alright then.

But I want a lift back after!"

Calloway nodded to Pavitt as he strode into the interview room. He'd got a call from Turner that they'd pulled Webb in to Ilford nick. So far, this young man was the only real lead they had. Webb sat drumming his fingers on the table. He glanced up at Calloway's entrance.

"Is this going to take long, mate? Only I've got places to be."

Calloway ignored the question, dropping a folder on the desk before dragging the chair back and sitting down. He didn't so much as glance at Webb, keeping his attention on the papers in the folder. Webb sighed again and crossed his arms. After a couple more minutes, Calloway looked up, directly into Webb's eyes.

"Drug dealer, eh?"

"Only the once. And I was just meeting a need. Market forces, innit?"

"Oh, so sorry, you're an entrepreneur, then? Forgive me, Mr Sugar."

Webb curled a lip. He was slim, smartly dressed, in light blue sta-press trousers and a checked, button-down shirt. His jet black hair hair was back-combed into a style Calloway hadn't seen in almost twenty years, and even then not that often in the back streets of Dundee.

"So I flogged a few dexies? I got done, didn't I? Paid my dues and all that."

Calloway glanced at the file again. "Suspended sentence, first offence. Lucky boy." He closed the folder and leaned forward, elbows on the desk. "What do you know about Patricia Clark?"

Webb shook his head. "Who?"

"Young girl, about your age. You were at a party with her in Seven Kings, August last year."

"Me and fifty other people."

"The other fifty weren't drug dealers, though. Dodgy business, I imagine. Turf wars. People grassing you up. Or not paying for their drugs, perhaps?"

"I wouldn't know." Webb's suede desert boot tapped on the concrete floor.

Calloway sat back in the plastic chair. "Suspended sentence. That's awkward for you. Hint of trouble and you could be back in."

"I ain't done nothing. Are you gonna charge me, or can I fuck off?"

"Mind your language, laddie." Calloway paused, as if thinking. "Listen. We're after information here. That young lady was shot yesterday. Dead. While walking her dog in the park. What do you know about that?"

"That was her? Yeah, I saw something about that in the paper this morning. And what, you think I did it?" Webb scoffed, shaking his head again.

"Could be. Who knows? Lovers tiff? Perhaps she disapproved of your drug dealing?"

"I'm clean. And I barely knew her. Saw her here and there, never spoke to her. Wouldn't want anything to do with her. Not with -" Webb paused and scratched his nose. "Nah, mate, nothing to do with me."

"Not with what?"

"Not with her being straight, you know. She wasn't into the

pills or nothing. Just the music."

Calloway looked doubtful. "Really? Is that why? Come on, Tony, you must have heard something. You must be in tight with the local gangsters. Someone must be saying something. Perhaps she upset someone? The jealous type, perhaps? Someone with access to a handgun?"

Webb gave a laugh. He mimicked Calloway's Scottish brogue. "*Access to a handgun?* That's virtually anyone who goes into a pub round here. Christ, you must be new to the area."

"Oi, watch your lip," Pavitt warned, taking a step forward.

Calloway waved him back, then smiled. "I've been here a couple of years, so not that new. And believe me, where I grew up makes this place look like Mayfair." He regarded the young man again, then stood abruptly. "Alright. Off you go."

Webb scraped his chair back and headed for the door, muttering. Before he could reach it, Calloway grabbed his upper arm in a grip that made the lad wince.

"But if you hear anything… and I mean, *anything*… you come and tell me, right? And if I find you dealing anywhere in this area, you'll be back in choky before you know it." It was his turn to mimic an accent now. "*All clear, my old china?*"

"Clear!" Webb snarled, pulling his arm free and hurrying out. Calloway sat again and lit a fag.

"Not him then, guv?" Pavitt shut the door behind the exiting figure.

"Doesn't seem the sort, does he? I mean I can see him shifting a bit of gear but a professional hit? He was nervous about something, though. Keep an eye on him. Any news on the ex?"

Pavitt leaned against the wall. "Out of the country, apparently. He's been working in Spain for the last few months."

Calloway exhaled smoke. "So not likely to be him, either. Still, see if you can get hold of him, will you? I'd like to chat to him." He drummed his fingers on the desk. "Day one and we're already out of suspects. We need to get down to this place she hung out at. What was it called again?"

"The Regency Suite, sarge. It's down the road in Chadwell Heath. My brother's band plays there sometimes. Friday night is mod night."

"That's handy. Alright, we'll go there tomorrow night. You, me and I'll ask WPC Smith, too. Let's hope something turns up."

Prior to finishing for the day, Calloway tapped on Denham's office door and popped his head round. His boss was just finishing up a phone call and waved him in.

"I know, I know," he was saying. "Look, he'll be fine. Chances are nothing will happen, it will all blow over. Okay, love, I'll be home in about an hour." He put the phone down and sighed.

"Alright, guv?" Calloway sat. Denham looked more worried than Cab had ever seen him.

"Margaret. She's worried. David's on the Falklands Task Force."

"Your oldest? Royal Marines, isn't he? Your old unit?"

"Yes. First in." He sighed again. "Give me a smoke, Cab, will you?"

Calloway was about to say "I thought you were giving up" but stopped himself. He offered his pack.

"Thanks." Denham lit and inhaled deeply. "So what's happening on the Clark case?"

"Nothing much so far, guv. Webb, the dealer, I don't think he's involved. But we're watching him anyway, he might know something. We chasing up the ex, too. He lives in Spain now. Apart from that…"

"Witnesses?"

"We have some decent descriptions but the guy sounds fairly nondescript, to be honest."

"What you'd expect? Pros rarely stand out. Sounds like he was efficient and well organised. This was planned."

"Aye, question is by who? Who'd want a young girl dead?"

"Indeed. Alright, get yourself home, Cab. Tomorrow is another day."

"Aye. And guv?" Calloway paused at the door. "Don't fret, I'm sure your lad will be fine."

Calloway hit the rush hour traffic on the way back and was starving by the time he reached his flat. Parking the car, he decided to grab a takeaway. There was a Chinese on the parade of shops on Manford Way. Two minutes walk, if he used the cut through alleyway. The usual group of youths was hanging around on the corner, the younger ones on BMX bikes, the older ones spitting and bum-sucking cigarettes. A few whistled the Laurel and Hardy theme tune as he approached. Calloway smiled and flicked up two fingers. He recognised a face.

"Hey, Kevin. How's your brother doing?"

A pimply youth puffed out fag smoke. "He got a not guilty, Mr Calloway. The jury cleared him." he grinned, prompting laughter form the rest of the group.

Calloway rolled his eyes. "Ah well, better luck next time. Stay out of trouble, kids."

Back home he served up the noodles, put a Charlie Parker album on the turntable, and popped open a bottle of red. The lack of leads on the case was bothering him. Seeing the grief of the parents only compounded his frustration. What possibly could their daughter have done to deserve such a fate? He pulled himself back from following that particular line of thought and focused on his noodles. As the guv had said, *tomorrow is another day*.

Spider had finished work that evening and was on his way out of the office. It was only a ten minute walk to his main doss, a room in a shared house, one of a few places he stayed in. Lighting a ciggie, he took the steps of the Ley Street railway bridge two at a time, still annoyed at that Scottish copper from earlier in the day. Trotting down the steps at the far side, heading for the High Street beyond, his attention was drawn to a car, parked directly in front of him. Unusually, for this part of town, it was a flash motor - a Jag, a black XJ6. The bodywork gleamed. As he passed it, the tinted driver's window hummed down and a gruff voice ordered, "Get in the back."

Spider swallowed hard but did as he was told. The rear door opened and he slid into the cool interior of the car, the door closing with a heavy thunk behind him. The driver was a large man, wearing shades. The man to Spider's left was older, though even larger. Even the roomy car interior seemed to struggle to contain him. He wore an expensive camel hair coat and smelled of good cologne. *Well-groomed* was the phrase that came to mind, though his face was heavy and lined; *lived-in*, some might say. To Spider he looked like a shaved bear in smart clothing.

"You know who I am, son?" the bear rumbled. Spider nodded. This was Eddie Pearce, a notorious enforcer, a major face in the firm that supplied Spider's gear.

"So you know who I work for, then? Good, that will save us some time. The young lady who was shot yesterday. What do you know?"

"Nothing. I mean, I saw the story in the paper, and that. But I didn't know her."

"You sure about that? You know what happens to people who tell me fibs?"

Spider had heard the stories. Most of them involved power tools and pliers. He suppressed a shudder. "Straight up, Mr Pearce. The last time I saw her was last year, at a party."

Pearce leaned in a little closer. The cologne was almost overpowering at this distance. "And what did you tell the Old Bill?"

"Eh? What? How did you know I'd been pulled in by them?"

Pearce's only response was to arch an eyebrow. Spider swallowed hard and replied. "Nothing. Just what I told you, that's what I told the Old Bill. I don't know any more. Honest."

Pearce remained close, staring intently at the young man, then suddenly sat back, the leather seat squeaking under his bulk. He quickly reached inside his coat, causing Spider to flinch. Pearce's laugh sounded like gravel being poured into a bucket. He took out a wallet in a huge, scarred hand, and removed a £20 note. With a surprisingly deft movement, he popped the note into the breast pocket of Spider's shirt.

"Here, buy your mum some flowers. Lovely lady. Is she keeping well these days?"

Spider mumbled a reply as his guts turned to ice. Pearce

continued. "Keep your ear to the ground, son. You move in the same circles as the young lady did. You hear anything, you let me know. Straight away, you understand?" He leaned back as Spider nodded frantically. "I hear you've been doing good business for us the last couple of years. Keep it up. And if you come through with some decent info, who knows? Could be some proper work in it for you. Alright, son, off you pop."

Spider virtually leaped out of the car. As it glided smoothly away, he leaned against a lamppost, hands shaking, breathing hard. *What a bloody day!*

Chapter 4

After another morning of fruitless witness statements and dead-ends, Calloway was halfway through a fried egg sandwich when Smith knocked and entered the office he shared with Turner.

"Sorry, sarge, you having your lunch?"

Calloway chewed and waved a hand. Turner called over from his desk. "Food of kings, eh? Fried egg and a Twix."

Wiping his hands, Calloway accepted the folder from the WPC.

"It's the autopsy report, just in. Oh, and Mr Clark has formally identified his daughter."

"Poor sod. Thanks. Let's have a look." He skimmed the page. "No surprises. Second shot killed her, to the heart. Third to the head was a formality. Precise shooting."

"Definitely a pro then, skipper?" Turner added. "Or a least someone with training. Former military perhaps? I've had a check through the files. No-one stands out. Most locals are banged up or away."

Calloway tossed the file onto his desk. "Aye, which leaves us with virtually nothing to go on. Let's get down to this Regency place this evening. Smith, how are you fixed to tag along with Pavitt and me? A female face might help with some of Patricia's friends. Sorry, I know you're not on duty tonight."

Smith pulled a fake scowl. "Well, I had planned a microwave dinner and Corrie, so being taken out clubbing sounds like a treat."

"Ah, that's great, thanks. We'll pick you up around eight. I might even splash out on a kebab after."

"You know how to spoil a girl don't you, sarge? You coming, Turner?"

"Nope, I don't get treated to nights out. I'm off away in a bit, following up on some of the witness interviews. There's a few people reckon they saw the shooter on a bus and later at Ilford station. Then I'm meeting Lynn later, it's dinner with her folks tonight."

"Ooh. Must be getting serious!" Smith grinned. "When's the wedding?"

Turner flushed and went back to his reports. Calloway chuckled. "Leave the poor boy alone."

The rush hour traffic had cleared by the time Calloway and Pavitt called round for Smith. The Regency Suite was in Chadwell Heath, a short drive from Smith's flat in Goodmayes. The venue was a large old pub with a mock Tudor frontage, sat right on the High Street. The car park was filled with scooters, some plain or stripped down to the chassis, others bearing an assortment of mirrors, leopard skin seat covers and chrome side panels. A group of suited youths eyed Cab's Rover suspiciously as he swung it into the car park. The suspicion only increased as the trio moved to the entrance. The smell of two-stroke fuel hung heavily in the air, with just a hint of cannabis underneath.

Calloway flashed his warrant card at the tuxedo-clad bouncer on the door, who waved them in. The sight of the card elicited low jeers and oink-oink noses from the crowd hanging round the entrance. The inside was split into two areas. To the left, a bar. Music thumped out through the doorway to the right. A young woman looking like something out of a Mary Quant advert told them, "It's three pound on the door," before seeing Calloway's ID. Cab nodded as he moved past her. The large, dimly lit room beyond was mostly taken up by a sunken dance floor, around which were arranged tables and chairs. To the right sat a low stage, at one side of which a headphoned DJ worked in his booth.

To Calloway's eyes the place looked like something out of Ready, Steady, Go. The fashions, the haircuts, even the music, *Martha Reeves and the Vandellas*, if he wasn't mistaken. Most of the people here were aged between eighteen and twenty, he estimated, mostly white with a few black youths, too. Dress-wise, only Pavitt fitted in, in his striped knitwear top and straight trousers. Cab was by far the oldest person in the room, and Smith the only one wearing jeans. The DJ had his back to them, taking an LP out of its sleeve. Calloway head for him, brushing his way through the dancers. Leaning into the booth, he tapped the lad on the shoulder and signalled for him to cut the music, prompting groans and boos from the crowd. He pointed to the mic the DJ passed it to him.

"Alright, alright, settle down." The mic whistled. Someone shouted "Fuck off, pig!" from the back. Pavitt stepped up to Calloway's side, glaring at the crowd.

"Pavitt, you wanker!" came another shout, followed by a rippled of laughter. Pavitt's face reddened and Calloway spoke again.

"Shush, now! Listen. We're sorry to interrupt your evening, but this is important. It's about Patricia. Tricia Clark. I'm sure you'll have heard, she was murdered yesterday. Shot."

There was an instant change in atmosphere. A low murmur filled the room, a girl in the corner began sobbing.

"All we want to know is, do any of you have any information that might help? Anything at all, no matter how small it might seem to you. Was Tricia seeing anyone? Did she have enemies? Has anyone threatened her recently? That kind of thing. My colleagues and I will be just outside, so you can carry on with your dancing here. But if anyone has any ideas of who might have done this or why, please do come and talk to us. Alright. Thank you."

He handed the mic back to the DJ, who nodded to him before addressing the crowd himself. "You heard the man, everyone. Let's find the bastard who did this."

"String 'em up!" someone called from the back, prompting shouts of agreement. Calloway motioned for Smith and Pavitt to leave and was just about to go himself when his eye fell on the DJ's record box. He leaned forward.

"Is that an original Verve?" he asked.

The young man pulled the album out. "Yep. It's actually the US release, 1964. Jimmy Smith, The Cat."

"Nice. What else you got in there?" He flicked through the sleeves. "Stanley Turrentine, Blue Note. Wow. I thought you guys were into the Who and all that?"

The DJ shrugged. "Well, I suppose. But the real mod music was always modern jazz, soul, that kind of thing."

"Where do you get this stuff?"

"Went over to the States last year, picked up some of these and a ton of Northern Soul. And then at record fairs here. There's one every month in Dalston. You should go if this music is your scene. Hold on." He turned and rummaged among his record boxes, then handed Calloway a flyer.

"Aye, it is, son, it is. Thanks, I'll check that out. I - "

He was interrupted by Smith tapping his shoulder. "Sarge? We've got some people to speak to?"

Calloway smiled. "Ah, yes, of course." He nodded to the DJ, folded the flyer into his pocket and followed the WPC outside. Pavitt was seated at a beer garden table at the side of the pub, a dozen of the mods crowding around. Cab and Smith joined him and began chatting to the group, taking notes, asking questions. A few more wandered out to talk but it was clear that there was little, if any, new information forthcoming. Calloway dropped Tony Webb's name in a few times, it either drew blanks or, in a few cases, instant silence. *Customers, no doubt,* he thought. After half an hour or so, it was clear no-on else was coming forward so Cab called it a night.

"Alright, let's wrap-up. I'll drop you back home Smith, then Pavitt back at the station."

The pair folded notebooks and followed him to the car. As they reached it. Smith tapped Calloway on the arm. "Erm, sarge? I believe there was mention of a kebab?"

Chapter 5

The next morning, Calloway was leafing through Smith's latest batch of witness statements when Kit Kat rang.

"There's a bloke at the front desk, Cab. Insists on seeing 'the man in charge of the murder investigation.' I figured that was you."

Calloway grunted a reply and closed the folder on the desk in front of him. Minutes later, a man in his early fifties was shown into the office. Almost on sight, Cab had his type pegged. The beige raincoat, despite the sunny weather, the peering over the glasses, the faintly supercilious air. He stood and extended a hand.

"DS Calloway, lead officer on the Clark murder investigation. You wanted to see me, Mr...?"

The man took Calloway's hand in a clammy grip.

"Gossage. Brian Gossage. I'm a neighbour of the girl who was murdered. Well, I say neighbour, Mother and I live three doors along. On the opposite side." He withdrew his hand and took the proffered chair, pursing his lips. Cab waited. When nothing was forthcoming, he raised an eyebrow and titled his head. The prompt did the trick.

"Ah, yes, well. This business, it's awful. Mother is very upset. We all are, the whole street. It's getting so you can't even go for a walk any more, terrible."

"Indeed." Calloway inwardly sighed. "Sir, do you have some information pertaining to the investigation?"

"Yes. Well, no, not exactly. I'm here to put in a complaint."

"A complaint?" The sigh turned into the beginnings of a dull headache.

"Yes. It's outrageous. The press. All day, every day, there's a pack of them outside the girl's house. And their language! Filthy! Mother was quite -"

Cab leaned forward. "I'm sorry, Mr Gossage, have you asked to see me to complain about the reporters?"

"Well, yes! All the neighbours feel the same. Naturally, they look to me to take action. I'm lead co-ordinator on the new Neighbourhood Watch scheme, you see?"

Yes, you would be, wouldn't you? Calloway sat back again. "Well, I'm sorry to be the bearer of bad news, Mr Gossage, but unless the press are breaking the law, there's nothing I can do to stop them congregating outside the house. If you want my advice, give it a day or two, and they will be gone. At the risk of sounding harsh, these cases come and go, they will be onto the next one soon enough."

Gossage stuck his bottom lip out like a disappointed child. "Well, I must say I'm disappointed by your attitude, Sergeant Calloway. Not only do we have the fear of a murderer on the loose, we have to put up with this kind of disruption, too. We're rate-payers, you know. Law abiding citizens. We have a right to feel safe in our own country!"

"I understand your concerns, Mr Gossage, but please be assured that we regard this as an isolated incident and are doing everything we can to apprehend the killer."

"Have you made any arrests yet?"

"I'm afraid I'm not at liberty to discuss details of the case."

"You should be checking the family at number seventeen, if you ask me."

I didn't, thought Cab, *but you're going to tell me anyway.*

"Coming and going all hours, then there's the music. And the drugs, no doubt. I wouldn't be at all surprised if they had something to do with it."

"And what makes you say that, sir?"

"Well, it's that lot, isn't it? You know?"

Calloway feared he did but pushed anyway. "That lot?"

At that moment WPC Smith came in with a blue folder under her arm.

"Sarge, here's the last of last night's notes, typed up. Oh, sorry, I didn't realise you were busy."

"That's okay, constable, thank you." He took the file and Smith left. Gossage looked outraged.

"Her lot," he hissed through compressed lips. "Darkies! I'm surprised you have one working here, I must say!"

Calloway suppressed the urge to knock Gossage's glasses across the room and spoke in a low growl, his Dundee accent thickening. "WPC Smith is an experienced and valued member of the team. The Met Police is not an organisation given to colour prejudice. Sir." He knew, however, that though that was the official stance, a line of racism still existed amongst certain officers. Still, he was not about to give Gossage the satisfaction of mentioning that. Cab stood abruptly. "So, if that is all, sir, I'll bid you good-day. I'll call someone up to guide you out."

Gossage stood, slightly flustered. "Well, I must say I'm not happy with your attitude, Sergeant. Be assured, I will be writing to my MP."

Good, let him deal with you, Cab thought but outwardly merely nodded.

"At the very least do something about the rabble at number seventeen. They are trouble, mark my words!"

"I'll have an officer check them out," Calloway ushered Gossage out, of the office, motioning to a passing PC . Even as the door closed behind him. Gossage was still muttering loudly.

Cab sat and took out a fag, shaking his head. Smith returned. "Did you hear that?" he asked.

"I heard enough," she replied. Then, under her breath, "Dickhead."

Calloway chuckled. "Dickhead he might be. But he's a dickhead who pays his rates."

"So you'll be checking that house out?"

"I doubt they have anything to do with it. Besides which, door-to-door would have picked up anything odd. I'll double check with Jones and Houlihan."

"Well, I have some better news. We've tracked down Tricia's ex in Spain."

"Hurst, right?"

"That's him. Apparently Houlihan called in a favour from a friend he has over there, and the local force tracked him down for us."

"Good. Let's set up a phone call, then. Not as good as a face to face and I'd love a trip trip to sunny Spain, but I can't see Denham stumping out for a flight."

"I'll get on it, sarge." Smith left, leaving Cab to return to the disappointingly thin pile of witness statements.

Following lunch at a seafront café, the killer was strolling back to his digs. It was a bright, sunny day, if a bit breezy, and the town was stirring with the beginnings of the holiday season. It was the second Saturday in April, and there were already a number of families here, either sat on the beach behind windbreaks or trailing their excited kids around the amusement arcades. He paused at the entrance to the pier, bemused by the display. A lurid sign that read WAXWORKS! CHAMBER OF HORRORS, sat atop a large window. Behind it lay the waxen figure of a man bound to a slab. Across him swung a large semicircular blade on a pendulum. The figure's head turned, as if the victim were watching the blade as it sliced across him. Already, the figure's belly had been cut, his clothing stained with blood. A number of children were pointing and laughing at the display, to the apparent amusement of their parents.

The killer shook his head. His old teacher had been right, the English were a very strange people. On the way back he stopped at a newsagent to buy some magazines. He specifically avoided newspapers, not wanting to read any potential stories about his victim. That was a slippery slope, he had been warned. He was halfway up the stairs at the hotel when the landlady's voice called from below.

"Cooee, Mr Petersons? Cooee."

He turned to the blousey figure below. She held a piece of notepaper in outstretched hand. "There was a phone call for you. A man. He left this number and asked that you call him back."

The killer put on his best smile. "Why thank you, Mrs King, that's very kind of you. It's probably my boss." He rolled his eyes for effect. "May I call him back?"

"Of course, you can use the payphone there."

He took the number and rummaged for loose change. The payphone was in the hallway, more public than he would have liked, and Mrs King remained hovering until a glance and a nod from him prompted a retreat. The call was answered and he fed in a coin.

"Yes?"

It was the voice of his employer, speaking in accented English. "We need to meet. Very soon. Choose a location."

The killer thought fast. The voice didn't sound happy. *A public place, then.* Though if they wanted him dead there would have been no phone call. Still, his nape was tingling.

"Southend Pier. The entrance. By the torture exhibit."

If there was any surprise at the description it didn't show in the man's voice.

"Very well. Monday morning. Ten o clock." There was a click and the hum of the dial tone.

The killer exhaled and replaced the receiver. He didn't like changes of plan. He liked the tone of voice even less. With grim humour he wondered if meeting by the pendulum victim was a good thing after all - it may give certain people ideas. Not that these people need any assistance in that area, from what he knew about them. Pausing only to wipe the handset clean, he returned to his room.

Chapter 6

The briefing was just being wrapped up when word came through that the phone call to Spain had been organised. Denham had sat in, saying nothing but not looking happy. There had been little to report. The visit to the Regency Suite had brought in no new information beyond Tricia's activities over the previous week or so. Still nothing out of the ordinary, no jilted lovers, no stalkers, no arguments with anyone. By all accounts she was a perfectly ordinary teenager. It prompted Denham's only contribution to the briefing.

"We're obviously looking in the wrong place, then. Perhaps this wasn't about the girl, perhaps it was something else."

"A random attack?" proffered Jones. "You think this could be some sort of serial killer?"

"Wouldn't be the first," Calloway replied. "Remember the Brighton case last year?" They all nodded. A series of murders along the south coast had eventually been pinned on a lone serial killer, choosing his victims at random, apparently in a twisted bid for some sort of fame or notoriety.

Turner spoke next. "But that guy was pretty messy wasn't he? Stabbings? This guy appears to be a lot more professional."

"True," Jones responded, "Doesn't make him potentially any less of a nutter, though. Or perhaps he's watched too many gangster films?"

"Alright," Cab stood and stretched his aching back. "Let's get a check on any recently released prisoners or psychiatric patients. Especially anyone with previous for violence."

At that moment that Bellotti the SOCO came in.

"Sorry I'm late, everyone." She nudged the door closed behind her and placed a number of items on the desk, including three bagged bullets. "I only just received the lab reports." She brushed back a lock of hair and opened a folder.

Calloway smiled at her, "No problem, we're just kicking the can around here. What do you have for us?"

Bellotti took the team through the crime scene findings, which comprised little more than the three bullets. "Ballistics confirm they were fired from a Beretta, probably a 92."

"Common model, then," Jones chipped in. "Used by law enforcement and military all round the world. Easy to source. Any sign of it?"

"No. We had all the bins in the park checked, but nothing has tuned up as yet."

"There's a boating lake in the park, sarge" said Pavitt. "And if he went out onto Cranbrook Road the gunman would have walked past it."

"Okay, let's ask upstairs if we can get the budget to have that dredged, then. He may have thrown the gun in on his way out. Anything else?"

Bellotti shook her head. "You already had the autopsy report, I believe. We carried out a search of the vic's flat, too. If anything turns up there, I'll let you know."

Denham called an end, everyone was standing and chatting when one of the station sergeants came in to let Calloway know about the phone call. He excused himself and hurried up to his office, readying pen and paper before picking up the receiver.

"Hello. Yep, right, you can put them through, thanks."

The next voice on the line introduced himself as Subinspector Martinez of Malaga Police and informed Calloway he had one James Hurst in attendance at the station and ready to speak. Cab thanked the officer and a hesitant, East London accented voice spoke next.

"Hello? This is Jim Hurst."

"Hello, Jim. I'm DS Calloway, speaking to you from Ilford Police Station. Thanks for talking to me today, hopefully I won't keep you long. I take it you have heard of the death of Tricia Clark?"

"Yeah. I saw it in some of the English papers and some of my mates told me. She was shot, right? What happened? Why did it happen? Who was it?"

"Those are all things we're working to find out, Jim. I understand you and Tricia were an item at one time?"

"Yeah, last year." He sighed heavily. "She was a lovely girl. I don't get why someone would do this to her."

"Aye, it's a terrible thing." Cab paused. "Jim, I have to ask. How did things finish between you. Any hard feelings?"

"How did they - 'ere, what, you think I had something to do with this?"

"No, but you understand I have to ask. Procedure and all that."

"Yeah, I suppose so. Well, we ended things okay. No stand up rows if that's what you mean. I moved over here soon after. We never kept in touch."

"And why did you split?"

"Well, to be honest is was all getting a bit heavy for me. I mean, you know, I'm not really up to getting hitched and all that. Her family were all for it though. Some of them, at least."

Calloway detected a change in tone. He pressed on.

"Her parents were putting pressure on you both?"

There was a pause. "No, not her parents. More her uncle. Look, is this really necessary? I don't see how it has anything to do with what happened."

"Probably not, but, again, I have to follow procedure. No stone unturned and all that. So tell me about this uncle."

A short laugh sounded down the line. "I'd have thought you know all about him already. He's the main reason I came out here. I heard he was right pissed off when me and Trish split. Like, real pissed off. And he's not the sort of bloke I want to be around when he's annoyed. I got an offer from a mate at the time to come over here and help him with his entertainment business, so I took it. It's all working out fine so far, what with the tourism here. Not to mention the ex-pats, they enjoy a - "

"Yes, yes, that's nice," Calloway interrupted, "But who's this uncle you're so scared of?"

"Blimey, you really don't know, do you? Tricia's uncle is Terry. Terry Taverner. Yes, *the* Terry Taverner. The biggest gangster in the East End."

"How the *fuck* could we miss this?" Denham was not happy. Calloway has taken Hurst's news straight up to him.

"Taverner's her uncle on the maternal side. We hadn't checked the mother's maiden name so nothing had been flagged up, guv. There was no obvious connection, other than the name."

"Well, you best get on it now! Call the team back in, pull all the files on Taverner. This has gangland hit written all over it."

"Yes, guv. Want me to go down and see him, too? Where does he hang out these days?"

"Yes, I do. He's stayed close to his roots, as far as I know. Most of them move out to Essex once they get a bit of cash, but our Terry still lives in Stratford." He glanced at his watch. "We have a press conference scheduled in an hour, I'll need you here for that. Get down and see him tomorrow. I can't imagine for a minute he'll want to cooperate with us but any information would be useful at this stage."

"You think this could be the start of a turf war?"

"I bloody well hope not. We have our hands full enough as it is. Yardies to the south, Turks to the north, Albanians in the west end and Taverner's firm all over. I best take this up to the Chief Super. Get everyone on alert in case. Alright, keep me informed."

"Aye, guv." Calloway turned to leave.

"And Cab…"

He paused in the doorway. "Yes, guv?"

"Don't drop another bollock like this. Clear?"

"Crystal, guv."

Chapter 7

Spider smiled in satisfaction as he added another fiver to the roll of notes in his pocket. Almost all the pills had gone, it had been a good night and the gig hadn't even started yet. He was working out of his usual pitch for this venue, a narrow alleyway not far from the Rainbow. Close enough for people to find him, far enough to be out of range of the venue bouncers. The only people making him nervous were the group of skinheads gathered outside a pub on the other side of the road. Par for the course at any mod gig, especially in London. It was funny, Spider's older brother had been an original skinhead in the early 70s. It was him who'd turned Spider on to ska and rocksteady music. These new skins were a different breed, bleached jeans, torn t-shirts, swastika tattoos.

Spider had been there that night at the Bridgehouse when the Hoxton mods had fronted up a group of National Front boneheads. "We're skinheads," their leader had proclaimed proudly. "No you ain't, "one of the Hoxton faces had replied. "You're just a glue sniffer with a crop."

Still, authentic skins or not, they were lary bastards. Mind you, they would be outnumbered tonight. Secret Affair, one of the leading mod revival bands, were playing a farewell tour, and this was their last London date. Everyone who was anyone would be here tonight, and most of them would be looking to get pilled up beforehand. Ilford Kenny had already scored his supply. Spider nodded over to Carl, the young lad who acted as his main runner. Any sign of Old Bill and Carl would take the money and stash and leg it. The police were unlikely to chase and arrest a fifteen year old. It wasn't long to the start of the gig, Spider thought he'd give it another ten minutes then go in. He'd drop the last few blues himself, Carl could find his own way home. Spider was about to take a last look around when he suddenly became aware of a figure to his right. He span, startled, flinching back from the tall figure who loomed at the mouth of the alleyway.

The heavy-set man wore a sheepskin jacket, hands thrust deep into pockets. He smiled but Spider took no comfort from that. The guy looked foreign, Greek or Turkish, perhaps, judging from the black hair and thick moustache. The smile was a jagged line across the sinister, pock-marked face. A voice sounded behind the intimidating figure.

"Serkan, step back, give the boy some room. I do believe you have frightened him."

The lead man obliged and another squeezed past him, forcing Spider deeper into the alleyway. Suddenly it didn't seem such a secure place.

"I do apologise," the newcomer was saying. He had similar features to the first, though somewhat less brutal looking. A shorter, leaner man, in a smart sports jacket and beige Farah slacks. He removed his Ray-bans and placed them in his breast pocket. "My name is Ismet. You are Mr Webb, no?"

Spider struggled to regain his composure.

"No. Yes. Who wants to know?"

"I will be direct, Mr Webb. I understand you have a lucrative business supplying certain merchandise to quite a large group of people?"

Spider made to deny but Ismet held up a hand. "It is alright, young man. We are not police officers. No, my friend and I are businessmen. In fact, we represent what you might call a large company, a family run concern. That concern is most eager to move into new markets, and that is why we have come to talk to you tonight."

"But how did you know I would be here? How do you know about me?" Spider remained flustered.

"Ah, we have many ears and eyes around, particularly here in north London. You might even say you are working on our patch." There was a hint of menace in the last phrase. Spider went pale but Ismet smiled and held up a reassuring hand again.

"Relax, Mr Webb, we only want to talk. To offer a proposition, in fact. In the future, you will buy your merchandise from us. We can offer you much better rates than what you currently pay. I am sure. And, all being well, in the future we can offer many other ranges of merchandise for you to sell to your customers. Ranges that are much more profitable than these pills you currently sell."

Spider's mind was racing. On the one hand, he knew they were right. Pills were okay but were bulky and you had to take a dozen to get a buzz. He'd heard about the increase in cocaine coming into the country, about how it was now filtering down from the lofty heights of aristocrats and rock stars to street level. And how much longer could the mod scene last? New discos and nightclubs were springing up all over. That was where the money would be in the future. But the vision of Pearce filling the back seat of his Jag threw cold water on his vision.

"You know where I currently get my pi- er, merchandise?"

Ismet nodded. "We are aware of that, yes. And, naturally, we would not wish you to get into difficulties with your current associates. But times change, young man. Businesses come and businesses go. Still, no need to make a decision now. Here, take this." He produced a business card from his jacket. It was blank save for a phone number. "Call me when you have decided. But don't leave it too long. My boss is a patient man, but only so far."

With that the pair turned and left, leaving Spider to lean his forehead against the cool brick wall and wonder if it was time for a career change.

Chapter 8

Calloway swore as the bike came out of nowhere, forcing him to break hard. Both he and Houlihan in the passenger seat were both jerked forward and back, the DC shouting "Twat!" at the back of the disappearing cyclist. They were on the Romford Road approaching Stratford. Word was that Taverner often enjoyed a Sunday lunch at the Carpenter's Arms pub, so that was where they were heading. The press conference yesterday had gone as well as could be expected. The Clarks attended, tearfully asking for anyone with information to come forward. Denham had fielded all the questions well, all Calloway had had to do was confirm that "several lines of enquiry are being investigated."

Houlihan pointed out a turning just before the Bow Flyover and Calloway spun the wheel, bringing the maroon Rover to a halt on the outskirts of the large estate.

"Best park here, skip," the big man advised. "Park too far in and we'll come back to a wreck."

Calloway squeaked the wheels against the kerb and the pair got out. It was a short walk to the pub, through the heart of the estate. A few tower blocks loomed over them but most of the houses were in neat rows, tidy little boxes with postage-stamp sized gardens. It was quiet, a few men were out washing cars, some kids kicked a ball around, a few curtains twitched. Soon they were at their destination, a typical seventies estate pub, set off nicely by the burnt-out wreck of a Ford Cortina outside. Houlihan led, pushing open the door, releasing a cloud of cigarette smoke and beery voices from within.

Cab had chosen Houlihan specifically for this job. This was the equivalent of going behind enemy lines. Going in mob handed would result in a riot. Going in alone was not advisable. Hopefully, the hulking Houlihan would be just enough to deter anyone who fancied belting a copper for fun. Hopefully.

The drone of conversation stopped, Calloway felt like he was in an old cowboy movie. Ignoring the sullen stares, he moved to the bar, nodding at the shirt-sleeved man wiping the counter. There were small bowls of cheese and cockles laid out, Calloway sat on a barstool and helped himself to cheese and pineapple on a stick. Houlihan remained standing, big hands clenched at his side.

"My name is DS Calloway, Ilford CID. I'm here to speak to Terry Taverner," Calloway told the barman, flashing his warrant card. That man shrugged.

"Never 'eard of him."

There was the scrape of a chair behind him. Calloway turned

slowly on the stool. One of the nearest group of drinkers was on his feet, a young track-suited man with a bubble-perm.

"Think you've got the wrong place, mate. Newham City Farm is down the road. That's where they keep the pigs." There was a ripple of laughter around the room. Houlihan made to step forward, Calloway laid a hand on his arm to stop him. He slid from the stool and stepped towards the joker.

"See here, laddie. That's not very polite. Did your mammy not teach you any manners? Or was she too busy jacking off sailors down the docks?" He mimicked the hand action. The man snarled and took a step forward, but Cab was ready for him. The gesturing hand was already up and forming a fist. He jabbed it sharply into the attacker's face, sending him flying back to land heavily in his chair.

"Anyone else?" growled Calloway. Several men stood, and the lad, wiping his face with a hand that came away red, stood and reached for his back pocket. They were all frozen by a stern voice from the back of the room.

"That's enough, Billy. Alright, Calloway. In here. Your monkey can stay there."

A face had appeared round the folding doors at the rear of the pub. Taverner. Calloway straightened his tie and walked over. He followed the figure into the back room, a space dominated by the snooker table at its centre. Taverner turned to face him. Two other men were at the far side of the table, one chalking a cue, the other stood with arms folded glaring at the newcomer.

"Lads, give me a few minutes with our friend here, will you?" Taverner motioned and the two heavies left. He was not a physically imposing man, being quite short and slim, but there was an air of danger about him. *The eyes*, thought Calloway, icy blue behind the bi-focals. The man was smart too, from the swept back greying hair, to the crisp, white shirt and waistcoat, to the highly polished, no doubt handmade, shoes.

"You're a bit handy, ainch'a? That was a nice jab."

"Boxed as a youth," Calloway replied. "Lochee Boys Club. Won a few, lost a few."

"Ah, boxing, the noble art. Drink?"

Calloway nodded and Taverner handed him a ready poured tumbler of whisky, indicating a chair. Cab sat as the older man poured himself a drink and perched on the edge of the snooker table.

"You were expecting me?" Cab raised the glass and took an appreciative a sip.

"I knew you were here the minute you set foot on the estate." The older man sighed. "Terrible business. I expected you sooner, to be honest."

"Well, to be honest back, we didn't find out she was your niece until yesterday."

"Ah, right. Well, Sue never did approve of my line of work. And that prick she married… soft as shit. Thing is, I've barely spoken to my sister for years. Tricia, though, that was different." His eyes glazed. "She'd come and see me when she could, once she was old enough. Never told her mum. And now… this." His knuckles tightened on his glass.

Calloway took another sip and leaned forward. "Listen, I don't expect any co-operation from you, or for you to assist us in anyway. But is there anyone you can think of? Any reason this would happen? You know it was a professional job?"

"I heard. Two in the chest, one in the head."

That information had not been released to the public but Calloway didn't ask how Taverner knew. He gave the man some space as he fought to contain his emotions.

"No. I don't. And yes, you're right. Normally I wouldn't be talking to the filth. No offence."

"None taken."

"You get used to rough stuff in this game, it comes with the territory. But this? To attack a man's family?" Taverner's face contorted, his voice lowered. "What sort of mongrel does that? What sort of absolute fucking animal shoots and kills a young girl?"

The tumbler in Taverner's hand shattered and he stood abruptly, looking vacantly down at his cut hand. He pointed at Calloway, blood dripping heavily onto the green baize.

"You find him, Calloway. Or I'll find him. If I find him first, you know how it goes. If you find him, I want him. I'll pay you whatever it takes. But I want him."

"I cannae do that Terry." Calloway stood. "But I promise you this. I won't be resting until the bastard is under lock and key. I'll be in touch."

He made his way back to the bar where Houlihan was stood on the same spot, still glaring at the punters.

"Come on, let's go." Calloway led them out of the pub, lighting a Marlboro and drawing on it heavily.

"Anything, skip?"

"No, I don't think so. I don't think the poor sod has a clue. And that makes him even more dangerous. I don't doubt he'll be pulling in every face in the area for questioning. If we don't sort this quick, we could have World War Three on our hands."

The barmaid had just finished bandaging Taverner's hand when Pearce entered the snooker room.

"Thanks, Debs," Taverner nodded and the woman squeezed past the leering Pearce. He focused his attention back to his boss. "Heard you had the filth in, T. Anything?"

Pearce was the only man to address Taverner this way. The two had grown together, coming up on the streets of Bow. The older Taverner had always watched out for Pearce as he had risen up the ranks of one of the old Kray off-shoot firms.

Taverner shook his head. "They know even less than we do. Our man says they have no witnesses, no suspects, no leads. Calloway virtually told me as much himself. All we know is that was a pro hit. Not one of the usuals, though. And there's no-one come forward to claim ownership."

Pearce poured himself a drink, loosened his tie and sat. "Well I got something that might be interesting. Ain't much but it might be an indicator."

"Go on." Taverner leaned on the table, fixing Pearce with a stare.

"You know young Tony Webb, Spider as he calls himself?"

Taverner thought for a second. "The pill dealer, right? Covers east, all the way out to Romford?"

"Yeah that's him. He shifts a ton of gear, makes good gravy for us. Anyway, he phoned me this morning. Apparently he was dealing over at Finsbury Park last night when a couple of herberts had a word. He thinks they were Turkish, maybe bubbles. Short of it is, they offered him work. Said they'd supply him with cocaine, apparently. Said our business was on the way out."

Taverner snorted. "Turks, eh? That'll be the Arikans. They've been sniffing round North London since the Tottenham lot went down. And now they think they can take us on?"

"Seems so, T. What d'you want me to do?"

Taverner thought for a moment. "Tell him to accept their offer. Tell him to get in with them. He might be able to find out more on the inside. Especially if they were connected with what happened to Tricia."

Pearce nodded. "I'll let him know. Could be dangerous, mind. If they find out he's still working for us it won't go well for him."

Taverner shrugged, face impassive. "Who cares? One less drug dealer in the world. Besides, like the coppers, we've got no leads. Could be a start."

"And if it turns out to be them what's responsible?"

"Then we torture and kill every last fucking one of them. They'll regret the day they ever set foot in this country."

Chapter 9

As he pulled his car keys out of his pocket, the flyer the Regency DJ had given Calloway came with it. He glanced at it and made a decision.

"Bob, do you mind making your own way back? There's somewhere I'd like to go but it's in Dalston."

"No probs, skip. My brother's playing football on Hackney Marshes today. I was going to pop over and see him anyway."

The drive to Dalston didn't take long and Calloway soon found the venue of the record fair, St Mark's Hall, off Dalston Lane. The event had been running for a couple of hours, so he wasn't hopeful of picking up anything rare. Still, he was soon enjoying browsing the boxes on the tables, and chatting to a couple of the dealers. He was even more happy, and surprised, to see Gemma Bellotti flicking through some old magazines on a nearby stall. He strode over.

"Mrs Bellotti? Hey, how are you? I didnae expect to see you here."

She turned and smiled at him. "Oh, hello. DS Calloway, isn't it?"

"Please, call me Cab. I'm not on duty now," he laughed.

"Alright, and it's Gemma. And it's Miss, too," she raised an eyebrow.

They shook hands. "I didn't know you were into record collecting?"

"Oh, I'm not really. It's just that my father wanted to come here, so I brought him." She indicated an elderly man browsing across the aisle. "He, er, gets a bit confused these days so I like to be with him when he goes out. No, this isn't my thing at all. All these boring middle-aged men rummaging through crackly old records, I - " she brought a hand to her mouth, eyes widening. "Oh my God, I'm so sorry, I didn't mean…"

Calloway's shoulders shook as he chuckled. "No worries. And you're right. I can't deny it, just look around. Still, I don't think I'm middle-aged just yet."

"No, no, you're not."

There came a slightly awkward pause, during which Calloway coughed and shuffled his feet. "There's a café just by the foyer. Fancy grabbing a coffee? Will your dad be alright on his own for a bit?"

Gemma tilted her head. "Yes, that would be nice. I'll just tell him. Give me a second."

As she turned and walked away, Cab swiftly smoothed his hair back and straightened his tie. He rummaged in his pocket for his Tic Tacs, popping one in his mouth just before Gemma returned. They spent the next twenty minutes or so chatting over coffee and a slice of cake. Gemma began by asking about the case.

"Any news yet? Oh, I'm sorry, we shouldn't be talking about work."

Cab glanced around before answering. "No, nothing, really. At least nothing substantial. And it's fine." He smiled. "You know what the job is like, especially with a case like this. Difficult to switch off when you go home. You been in it long?"

"About three years now. I was based at Basildon, then transferred to Ilford when I moved back here. I'm originally from Leytonstone. I came back for Dad. Since Mum passed away he's been on his own, so I moved back in with him. I've been trying to sort out a care home but it's not easy."

"I imagine they cost a fortune?"

"That's only half of it. Biggest difficulty is getting him to agree. Dad's old school, from a big Italian family, all very independent minded, all as stubborn as hell. But he's getting worse. Half the time he forgets Mum has gone." She paused and took a sip of coffee. "Anyway, that's enough of my troubles. What about you? You're not from round here, are you?" She smiled. Cab decided he liked it when she smiled.

"What gave it away?" He laughed. "No, I was dragged up in the back streets of Dundee. Not much to say, really."

"How did you end up in the police?"

"Ah, that was all down to a chap called Joe Lynch. He was a trainer at the local boxing club. I was a bit of a tearaway until I started training there. Old Joe sorted me out, got me on the straight and narrow."

"You were a boxer? You don't have broken nose."

"I was always good at dodging, " he chuckled. "Besides, I only had a few fights, it was more for the training and discipline. Joe was an ex-copper. I suppose that's what got me into thinking about joining. Besides which, there wasn't much else around. Most of my pals went into factories or the army. I never fancied either, so, here I am."

"But how did you get down here? Was Dundee that bad?"

"Well we moved to Glasgow first. My wife and I."

"Oh." Gemma's face fell slightly. "I didn't realise you're married."

"Was. After we divorced, I decided on a clean break and transferred to the Met."

"Oh, right. Happens a lot, right? I had plans to get married back in Basildon. But, you know… Did you not have any kids, then?"

Cab waved over Gemma's shoulder. "Here's your dad. Hello, Mr Bellotti ."

Gemma twisted in her chair as her father came over, smiling. He was clutching a plastic bag to his chest and began talking excitedly.

"Three old 78s! Giuseppe Krismer, so good. You momma will love hearing these."

Sadness flashed over Gemma's face for a second. "That's nice, Pops. Alright, we best get you home." She stood and reached into her bag.

"No that's okay. These are on me," Cab gestured.

"Ah, so it's not true what they say about Scotsmen?"

Cab laughed. "That depends on what they say. See you in the office?"

Gemma nodded, waved and was gone. Calloway grinned. This morning aside, not a bad day. And still some browsing to do amongst the old records.

Chapter 10

Spider was up and on the move uncharacteristically early for a Monday morning. After speaking to Pearce yesterday, he'd called the number on the card. This mob didn't hang about. He was given an address in Wood Green and told to be there at 11am that morning. The place turned out to be a Turkish restaurant on Green Lanes. Eventually finding an empty spot, he parked up his Mini and walked round the corner to knock on the curtained door. It had been pulled aside to reveal a weathered, suspicious face.

"I was told to ask for Yousuf. They said you'd be expecting me? I'm Spider."

The man nodded, unlocked the door and allowed Spider in. He was taken to an upstairs room at the back of the property. There, a younger man, Yousuf, he presumed, opened a briefcase and took out a bag of white powder.

"Ever seen this before?" he asked.

Spider bluffed it. "Yeah, of course, loads of times."

Yousuf look doubtful. "Right. Well, what you've got here is a monkey's worth of the good stuff. How you sell this is up to you. Best way is split into small deals, knock it out for a tenner a bag. If you want to spread it more, you can mix it, of course. But this has been cut already, and you also need to be careful what you mix it with. This is about repeat business, not ripping people off or killing them. But you know all that, right? You've done this before."

Spider squirmed in the chair. "Well, yeah, but I've been flogging pills, mostly. It's a bit different."

"It is. You'll need some decent scales and zip-bags for a start. And forget the pills, they're nothing. This is the future. Play this right and you'll be sitting pretty in a year or so. "

"Got it. How much do I have to pay for this?"

"Pay?" Yousuf smiled. "No pay. This is a gift. Call it a welcome present."

"Oh, right. Erm… thanks."

"When you've sold this, if there's no problems, you can start buying from us. You have an existing clientele, it should be easy. Just don't get caught. And if you do, you keep your mouth shut, understand?"

"Got it. "Spider nodded. "I know the score."

"Make sure you do. The people you are working for now are very nice if you do well by them. Cross them or cause problems, and you'll pay. Big time."

"Right." Spider reached across to take the bag. As he did so, Yousuf clamped down hard on his arm and stared him in the eye.

"No-one is beyond their reach. Remember that."

Calloway was finishing up his morning report to the team on

yesterdays' chat with Taverner when Smith came into the incident room. She nodded and sat, placing some exhibit bags on the table in front of her. She waited for Calloway to finish, then stood.

"If I could, sarge? We've had a bit of a result. A search of all the bins in the park brought up something interesting. This photo was found in a bin at the park entrance closest to the crime scene." She held up the photo in its plastic bag and it was passed around the group. Calloway studied it.

"Interesting." he remarked. "A young woman, looks to be around the same age as our vic. In fact, looks somewhat similar to her. Very similar."

"She does. It was missed at first. I guess the people picking through wouldn't have known. I only saw it by chance, the likeness caught my eye. And there's more. I asked Jonesy to follow up. I believe he has some more info?"

"S'right." Jones flicked open his notebook. "Using that entrance as a starting point, we started door-to-door on the surrounding houses. In particular, we called on all the B&Bs. There's quite a few in those streets. Anyway, the punchline is we got a positive on our hit man. At least, someone who matches the descriptions from all the other witnesses."

"Great!" Calloway responded. "Too much to ask that he paid by cheque, I suppose?"

"It is. Cash. That's not unusual in these places. What was unusual, what made this guy stand out, was he's a lot younger than most of the lorry-driving crowd. Also, he didn't stay for breakfast and had no luggage other than an Adidas holdall."

"Okay. Well, it's not a lot but it's more than we've had so far.

Let's get that owner in for a photo-fit session, and see if we can ID the girl in the photograph. Has the photo been tested for prints, Smithy?"

"It has, sarge. Nothing clean, just a few partials. Forensics have no match."

"Okay. Anything else from witnesses?"

Turner answered. "We've had a late one come in. A woman reckons she saw our man at Ilford station. Said she would have come forward sooner but she's been away for a few days. Reckons she saw him going down the steps to platforms one and two. The Adidas bag is the clincher."

"Right, and where would he go from there?"

"Platform One takes you into Liverpool Street, Platform Two is the Southend line."

Calloway scratched his chin. "Get onto Essex then, get the description over to them for circulation. If someone saw him at this end, someone will have seen him when he got off. Get onto BTP too, in case he went the other way."

"If he went to Liverpool Street he could be anywhere," Pavitt pointed out.

"True." Calloway nodded. "But if he went the other way, his options are severely limited." He stood and walked to the large map on the wall, tapping it with his pen. "Southend, eh?"

The killer arrived an hour early at the pier. Having conducted the standard counter-surveillance routines on leaving the hotel, he stopped off at a shop, buying a baseball cap before strolling down to the the seafront. If there were any watchers in place around the pier, they were extremely good at their job. He doubted that the outfit he was dealing with had that level of skill. They were brutal and cunning, ruthless, certainly, but fieldwork was not their area of expertise. Satisfied, he sat on a bench and waited.

At three minutes to ten, two men approached. Both looked Turkish in origin. One was large, the obvious muscle. For protection and intimidation, no doubt, though the latter did not concern the hit-man. He had taken larger men down and this one, while big, looked dumb as an ox. He held an ice cream cone in his hand, licking at it like a child. The other man, smaller, smarter, sat next to him on the bench and nodded.

"You have my money?" the hit-man asked.

"Not exactly," the man replied, a gold tooth glinting in the sun."You see, there is a problem."

The hit-man did not like the sound of this. He slowly leaned forward, ready to leap to his feet if required. His right hand moved subtly towards the knife at his belt. His face was impassive. "Problem?"

"Yes. You see… you killed the wrong girl."

Chapter 11

The killer was livid. Not that had face showed any sign of his inner turmoil. Having said that, the meeting could have gone a lot worse. His clients were angry, of course, but there had been, as they had put it, "a silver lining." It turned out that the girl he had shot had been a close relative of a rival. A big gangland name, though it meant nothing to the hit-man. So while the hit was not the one required, it had not been without its uses. If nothing else, it achieved the aim of directly hurting a man who stood in direct opposition to his client's business expansion. The killer could guess what that business was. Drugs, most likely. Cocaine and heroin were flooding into Europe, they would be the next big thing. He had no thoughts on the subject, in much the same way he had no thoughts about shooting an innocent girl. Any thoughts were concerned only with himself and his embarrassment and anger at having made such an elementary mistake.

The words of his last instructor came back. *Never underestimate. Never take for granted. Always check, check twice, then check again.* The old bastard would have dished out a beating for a mistake such as this. Or worse. Still, as a freelancer, at least he had no concerns on that score. His clients, though, that was a different story. Fortunately, the hit had suited their purposes. Furthermore, the actual target was still in circulation, it appeared that no connection had been drawn between the two. Why would it? It was agreed, then, that the rest of the money would be forthcoming on completion of the original hit. That had been only fair, he could take no issue with that.

Irritatingly, though, it did mean spending more time in this country. He preferred not to spend too much time in any one place outside of his forested retreat back in France. The longer you stayed in one place, the more visible you became. But there was nothing for it. He would have to return to London.

Calloway nodded thanks to the court clerk as he walked over to the table in the canteen to let him know, "They're coming back in now."

Cab hastily finished his coffee and headed down to Court Four to hear the verdict. He'd been at Snaresbrook Crown Court for the whole of Tuesday and Wednesday. As arresting officer on a Handling Stolen Goods case, his attendance had been mandatory for questioning. The verdict came in as guilty on both men. Why they had pleaded not guilty, he couldn't work out. Most likely, they'd ignored the advice of their brief, hoping to rely on the sympathy of a local jury. But being caught with a van load of nicked car stereos, combined with the fact that people were getting fed up with having their car stereos nicked, obviously outweighed any anti-police sentiments.

Happy at the result, Calloway glanced at his watch as the court room emptied. Not worth going back to the station, and if anything major had come in, the team would have let him know. *Might as well grab a takeaway and get home.* Getting out of the building wasn't so easy, though. Snaresbrook was a big old Victorian pile, originally built as an orphanage. In the late 1930s it had been converted into a school; in fact Churchill had been a governor here. With the setting up of the Crown Court system in the seventies, the grand old building had been earmarked and converted for its new use. Plenty of the old building still remained, though, including the grand entrance lobby. A lobby that Calloway now tried to push his way through, the space being filled with a heaving mass of reporters and photographers. There was some sort of commotion going on outside, the court staff doing their best to maintain order and prevent a crush.

Calloway saw a familiar face among the press and called him over.

"Sammy! Sammy! Over here."

The young man elbowed his way clear of the scrum and grinned.

"Alright, Cab? What brings you here?"

Mark Samuels was one of the new breed of journalists, a change from the rakish boozers of the golden age of Fleet Street. Rather than a little black book, Sammy carried a Filofax, the latest must-have accessory from a company based just up the road in Barkingside. A sharp suit, a fashionable highlighted mullet, an expensive Rolex… he could have been a city banker rather than a journo. Cab had known Samuels for a few years, one of the first major contacts he'd made when moving down here. Most detectives had a tame reporter or two, it was something of a symbiotic relationship.

"Usual. HSG, nothing major. Got a result, though. You?"

"Part of the frenzy," he tutted. "You'd think a major celeb had killed someone, but it's just the local MP's daughter. Called in as a witness, her boyfriend's up on a charge. Bit of a wild child, by all accounts."

Calloway raised his eyebrows., "Really? Slow news day then?"

"Pretty much. Here, aren't you on the shooting of that girl in Valentines Park? Anything you wanna tell me?"

"Wish I had, Sammy. To be honest, we've hit a bit of a brick wall. No motive we can work out, aside from a family connection to Terry Taverner. You heard anything?"

"No, I haven't. And as far as Taverner goes, no-one's talking. Even the old hands on the paper won't go snooping around his outfit. Mind you, they're still scared shitless of Ronnie and Reggie. I keep telling them that times have changed, but, you know?"

"Aye, I know. Well, if you do hear anything."

"I'll give you a bell. And you likewise, eh? Usual arrangement?"

"Usual arrangement. Now, let's see if we can get out of this place…"

Spider patted the roll of notes in his pocket and smiled. His new friends had been right, the coke was flying out. He'd started with the Monday night session at the Regency. Usually a quiet one, but once word got round, he'd sold all the gear he'd taken there in half an hour. More important, he'd established himself as a supplier for people looking to graduate up from a few blues and the odd toot of whizz. Plus, a few of the lads who'd bought from him had links into other groups and gangs, which meant more business. He could even afford to give them a discount with the amount of potential trade they'd bring in. Now he was hitting the rest of his regular selling haunts and trade remained brisk, in fact he'd just sold all but two of his remaining bags.

Still, the figure of Pearce loomed large, even though he'd given the go ahead to get in bed with the Turks. Spider had got word to the big man detailing his activities, nothing had come back, so he presumed he was okay to sell. Despite that, he still felt a lurch in his stomach as, on this rainy Wednesday night, the Jag pulled into the car park of The Plough pub on Ilford Lane, just as he was leaving. He slipped into the rear door as it opened.

"Alright, son?" the bear-like form of Pearce growled in the semi-darkness.

"Yeah, all good Mr Pearce."

"So, you been doing some selling then?"

"Yes. Just like you told me, I phoned the Arikans, went along with what they said. They gave me some bugle to sell."

"Let's see it, then."

Spider's lip twitched. He had a horrible idea what was coming. He fished a remaining bag out of his pocket and handed it over. Pearce dipped his finger in as though it were sherbert. He nodded in appreciation.

"Good stuff! How much money have you made?"

Spider knew there was no point in arguing or lying. He removed the roll of notes from his other pocket and Pearce beckoned for it to be handed over.

"For fuck's sake," the expression was out before Spider realised he'd said it. Pearce scowled as he took the money.

"Perhaps you're forgetting who you work for, son?"

"Sorry, Mr Pearce, I didn't mean it. It won't happen again."

"See that it don't. Anyone who disrespects me pays for it. Remember that." Spider mumbled another apology as Pearce removed the rubber band and made a quick count. Withdrawing a few notes, he put the bundle in his own pocket. The few, he returned to Spider.

"Alright. You've done good. Here you go, this is for you. Keep it up. Now, listen. I want you to find out where they're shipping the stuff in from, alright? Where did you go to get the gear?"

Spider gave the address. "But Mr Pearce, if you hit it, they might suspect me. What with me being new and all that."

Pearce grunted. "You just worry about selling the gear, son. Leave the rest to me. Keep in touch!" He waved Spider out of the car and it slid off into the night, leaving a damper, and poorer, Tony Webb to tilt his head up into the rain and swear.

There was better news when Calloway got into the station next morning. The team had spent the last couple of days liasing with Essex Police and sifting through new witness statements. With the case being so high profile, the photo-fit from the B&B manager had gone out on TV, and local uniform had been out canvassing commuters at each station all the way down to Southend. Smith presented Calloway with the results, a number of possible sightings, particularly at Southend. After reading through them, Calloway nabbed Turner and the pair were soon driving east on the A127.

At Southend Police Station they interviewed one of the key witnesses who had come forward, a Mrs King who ran a hotel on the seafront. She enthusiastically told them about a "Mr Petersons" who had lodged with her until Monday just gone. "A foreign gentleman. I always thought there was something suspicious about him. What has he done?"

That done, and other statements checked, Calloway decided on a walk around the area. The pair now stood at the entrance to the pier, Turner trying to prevent the ice cream from his cone dripping on his suit.

Calloway glanced around. "So this is where cockneys come for a holiday?"

Turner lifted the cone away from his jacket. "Not so much any more. More likely to go to Malaga or Ibiza. These days Southend is more a day trip for the oldies. Or the kids." He nodded towards the Peter Pan Playground, where pumped out music competed with the joyful screams of children.

"So why would our killer come here? Jump on a boat over to the Continent? Southend Airport?"

Turner shrugged. "We checked at the airport, zero sightings of our man there. He could easily have slipped away on a boat, mind. Plenty of smuggling still goes on here. Dope, pills, people. And no-one involved in that is going to be phoning us up. "

"In which case, we're screwed." Calloway took out and lit a cigarette. "Sod it. Let's get back to London."

The hit-man was well settled into his new digs. Catching a train back to London, he'd first moved first to a cheap hotel in Seven Kings, close to the station, only to discover the place had been what they called locally a "knocking shop." After a couple of sleepless nights, he'd moved to a slightly more upmarket place in Newbury Park. More pleasant but further from his target. The presumption was that the target was still following her usual routine, though he was waiting to hear from his employers if that were the case. He wondered if it would not be easier for them to do the job themselves, seeing as how they obviously had surveillance on the girl. *Perhaps even hardened gangsters have their limits,* he thought.

Worse news came when he'd flicked on the small TV in the room in the brothel. As was his habit, he hadn't looked at any newspapers, so seeing a photo-fit of his face flash up on the local news program had come as a shock. It wasn't a total likeness, and he lacked any distinguishing features - unless you counted being described as "distinctly average." That was exactly how he liked it. Still, the image was close enough to prompt a stab of fear, followed by a flash of anger at the situation. The Adidas bag was also mentioned and he resolved to dump it immediately.

That evening he'd gone to the phone box outside the hotel and thumbed through the Yellow Pages. His first step the next day had been to visit a local fancy dress shop. The wigs were way too cheap and obvious for his purposes, but he did buy some fake glasses and facial hair. That, and a change of clothing, was a good start. Those he bought at a nearby department store, being sure also to buy an unbranded holdall in which to put them.

Now, in a new brown leather bomber jacket, black jeans and Dealer boots, he'd caught a bus up to Newbury Park to these new digs. Giving the name "Mr Wozniak," he booked in and now sat in the small room eating fish and chips from the local takeaway.

He'd bought a couple of national papers to flick through too, cursing at the coverage the job had got. Normally, that wouldn't be a problem, he'd be out of the country by now, but as he still had to operate in the same area, it could present difficulties. First step, relocate the target. The park may not be the best place for the hit, now. He consulted the intel notes, checking his AtoZ for her work address. That may be easier. Busier, plenty of places to slip away. But maybe too busy. Her home, then? A break-in, perhaps? That would take some surveillance but would give him more control over timing. *Yes, a break-in.* But best to lay low for a few days first, given the coverage. He threw the vinegar-soaked wrapping in the bin and began making plans.

Chapter 12

The mood at the Friday morning briefing had been improved, largely due to news of two more possible sightings that had come in overnight. Jones provided the details, one from a ticket clerk at Southend, the other from a passenger on a west-bound train.

"So judging from the times of each of those sightings, our man has headed back to London," Calloway said. "Question is, why? Another hit?"

"We still don't know why he did the first one," Pavitt pointed out.

"Aye, true." Calloway turned to face the evidence board again. "Though a hit on Taverner seems the likeliest explanation. Perhaps he's back for the man himself?"

"Should we let him know, skip?" asked Turner.

"I suppose so. At the very least, we need to get some eyes on him."

"Not easy," Jones leaned back in his chair. "I was part of an op a couple of years back. We were trying to get something on our Terry as part of an anti OC operation. His estate is like a fortress, eyes and ears everywhere. He always has at least one bodyguard with him, not to mention Pearce."

There were nods and mumbles around the room at mention of that name. Calloway held up a hand. "What's the deal with this Pearce? Why the long faces?"

Houlihan answered. "He's Taverner's enforcer. Guy's a total psycho, skip. One step beyond your average thug. Intimidation, violence, torture. Always managed to stay out of our reach, though, apart from a couple of minor charges years back. The locals are terrified of him and not without reason. I wouldn't want to go up against him."

Calloway was momentarily silent. A man who could daunt Houlihan was not a man to be taken lightly. "Alright. Well, regardless, let's see if we can get some type of surveillance going. Jonesy, I'll leave that to you and Houlihan. Pavitt and Turner, you can check the witnesses this time, get all the statements back to Smith. Have a scout around the stations, too. Our guy was seen on a west bound train, so check everywhere from, say, Brentwood to Liverpool Street."

Denham came into the room at that moment. "Morning all. Everything alright?"

Calloway nodded. "Morning, guv. Yes, we have some new sightings, we're checking them out now."

"Good. Listen, Cab, I don't like to to do this, but can you spare me one of your team?"

"I guess so," Calloway frowned. "If it's something urgent."

"It is, and it shouldn't take long. Pavitt?"

The young DC came over. "Guv?"

"You were a Crime Reduction Officer, right?"

"Yes, guv. After probation, I was a CRO for six months before applying for CID. Why?"

"There's a little job I want you to do." He handed Pavitt a yellow Post-it note. "Go to this address tomorrow first thing and give it a security review. A proper going over. They'll be expecting you. Be on your best behaviour, this is a friend of the Chief Super. Good golfing buddies, apparently."

Calloway grunted. "Oh, you mean...*golf*." He mimicked a funny handshake.

Denham shook his head. "That cynicism will get you in trouble one day, Cab."

Calloway turned back to the team. "Turner, you're on your own it seems. If you need any help, take Smith with you. Alright, folks, you all know what you've to do, let's get out there and do it."

On the way back to his office, Calloway bumped into Gemma carrying an armful of papers.

"Oops, sorry!" he held his hands up then bent to help pick up the folders.

"No, my fault, I was miles away."

"Anywhere nice?" He smiled and stared straight into her emerald green eyes.

She gave a musical laugh. "Leytonstone. Hardly the Bahamas."

They both stood, Calloway touched her arm. "Your dad?"

Gemma bit her lip. "Yep, still having trouble getting him in anywhere. He's been worse these last few days, too."

Calloway grunted, a silence hung between them for a moment.

He coughed. "Well, I can't do anything about that. But if you fancy a break, I can't manage the Bahamas right now, but how about we go out for a meal or something? I'm catching up on paperwork this evening, but how about tomorrow night?"

"That would be nice." She laid a hand on Cab's forearm. "I can't go very far, though. Or stay out for long. I don't like leaving Dad on his own."

His face fell. "Oh aye, well, if you'd rather leave it for another time?"

"No, no," she reassured him. "Tell you what. Do you know the Walnut Tree on Leytonstone High Road? They do nice food there."

"I'll find it. What time?"

"About seven thirty?"

Calloway grinned. "Great! See you there!"

Spider drained the pint glass and plonked it on the bar. He waved to a couple of associates as he left the pub. Turning up the collar of his new jacket, he crossed the street, heading for the home of one of his girlfriends. She'd promise to cook him a nice dinner... and more. The thought of a leg-over brought a grin to his face. It had been a good day. Even minus Pearce's cut, he'd made a solid wedge from selling the coke. He'd decided on a trip up West earlier that day, spending most of the Saturday browsing the clothes shops round Carnaby Street.

He'd decided on some new clobber. The football lads at Upton Park were drifting away from the sixties look and Spider decided to drift with them. Besides, the mod thing looked to be on its way out, there were too many kids and third class poseurs getting into it now.

The new look was all about sports casual, designer labels, flash trainers. The top ICF faces were all sporting Sergio Taccini, Ellesse, Lacoste, a far cry from the old boots and braces look. And where the faces led, others followed. Besides, the new look would allow Spider to fit into places easier, allow him to spread his sphere of operations beyond the mod scene.

So here he was, decked out in his new gear, minted, and heading for bit of the other. There was only one cloud in his sky - the van. He'd noticed it earlier, as he'd walked to the pub. He could make out a vague face behind the wheel, not one that he recognised. For some reason, he had a vague tickle at the back of his brain. Spider had been on the street long enough to know that you always listened to your instinct. And here the van was again, still parked outside the pub. *Old Bill?* Maybe. Still, they had nothing on him. He dismissed the concern, the van could sit outside his girlfriend's house all night for all he cared.

Nonetheless, he picked up his pace and ducked down a side alley as a short cut. He was almost at the far end when a car screeched to a halt across it, a silver BMW. Two men jumped out of the back. Spider didn't wait to see what they wanted, he turned and ran. The alleyway had bins along it, Spider tipped a couple over as he ran, hoping to buy some time. He heard swearing behind him or, at least, gruff words in a foreign language. The pounding footsteps didn't stop, though.

Spider felt a hand grab his collar, without thought he span and fired out a couple of punches. One connected hard, the pursuer stumbling back with an *ooof.* Spider gave a bark of laughter and turned to run again. His face dropped when two more men stepped out at the alleyway entrance. He recognised the larger one - Serkan, Ismet's minder. The first punch from him brought sparks to Spider's eyes. The second one brought oblivion.

Cab allowed himself a broad smile as he drove home. The date that night had gone really well. The couple enjoyed a nice drink and meal at the pub and then he'd walked Gemma back to her flat. At the entrance she'd halted and turned, looking up at him.

"I would invite you in for coffee. But Dad, you know?"

"I understand, it's fine. Maybe next time you'd like to come over to mine. I make a passable spag bol, I'm told."

"Yes, I'd like that." She stood on tiptoe, put her arms around his neck and kissed him. Then she was gone.

Tapping his hands on the wheel in time to the Miles Davis track, he swung the car into his street and, eventually, found a parking space. Swinging his keys around his finger, he was heading for the entrance of the flats when five shapes detached themselves from the shadows and barred his path.

"Hello, pig," growled one of them.

Calloway stopped and swore under his breath. It was the lad from the Carpenter's Arms, Billy, a piece of tape across the bridge of his nose. His friends spread out, two on each side.

"Now, let's think about this, lads." Cab raised his palms. "No-one wants any trouble." Nonetheless he shifted to the balls of his feet, dropping his weight slightly. "Remember what Mr Taverner said, right?"

"Mr Taverner won't find out," Billy hissed. "And you won't be in any state to do anything at all."

Calloway stalled for time, it seemed his the only option. "And how did you know where I live?"

Billy gave a low chuckle. "Half your lot are in our pocket, copper. Dirty filth. We know everything that goes on."

The lads came forward slowly, spreading across the paved area in front of the flats. Calloway took a few steps back, trying to keep each of the gang in view. He'd been in a few rucks in his time, but five to one was not good odds. Best he could hope for was a beating. Still, he was not the type to go down without a fight.

With a shout Calloway shot forward and right, throwing a fast jab that caught the nearest lad square in the face. He span on the spot, throwing a hook at the second attacker as he rushed forward, but this one was prepared, He ducked back, avoiding the punch, lashing out with a kick. His distance was off but the kick still caught Calloway a glancing blow on the thigh. It gave the other three the opportunity to swarm forward and Calloway found himself under a hail of blows. He dodged and weaved as much as he could, and felt at least one of his own hits land with a satisfying thud. But it was hopeless. A fist caught him in the kidneys, another glanced off the side of his head. Half stunned, he staggered back, into the low wall behind him.

There came a pause. One of the attackers was bent over, hands on knees, wincing. Calloway took some satisfaction in seeing that Billy's nose was pouring with blood again but the end was in sight. Trying to catch his breath, Calloway was horrified to see Billy's hand disappear and reappear with a knife, it's cold blade glinting in the glow of the street lights.

"Gonna carve you up, copper." Bill grinned, teeth showing white against the dark red.

Calloway swore again. He had nothing on him to use as either a weapon, or for defence. He straightened up, coughed and spat, growling out his defiance. "Come on then, you wee cockney shite. I'll give ye a pasting yet."

The group advanced and Calloway swallowed, gritting his teeth in preparation for the final assault. Suddenly a vague shape streaked out of the shadows. The man at the rear of the group gave a short, choked cry and fell heavily to the ground. His friends turned to confront this newcomer, but the figure was like smoke, darting in and out of the group. Another one was down in an instant, face contorted in agony. The next swung at the attacker, who seemed to flow under the strike, coming up inside it to deliver three short, sharp hits that sent the lad reeling back. But the figure had not paused, he span like a dancer to deliver a face kick to the bent over lad, sending him tumbling back in a heap.

Billy snarled and slashed out viciously with the blade. Again, the man did that weird movement, weaving around the slice, simultaneously trapping Billy's elbow. There was a sickening crunch, a high pitched scream and Billy fell to the floor, clutching his arm. Calloway's unknown saviour moved to his side, grabbing him, pulling him towards the front door.

"What - who - wha-?"

The only response was a heavily accented whisper. "My name is Sergei. We need to talk."

Chapter 13

Calloway winced again as he sat down.

"I don't think anything is broken," his guest smiled. "But you might want to take it easy for a few days."

They had rushed inside and up the stairs following the fight. The gang had fled, dragging their wounded with them. In the flat, Calloway got his first good look at his rescuer. Dressed in stone-washed jeans, trainers and an olive green bomber jacket, slim, not a tall man, barely up to Cab's shoulder. But he carried himself with an air of confidence and moved with a compact litheness that put Calloway in mind of a gymnast. This Sergei had short fair hair and an easy smile. In fact he seemed totally nonplussed at having despatched four attackers within as many minutes. Calloway noticed that he'd eyed the whisky bottle on the side, though, so he poured both his guest and himself a stiff measure.

Now they sat at the kitchen table, each with a half-full tumbler in hand.

"You said we need to speak. So who are you and where are you from? Oh, and thanks, by the way."

"You're welcome. Nice to meet you." He raised the tumbler in salute. "As I said, my name is Sergei. I am from Moscow. I am here for same reason as you, Mr Calloway. To find killer."

"Well I hope you are having better luck than we are, Sergei. But why here? Why me?"

"You are leading the investigation, yes? It was easier to meet you here at your home rather than your place of work. Too many questions there." Sergei smiled again.

"Jesus, does everyone know where I live?" Calloway took another swig of the fiery liquid.

Sergei shrugged. "Such things are easy for us to find out."

"And who is *us*, exactly?"

Sergei's expression suddenly turned to stone. "First, you have to promise that you will repeat nothing of this conversation. Not a word, even to your superiors."

"As a serving police officer, I can't promise that, Sergei." Calloway paused and rubbed the bump on his head. "But... seeing as how you saved me from a beating, maybe even worse, I'll promise this. If what you tell me doesn't break any major laws, I can overlook any... irregularities. You have my word." He held his hand out.

Sergei stared him directly in the eye for a moment, then accepted the handshake.

"Very well. My name is Sergei Baranov of the GRU. I am in this country, how to say... *unofficially*? My superiors assigned me job of tracking down a certain operative. The man I believe was responsible for the murder you investigate."

Calloway's eyebrows rose in surprise. "GRU? That's what,

something like the KGB? Spetsnaz?"

Sergei nodded. "You might say so. Yes, I am Spetsnaz."

"And who is this man? Why are you after him?"

"His name is Andrejs Laçis. He is from Latvia and, like myself, was Spestnaz trained. For a time he worked in various roles for my government. Later, he… left and now hires himself out as an assassin to criminal elements. Here." He reached into his jacket pocket and withdraw a plastic folder. He removed a photo from it and slid it across the table. Calloway picked it up and nodded.

"Aye, I'd say that was our guy. Or, at least, it matches the photo-fit. But how does a Latvian hit-man turn up in East London?"

Sergei sat back in his chair, swirling the remaining whisky in his glass. "We guess he has been recommended by a major drug cartel to a group here in London. One we presume is trafficking drugs for that cartel. Your capitalist countries are awash with drugs, no?" He gave a sardonic smile.

Calloway had to concede the point. "That they are. And it's growing worse. Okay, but why shoot a young girl? The only connection we can draw is to her uncle, a local gangster."

"This I do not know. And to be honest, is not my concern. My task is to find and neutralise this man."

"So you're a hit-man for the hit-man?" Cab replied. "Seems your communist countries are awash with trained killers?" He arched an eyebrow.

Sergei smiled. "Indeed. And we are keen to put an end to the activities of this one. It does not look good for our security services to have such a rogue element at large. My superiors like to keep things… tidy?"

Now Calloway smiled. "I can relate to that. My superiors are much the same."

"And it is men such as us who are expected to deal with the trash, yes?"

"Aye, that it is, Sergei, that is is. But what now? I understand you wouldn't wish your activities to become known to the authorities. But why should I help you?"

Sergei nodded. "It is fair question. And yes, should your authorities become aware of my presence in your country, I would no doubt be apprehended and sent home - or worse. However, I think without my help you will find it very hard to find this man. And should you find him, even more hard to deal with. He was one of our top operatives. He is very capable."

"Capable is not the word I'd choose for a man who can shoot a teenage girl in cold blood, but I take your point. Okay, Sergei, what next?"

"I would like to shadow your investigation. I will not intervene, though I will offer any information where it might help. You should remember that I can operate without restriction. And I know how this man thinks. I know how he has been trained."

"And in return?"

"I realise that this may be difficult for you. Once located, I shall neutralise Laçis."

"By neutralise you mean kill?"

Sergei raised his palms. "I would like to return him alive. I doubt he would be happy to go with me, though."

Calloway sighed. "You're right. That is difficult for me. Impossible. You're asking me to sanction murder. That's not how we do things here."

Sergei tilted his head and raised his eyebrows. "You think not? That scientist who caused so many problems for your government recently. The one found hanging from a tree. You think that was suicide? Or Bulgarian man found in the Thames last month, his pockets full of bricks. Accident?"

"Alright, alright. So no government has clean hands. But I'm not the government, I'm a copper. This is my patch and I'll not have cold-blooded executions, no matter how well deserved." He took out a pack of cigarettes, offering one to the Russian. Sergei shook his head.

"I understand. This is your duty. Well, perhaps we can, what is the expression? Go over the bridge when we arrive at it?"

Calloway lit the Marlboro and took a long drag. "Shite. Okay then. We help each other out. But when he is found, the bastard is arrested and charged. What happens after that is out of my hands."

Sergei smiled. "Thank you. I will be in touch." He finished off the whisky and stood.

"Where are you staying? Are you local?"

"There is a Russian businessman based in London. He provides a place in -"

"Okay, I don't need to know. How do I contact you if I need to?"

"No need, I will not be far away." He took out a card and scribbled a number on it. "But if it is urgent, call this number and say only *can I borrow a match?* That is all."

"Jesus, what am I getting into? Alright, then. We'll speak soon."

Chapter 14

Spider came to and panicked. He couldn't see, he couldn't move, he could barely breathe. The bag was ripped from his head and he blinked against the sudden light shining directly in his face. His wrists and ankles were gaffer taped to the stout wooden chair beneath him. Two vague shapes, silhouettes, moved around him. His jaw ached, one of his teeth felt loose. He coughed and spat blood.

"Where am I? What the fuck is this?"

He stiffened in fear as the face of Yousuf loomed into view. "You are in our place, that's all you need to know. I have some questions for you."

"I don't understand. What's going on?"

The backhanded slap snapped Spider's head back. He cried out, in pain and fear.

"I ask the questions. One thing I said to you, don't cause problems, remember? And what happens last night? The restaurant... the place where you came to pick up the merchandise. It was hit last night. Professional job, a group, just at closing time. They smashed the place up, then cleared out the upstairs. Luckily, there was little merchandise there but three of our people are in hospital. Now, who would know that we use the upstairs of a nondescript restaurant as one of our storage places? Who, Spider?"

"I don't know, I don't know anything about this. I mean, yes, obviously I know about the restaurant. But I never told anyone about it, honest." He flinched as Yousuf bent forward again. But there was no hit this time, just a hissed response.

"That remains to be seen. You know what I think? I think you went running off to your East London friends. I think you told them all about our meeting. I told Ismet this was a mistake."

"No, I didn't, honest! I never said nothing! Cross me heart."

"And hope to die?" Yousuf sneered. "You'll understand we won't take the word of a lowlife drug dealer. No, we must be certain. We must find the truth."

He stepped back and Spider was able to make out more of the room. A typical garage workshop, tool benches, an inspection pit. As he watched, an older man came though the small door in the closed shutter at the front. He walked over to a large car battery on a trolley, removed an object from the holdall he was carrying, and began wiring it up. Spider swallowed hard but dare not say anything. Yousuf nodded and the trolley was wheeled over next to the chair. Spider began to struggle, to no avail, the tape held him firm. The older man was now standing behind him, just out of view.

"So let me ask you again, my friend." Yousuf spoke quietly. "Who did you tell?"

"No-one, I -" he screamed in again as pain surged throughout his nervous system. The skin on his neck burned from where the cattle prod had touched him.

"You know, old Mehmet here is an expert at this sort of thing.

Years of experience in the police force back home. He can make this last for hours. Days."

Spider struggled against his bonds again, eyes stinging with tears. "I swear, I don't know!"

Yousuf nodded to his other accomplice, the man knelt and quickly removed Spider's trainers and socks. He cut through the tape on one ankle with a knife, then pulled Spider's leg out straight, exposing the sole of his foot. Mehmet advance again, prod extended, a cruel smile on his pock-marked face.

"No! *No!*" Spider squirmed, trying to push back in the chair. It tilted but Yousuf held it steady, bending to whisper in his ear.

"Last chance or you won't be walking for months. No?" He nodded.

The door in the shutter burst open and three large shapes surged into the garage. One smashed the man holding Spider's leg over the head with an iron bar. Mehmet was grabbed and pulled back, disappearing out of view. The third hammered Yousuf in the side of the head with a ring-laden fist. Spider pushed back again, this time the chair tipped completely over. He found himself staring an unconscious Yousuf in the face. A familiar gruff voice barked out orders.

"Get the lad up. Put that one in the chair."

Spider felt his bonds disappear and he stood unsteadily. A wave of nausea over came him and he turned, bent and retched. Pearce's heavy hand fell on his shoulder.

"Looks like we got here just in time, son," he chuckled.

Spider straightened, wiping his mouth with his track suit sleeve.

"Mr Pearce? But how did you get here? How did you know?"

Realisation hit him. One of Pearce's men was the driver of the white van he'd spotted earlier. "You were following me. You set me up. You used me as bait! You cunt!"

The word was out before he could stop it. Peace's eyes narrowed and the paw moved from Spider's shoulder to the top of his head. He moved his face so close, Spider could smell the whiskey on his breath.

"You already had one warning about disrespecting me, boy. Tread carefully."

"Yes, Mr Pearce. Sorry, Mr Pearce."

"Alright. Let's get you away from here. Danny, stick him in the back of the van."

"Righto, boss. What about these three?"

"Give that pair a good shoeing and dump 'em in the pit. This one," he nudged the slowly rousing Yousuf with the toe of his handmade brogue, "Get him in the chair and bind him up."

Danny motioned to Spider who wasted no time in heading for the exit. He paused as he got there. "Oh, hang on." Danny looked at him quizzically. "Me trainers. They cost fifty quid!" Spider explained, heading back to grab the shoes. His last sight before heading out the door was of Yousuf, eyes widening in fear, being forced into the chair as a grinning Pearce weighed the cattle prod in his hand.

Andrejs Laçis cursed softly as he walked past the house again. Despite it being eight in the evening, the girl's house had a small group of people outside it. He had thought maybe they were waiting to go in, or perhaps waiting for a cab or something. But a ten minute walk around the block, and they were still there. He had stolen a bicycle to get down here from his hotel, it was quick ride down and more covert than public transport. He wheeled the bike slowly past the group, pausing to switch off the Walkman as he reached them. All men, most with cameras. Newspaper reporters, then? But why? With his face having been in the local press, he didn't want to risk speaking to them, even with the fake moustache and glasses. Instead, he pulled the baseball cap forward and walked on. There had been a burger bar on the way here. Swinging a leg over the saddle, he pressed play again on the Walkman and set off for it.

As he ate his bland burger and chips, Laçis pondered his options. Just leaving the country had crossed his mind. The problem was that this might have consequences. Not from his clients, their reach would not extend so far. But the cartel that had recommended him, that was a different story. Although he was extremely careful as to who he spoke to and how he communicated with them, with how he was paid and how secretive his forest home was, he was not naive enough to imagine he was beyond their reach. To them, such an act would be seen as a grave, personal insult. He doubted they truly cared anything for the opinions of the London gang, but such an affront could not go unpunished. No, leaving was not an option. Still, the longer he remained here, the more vulnerable he became, both to the local authorities and to those who may wish him ill.

He laughed briefly to himself as he swilled the remaining chips down with a swig of Coca-cola. Of course, any hit-man would have enemies, that went without saying. That was one reason for his secretive lifestyle, but it went deeper than that. During his time in service, his special forces training had been put to good use in a variety of roles. But that all changed on his last mission for the Soviet regime. An argument with a senior officer over the fate of a prisoner had led to the idiot drawing a pistol on him. It was the last thing he ever did. Laçis gunned the man down on the post.

Forced to flee, he had naturally headed west. Not as a defector, he had no interest in politics. It was a Serbian gang, the Magaš crew, who had first taken him in. They had put his Spetsnaz experience to good use. In turn he had been well hidden and paid, earning enough cash to eventually buy his own place. Word of his skills spread until, one day the cartel had come calling. Since then, Laçis had largely worked for them directly, or their business partners.

The arrangement suited him. The cartel paid significantly more than the Serbs, allowing him to insulate himself even further from prospective avengers. Despite that, there was always that tickle at the back of his mind, that knowledge that his former Soviet employees would by very keen to find him. Desertion was bad enough, murdering an officer prior to doing so meant a death sentence. He wondered if even the cartel protection would be enough in that case? In a way, he was surprised that the cartel were doing business with such a small London outfit, he reasoned there must be a connection back via the larger Turkish mafia groups.

Still, that was all history and speculation. Here and now, he had a job to do, with seemingly few opportunities to do it. Home, work, park, social life… these were all potential access points to the target, though each came with difficulties. He had a sudden thought of another. *Parents*. Presumably the girl had family? That might be worth looking into. He resolved to speak to Ismet for more information.

Chapter 15

Calloway found himself wincing again, this time as he slid out of his jacket to hang it over the back of the chair.

"Not often we see you here on a Sunday. Blimey, what happened?" It was Denham, stood in the office doorway, pack of mints in hand.

"Slipped on the steps at home last night." Calloway lied. "Just a few bruises, I'm fine."

"Bang your head as well, did you?" Denham gestured to the bruises on Calloway's face.

Cab forced a smile. "Aye, that I did. Bit pished, I guess."

Denham arched an eyebrow. "Okay. Anyway, I hear you got a result on the car stereo mob?"

"I did, they're up for sentencing next month."

"Good, good. Oh, by the way, it's the Clark girl's funeral tomorrow, would you mind going? It's at ten hundred at the City of London."

"Of course, guv. No problem."

"Speaking of which, any news on the case?" He moved into the office and sat down, popping a Polo mint into his mouth. Cab thought for a second about last night's meeting with Sergei. By rights, he should be telling his guv all about it, or at least the name of the hit-man, but something held him back. Not that he mistrusted Denham, he was sure the man was clean. But if walls had ears, he wanted to keep this info under wraps for the moment; give the Russian time to dig around, see what he could find out. He tapped the folder on his desk. "Just these. More witness statements to read through. Nothing major, though, from what Smith said."

"Well, here's something you might find interesting. There was a report came in last night of an abduction in Barkingside."

"Abduction, guv?"

"Yes. Three people phoned it in. A young man, apparently being assaulted and forced into the back of a car."

"Unusual for Barkingside. But what's the interest?"

"The description matches our man Anthony Webb. And, it seems, Barkingside is where he has one of his haunts."

"I see. Any description of the attackers?"

Denham nodded. "*Foreign*, apparently. One witness said Middle Eastern, another said Turkish looking."

"Oh Christ. What's he got mixed up in?"

"There's more. Turns out that on Friday night, a restaurant in Wood Green got turned over. Proper job, from the sound of it. A Turkish restaurant. It flagged up on the system, I only noticed it this morning."

"So this is the start of the war, then? Taverner against the north London crowd?"

"Looks like it. The Arikans are the biggest mob in that neck of the woods. Turkish-Cypriots, I think. Perhaps they're muscling in on Taverner's drug market, and this Webb got caught in the middle? You might want to give Wood Green CID a call."

"I will. Ties in what I've heard." Cab agreed. "There's been tons more coke about this year. I'm not sure that's Taverner's scene. I mean you need good international connections for that, he's largely local. A bit of puff from Amsterdam, perhaps, but high-grade coke? That has major cartel written all over it... and that spells trouble."

"Times are changing, indeed." Denham drummed his fingers on the desk.

"And speaking of Taverner," Calloway continued. "Guv, I've heard things from a couple of places. Word is that Taverner might have, er... eyes on us, if you know what I mean? Someone on the inside, so to speak."

"You mean a bent copper?" Denham narrowed his eyes.

"Aye, I suppose. Just what I've heard."

"Anyone in mind, Cab? It's a serious allegation."

"No, guv. Just general rumours."

"Well, you always get those. But to be fair, it's not impossible. That's one thing that comes of having all your coppers local, they grow up rubbing elbows with the villains. And there's always someone open to a bung. You've heard all the talk about Hackney?"

Calloway nodded. He had, they all had. You couldn't miss it. The rumour mill was buzzing with stories of drugs being confiscated then sold out of Hackney police station - and worse. "I have, guv. What a mess. Seems you can't trust anyone these days."

"Is that why you're not telling me everything?" Denham crossed his arms.

Calloway sighed heavily. He should have known better than to try and put one over on someone as shrewd and experienced as Denham. "No, guv. It's not that at all. It's just a bit… complicated. Give me a few days."

Denham stood, brushing an imagined speck of dust from his sleeve. "Alright. I'll take that as a vote of confidence. I'm off on a conference for three days. That's the time you have, Cab, that's it. I'll have a word with the Chief before I go. I'll relay your concerns to him, then it's up to him to proceed with any potential corruption investigation. In the meantime, you crack on. Upstairs is going mad on the Clark case. We need a result."

Sergei sipped the coffee and peered again over the top of his shades. From his vantage point of the table by the window, he had a good view of the house on the corner. In particular, he could spot anyone coming in and out of the front gate. He was in Seven Kings, following up a possible sighting of Laçis. The place was a brothel, and word had come through by certain channels to his case officer that a man fitting the hit-man's description had stayed here. It was a long shot, but the geography was right - and this was a not generally a house where men stayed for more than an hour.

He thought back to last night's meeting with Calloway and smiled. The policeman had been prepared to fight the gang confronting him. The man was a fighter. No surprise, given he was Scottish. Sergei had once been told, rightly or wrongly, that the Scots had been involved in more battles and wars than any other nationality. Given that, and their propensity for strong drink, it was no wonder that Russians felt an affinity. Still, very few men could take on so many attackers and prevail, particularly if blades were involved.

Sergei had timed his entry for maximum effect. *When outnumbered, hit fast, hit hard. Don't stop moving. Bang! Bang Bang!* He heard his instructor's raspy voice again. The old man had been a veteran of the Great Patriotic War, member of a long-range patrol team. He'd carried out numerous missions behind fascist lines before being recalled to Moscow. There, he had been instrumental in setting up and training what would, in the 1950s, become known as the *Spetsnaz*. Specialist troops designed to infiltrate, reconnoitre, carry out sabotage, assassinations and similar missions. During the Cold War their role had expanded, even more so with the advent of the invasion of Afghanistan. That was not a time that Sergei liked to dwell on. Occasional nightmares still plagued him from those days.

This was his third coffee. He reasoned he couldn't sit here much longer. A golden rule of surveillance was to be unnoticed. Not unseen, not hiding, just unnoticed. Building a hide was fine in the *taiga*. Urban camouflage was a different skill, the ability to blend, to not stand out in the crowd. His instructor's voice floated up from the depths of memory again. *You should be able to follow a man for two weeks. Every day, you stand next to him on the train. You are three behind him in the queue. And it is fine if he sees you, that is to be expected. But he must never **notice** you.*

Sergei drained the cup and stood, folding the Sunday paper. Tucking it under his arm, he strode outside. As he did so, the front door of the house opened, and a figure hurried out. Despite the warm, spring weather the man wore a long coat, the collar pulled up around his ears. *Concealment or embarrassment?* Sergei paralleled the man's course on the opposite side of the street, matching his pace. Unless the man looked round, he would be unable to see his face. He was not so concerned about Laçis seeing him as such, there was no reason that the man would know or recognise him. And true, it was always better to remain hidden for a long as possible, yet Sergei needed to be sure.

He picked up his pace, getting ahead of the figure opposite. The man was heading up towards the station. If that was his destination, he would be crossing the road. *Yes!* The man glanced over his shoulder and stepped off the kerb. Sergei halted, opening the paper as if checking something. The man crossed and passed right by, not even glancing at the figure leaning against the brick wall than ran down this side of the station road. *No, not him.* A flushed man in his fifties, no doubt rushing back to his wife for Sunday lunch. Sergei folded the paper again and sighed. His gut instinct told him his man was not at this house - if he ever truly had been. Maybe for a night but it was not a place an experienced operative would choose as a base. Too many people coming and going. *Or coming, then going*, Sergei chuckled to himself. No, he would most likely be holed up somewhere a little more upmarket, though not too much.

He spotted a red phone box outside the station and slipped into it. Wrinkling his nose, he opened the Yellow Pages. *Why did these places always smell of urine? Could English people not use a lavatory?* Thumbing through the pages, he scoured the entries for Bed and Breakfasts and hotels. It was as he feared, there were dozens listed within a mile or so radius. *Like looking for the wind in a field*, as the expression went. This called for another strategy. He would return to the small flat he had been allocated and gather more intelligence.

His handler's team would be scanning local police frequencies and intel was no doubt being gathered by other agents. Everyone was operating under a tight budget these days, and Sergei felt that scant resources had been allocated to him for this job. He had even dared to put in a complaint about it, which appeared to have been ignored. Still, perhaps something more concrete would emerge. He dropped the newspaper in a bin and, taking one last glance around, disappeared into the station.

Chapter 16

"Get in there, son!" Taverner shouted from the touchline. His two minders stood a discrete distance behind him, ignoring the wary glances of the other spectators. Out on the pitch, his grandson swerved one defender and kicked for goal. The keeper was well placed, though, and easily saved the shot.

"Unlucky! Good boy, Billy!" Seconds later, the final whistle blew and the schoolboy teams ran laughing from the pitch. Billy headed straight for Taverner. "Did you see my shot, Grandad? Did you see it?"

"I did, son. Well done. You were unlucky not to get a goal there." Taverner turned as he saw Pearce striding across the playing field out of the corner of his eye. "Tell you what. You run along with your mates and get changed, then I'll take you for a burger. Alright?" He ruffled Billy's hair.

"Yeah, great!"

Pearce waited for the boy to leave before approaching.

"Well?" Taverner nodded.

"It worked. They snatched Webb, we followed."

"The Turks, then?"

"Yes, T. The Arikans. The geezer I had a chat with is one of their cousins, name of Yousuf."

"A chat you say?"

Pearce gave a shark-like smile. "Bit of instant justice, T. I just gave him what he was giving the lad. Took a while but he spilled his guts in the end. They always do."

"And?"

"Turns out they've got a hit-man in. Top bloke, apparently, East European."

"And it was him who killed my Trish?" Taverner scowled.

"Yes, T. We've got everyone out looking. The old bill put a photo-fit out already. If he's still in London, we'll find him."

Taverner exhaled heavily. "Right. It's the funeral tomorrow." He looked down to the floor.

"Yeah, about that..." The big man moved in closer, speaking softly. "If they have this shit-hot feller working for them, it might be best you lay low. The Turks are bound to know about the funeral. What if they send this guy there? Might be best to..."

Taverner's head snapped up, his eyes glaring coldly into Pearce's. For the first time in many years, the big man felt a shiver of fear up his spine.

"I'm going. That's it. I know my sister won't be happy about it, but I'm going. If this cunt wants to come and have a pop at me, then bring it on. Besides, you can secure the place, right? Call in whoever you need. You're my guard dog, so guard. See to it!"

With that he strode off towards the dressing rooms, his minders trailing in his wake, leaving a scowling Pearce at the touchline.

Laçis was on his feet as soon as he heard the soft knock on his door. He opened it a crack to reveal the landlord.

"Mr Wozniak? There's a phone call for you downstairs."

He thanked the man and followed him to the hall. The familiar, accented voice spoke instantly.

"We need to meet. Today. Now."

"Very well. One second." He thought for a second. "There is a park near to here. A small memorial gardens directly on the A12."

"Be there. Thirty minutes."

Laçis returned to his room, took a few things, then went straight to the gardens. He was less concerned about trouble than his last meeting, but old habits died hard. The place was public but would be quiet on a late Sunday afternoon. He had walked there once or twice over the previous days, it was little more than a large patch of grass around a war memorial. Within minutes he was there again. As expected, there was a sole dog walker who was soon gone. Laçis stood for a moment in front of the monument, a tall cross, before which a bronze soldier stood to attention on a plinth. He read the words carved below the sentry, the dedication to the dead of the Great War and World War Two.

His mind flashed back to the beginnings of his own military service. Like those men of the Great War, he imagined, he'd had little choice about the matter. The training had been brutal but it awoke something within him. Something that his officers had seen. A calm efficiency. Where others acted tough or responded to every threat with aggression, he was calm, cold. Remote even. That had been apparent on his active service - though, small mercies he thought, he never had to face the hell of trench warfare as his grandfathers had. Still, his actions had been enough to earmark him for special training in covert ops and assassination techniques. And so began the next phase of his service, though he never quite knew which group or agency he was being tested for, most of them were known simply as *Special Purpose Brigades.* That's when he'd come under the wing of the Old Bastard.

Laçis snapped out of his reverie. *Damn, spent too long in these soft surroundings, getting far too introspective.* He completed a circuit of the gardens, now empty, selecting a bench on which to wait. He didn't have to wait long. The pair he had met at Southend, the small one and the gorilla, soon appeared at the gate and walked over to him. They nodded and the older man sat. Laçis scanned the area again as he did so.

"Our target?" Ismet asked, as Serkan took up position behind the bench.

"There are reporters at her house, but I do not think she is there. I also watched her workplace. She has not been there either."

"No, and as you suggested, we checked. We are quite sure she is staying at her father's house. But put that aside for now. We have another target for you."

Laçis raised an eyebrow. "This is most irregular. I do not negotiate direct, and my primary target is still active."

Ismet waved a hand in annoyance. "We don't care about that. Listen, one of our men, one of our cousins was killed last night. Tortured and killed. " His face contorted in grief and rage. "I found him myself. Such a beautiful boy, what am I to tell his mother?" He took a moment to compose himself.

Laçis sighed inwardly. The last thing he wanted was to get involved in these peoples' feuds and gangland wars. He was a professional, not a street thug. However, he had failed in his first attempt, this secondary mission might go some way to wiping away the stain of that failure.

"Who is it? " He asked quietly.

"His name is Taverner. Terrence Taverner. He is the uncle of the girl you killed. He is a bad man, a gangster."

And you are no Sunday school teacher, Laçis thought. "I see. And you want this man terminated?"

"Yes. It was he who was responsible for the terrible and dishonourable death of our cousin, so he must pay. Blood calls for blood."

Laçis made no attempt to rationalise the logic, he just quickly gave a four figure sum. As he expected, Ismet accepted immediately, then gestured to Serkan. The large man withdrew a folder from inside his coat and passed it over.

"Here are all the details. We know that he will be at the funeral of his niece tomorrow. That might be a good opportunity?"

Laçis accepted the folder and quickly scanned through it. "A public event where there are likely to be police present? Probably not. Leave this with me. I will do it."

Ismet leaned forward on the bench, hissing directly into Laçis' face. "See that you do, this time. See that you do!"

Chapter 17

Cab turned the Rover into the main car park and flashed his warrant card at the attendant. The City of London Cemetery was the largest in the area, the final resting place of generations of East-enders. It had been opened in the 1850s, during the second wave of the great Victorian metropolitan cemetery scheme that had already seen the opening of Highgate, Kensal Green and the rest of the Magnificent Seven, as the new necropoli became known. Their construction had been driven by the fact that London's old church cemeteries were filled to overflowing; burials were being stacked on burials, bodies were being removed and placed in pits to create space and the city's water supplies were becoming tainted with run-off from the churchyards.

Cab had heard the phrase *built on bones* used to describe London. As he parked up, he thought how true that was. Along with the old churchyards, London was dotted with plague pits, not to mention the layers of history before that, going back to pre-Roman days. Even this place, out on the edges of the city proper, was said to hold the remains of half a million people.

He mused on the local legends of other, less formal internments, such as the unfortunate individual said to be entombed in a support column on the Bow Flyover. *Built on bones*, indeed.

Uniform were already here. He strode over to one of the Ilford sergeants who was chatting with a cemetery attendant.

"Morning, John," he nodded. "Busy one today?"

"Alright, Cab? Yeah, just finalising things with Freddie, here."

The uniformed attendant stuck his thumbs in the edge of his fluorescent tabard and nodded sagely.

"Always get a big crowd with the young 'uns. They have lots of friends and family, see. Older ones, not so much. Barely a handful, usually. Sometimes not even anyone."

Cab digested this gloomy information and coughed. "Right."

The sergeant stepped in. "Well, anyway, we're expecting a large crowd of mourners. Then there'll be the press, of course. I'll get a cordon set up here, we'll try and keep them back as best as we can." He pointed to the five officers gathered around a van, talking quietly amongst themselves.

"There's something else," Cab leaned in. "We have reason to believe there's a direct threat to Terry Taverner's life."

"Taverner. He's the uncle, right?"

"Right. Ideally I'd like a sweep of the perimeter." He looked over at the group again. "Is this is all we have?"

"It is, Cab. And they'll have their hands full with the paps."

"Shit. Alright. I'll see if I can get a couple of my team down here." He looked through the arched gate at the landscape beyond. "That's quite a size."

"Almost two 'undred acres, to be precise." The attendant bounced on his toes. "We have procedures in places for such events. We've had a few famous people laid to rest here. Two of old Jack the Ripper's victims were some of the earliest. Dame Anna Neagle a few months back, that was a big one. We'll direct mourners to our main car park over there. From there, we'll form them up and walk them to the chapel. It's family and close friends priority, the rest go in the overflow chapel or wait outside. Then it's down to the burial plot for the internment. Again, we'll organise as best we can. Main thing is the chief mourners don't feel crowded or rushed. Afterwards, we'll stagger the remaining mourners in to pay their last respects."

"Okay, good. Do you mind if I have a stroll round? How secure its the perimeter?"

"No, sir, that's fine." The attendant glanced at his watch. "People won't be arriving for at least an half hour or so. As for the perimeter, we've got a golf course over to the east, a riding school to the north. I suppose they might be considered what in the army we used to call *porous*. I was in Malaya, you know. Now there was nightmare, trying to establish a perimeter in the jungle was - "

"And how about the other borders?" Cab interrupted.

"Ah, right. Well, the other edges are bordered by roads or houses. I suppose people could climb over the wall, but they'd have to get into a back garden to do so. There's the new estate to the north-west, though the wall there is topped with wire. We had problems with kids, you know? Bloody kids today, no respect."

"Indeed." Cab considered his options. By the time he got anyone else down here, the funeral would be underway. Still, he'd put a call in to Turner, in any case. "Well, I'll leave you two to get on with it. John, if you could mention it to your people. I doubt an assassination attempt is likely, but if they do spot anyone suspicious…"

"No worries, Cab, I'll let them know." The sergeant gave him a thumbs up and continued chatting to the attendant.

Cab walked through the gate, heading to the edge of the cemetery grounds. It was a bright, spring day, the carefully tended grounds looked immaculate in the sunlight. Soon he was at the eastern perimeter. The old boy had been right, the boundary here was little more than hedges and fencing. Beyond, through the trees, he could see pastel-garbed figures strolling across the golf course. He began walking northwards, looking around for he was not quite sure what. The cracking of twigs underfoot drew him up short. A large figure was coming through the undergrowth ahead. Cab crouched again the bole of a tree, one hand going to his radio, the other forming a fist.

A burly young man stepped out onto the trimmed grass, brushing down his dark-blue track suit. He looked up at Calloway in surprise.

"Police! Don't move! And who might you be?" Calloway growled?

"It's alright, copper," a deep voice rumbled behind him. "He's one of mine."

Cab span on the spot, heart pounding. From the mugshots back at the station and his sheer size and presence, this could only be one person - Pearce. *How on earth had the big man crept up so quietly*? He cleared his throat, trying to mask his surprise. "Oh, right. Well, that's okay then, I suppose."

Pearce, in an immaculate black suit, motioned to the younger man. "Carry on, Gavin. I want you and the others working up and down this line all the way through the funeral."

"Sure, boss," the man nodded and moved off.

"So I'm guessing you're Calloway, then?" Pearce regarded Cab's shabby suit with disdain.

"Aye, that's me. So you're worried there might be a hit?" Calloway took out his packet of Marlboros and offered one to Pearce. The minder declined.

"I'm trying to give up. And to be straight with you, yes, I am. But you're checking here, too. What have you heard?"

Calloway weighed up his options. Sometimes you had to throw a little bait out to get the fish interested.

"Professional hit man. East European. Former military."

Pearce considered this and nodded, fixing Calloway with an intense stare. "That's what I heard, too."

"I won't ask where from." Calloway lit his cigarette and took a drag. "Question is, who hired him?"

Now it was Pearce's turn to consider. "Fair enough, as we're laying cards on the table. It was the north London mob. The Arikans. They're shifting in coke. It's the new big thing, apparently. Times are changing."

Cab never thought he'd find himself agreeing with someone like Pearce. Nevertheless, he ran a hand through his hair, replying, "Can't argue with that. Times are changing. Family used to be off limits amongst your lot, right?"

"They did. We had rules. Not with this crowd, though. Scum. They'd off their own grandmother for a cut of the pie. Or even take a whack at someone at a funeral. I told him, but he insists on being here today."

"Well, it looks like you've got everything covered. Seems that for today, at least, we have the same goal in mind. But I want this thing contained, Pearce. I won't stand for open war on my streets. Got it?"

"Oh, I get it Calloway. And don't you worry, I'll get this sorted. Better than you lot could."

Calloway shook his head and flicked away the half smoked fag and made to leave. He paused. "Oh, the lad. Webb, is he alright?"

"He's being looked after. No need to worry about him, he'll be fine."

Now it was Calloway's turn to stare. "See that he is, Pearce. See that he is."

Spider yawned and stretched as he walked into the bathroom. He'd hit the vodka pretty heavy last night and was paying the price this morning. Thing is, there was nothing else to do in this poxy flat other than drink, eat and watch TV - there wasn't even a video player. Danny had brought him here after the rescue. He wasn't exactly sure where *here* was exactly, he thought maybe Hackney. He'd been shown in, told there was some grub in the small kitchen, told to stay put, then left on his tod. To be fair, he'd slept most of the time. The shock of the questioning had hit him once he'd sat down on the threadbare sofa. His neck was still store, there was a dull throb in his head, he felt like shit. Mind you, that was mostly down to the bottle of voddy he'd found at the back of a cupboard.

A piping hot shower cleared his head, and after beans on toast, he began to think about what to do next. On the one hand, given what had happened, the north London lot would be out for him even more. Hard to plead innocence when Pearce had rocked up to rescue you. On the other hand, time was money. Every day he was out of circulation meant a day not hustling, not earning, not to mention the trouble he'd get in at work. *Nah, screw them.* This coke business had opened Spider's eyes to the amount of cash he could be making. Should be making. Nine to five was for mugs. He glanced at the phone again. He needed gear to go out selling, whatever it was. Dare he ring some of his contacts? Recent events had upped his paranoia levels… the line could be tapped. While Pearce's crew had rescued him, they'd also dropped him in the shit in the first place.

He decided to play safe and rest up for another day or two. Let the dust settle. Maybe by the end of the week the big boys would have sorted things out. A sharp rap at the door brought back the fear. Spider crept quietly into the tiny hall, noticing, with disgust, that his hands were trembling.

"Who is it?" he hissed.

"It's Danny." Before he could open the door, Danny had unlocked it, in any event. The wide-shouldered young man moved in, almost filling the space. He had a couple of carrier bags. "Brought you some more stuff. Figured you'd have finished what was there already. There's bread, milk, few other bits and pieces. Oh, a newspaper too."

He followed Spider into the kitchen, placing the bags on the counter.

"Oh, right. Ta." Spider took the Sun out of the nearest bag and flicked his eyes over the front page. "So what's happening then?"

"Shit is what's happening," Danny replied. "Apparently the Turks bought some assassin guy in from Europe. That's who done the boss' niece."

"Fuck, that sounds heavy."

"Don't it just. You're alright, though, there's only a couple of people know you're here. Mr Pearce said to keep you here until things blow over. Is there anything else you need?"

Spider glanced through the contents of the shopping bags. "Some Aspirin would be good. My head still aches."

"It will after a knock like that. Anyway, you should be happy. Mr Pearce said you done good. Kept your mouth shut. He liked that."

"Oh. Great." Spider sounded less than enthusiastic. Danny laughed.

"Tell you what, I'll pop back a bit later with some Aspirin, maybe a few tinnies, eh? Or even better," he leered, "I'll get one of the girls from the strip club to drop them round. That'll cure your headache."

He continued chuckling all the way out the front door. Despite the prospect of food and beer, and maybe more, Spider couldn't help feeling that it sounded like a cell door slamming.

Chapter 18

Calloway was back at the cemetery's main gate. The press had turned up, a scrum of them trying to get access to the service, all eager to get close up shots of the grieving family. Uniform and the attendants were having a hard time keeping them out. The figure of Pearce strode out from somewhere, flanked by two of his lads, heading straight for the press pack. He stood for a moment and waited for quiet. Even the police stopped talking.

"Here's what's gonna happen." He pointed a finger at the group, sun glinting off a cufflink. "You lot will wait here. You ain't coming in. Any pics you want, you take from here. That's it."

Only one reporter spoke up, a young, long-haired guy with a Welsh accent. *Must be new to the area,* Calloway thought to himself.

"You can't do that. We're perfectly within our rights to go in. This is a public space, see?" His older colleagues edged away from the man, who suddenly found himself alone facing the gorilla-like form of Pearce. One massive fist balled itself into the journalist's sweater and pulled him forward.

"You take one step through those gates, son, and there'll be more than one burial today? Do you understand me?"

He pushed the man back into the group. The reporter was outraged. "He just threatened me! Did you see that? He just threatened me!"

His colleagues all suddenly had reasons to be looking elsewhere or checking their cameras. The man turned to the police line. "You saw that, right? He threatened me!"

The sergeant shook his head. "Not me. If I was you I'd move back, sir. The mourners will be arriving soon."

Calloway had to smile. No-one liked the press, bar the odd useful reporter. The tension was broken by the sight of the funeral cortege approaching, followed by the sound of high-pitched engines. The group moved aside as a hearse and five cars came through, followed by a group of around thirty or forty scooters. The attendants moved in, directing people where to park, allowing them to walk into the cemetery in small groups at a time. The press were already clicking away, though Calloway noticed that none of them made a move towards the gate. Turner and Jones appeared at his side.

"Alright, skipper? Big crowd. I parked down the road and walked up. There's more still coming. Sad day, eh?"

"Yes, Turner, a sad day, indeed. Listen. I want you two to float about. Keep your eyes open for anything odd."

"You think the killer might turn up?" Jones asked.

"Who knows how that sort of mind works. I can't imagine this is a good place for a hit, but he might want to gather intel. Or he might be the sort of sick, twisted bastard that gets a kick out of attending the funerals of his victims. Any case, go mingle. We'll meet back here after."

The pair left and Cab fell in behind the mourners walking up to the chapel. The coffin was already being carried in, the tearful parents and other family following. He he caught sight of Taverner, head down, at the back of the group. His face looked pale and drawn. Calloway rushed up as fast as was decent, flashed his card at the attendant, and squeezed into a space at the back of the chapel.

The increasingly large group gathered around the graveside. The service had been moving, a number of friends and family making emotional eulogies. Cab noticed that Taverner hadn't got up to speak. Outside, he'd moved to get as close to Taverner as he could, without being too obvious. Jones nudged his elbow as the vicar began the burial.

"No sign of anything, skip," he whispered.

"Alright. Keep looking."

The ceremony passed quietly enough. It had almost drawn to a close when Calloway became aware of another presence at his side.

"Is sad occasion," the voice said quietly.

Calloway jumped for the second time that day. He turned. "Sergei." he nodded. "Surprised to see you here."

The Russian, dressed in a green flight jacket jacket and carrying a crash helmet, shrugged expressively. "I had same idea as you, I imagine. Perhaps this man will try to kill here."

"You think it likely?"

"It is not what I would do. Too many people. And also police."

The ceremony had finished now, the family were gradually drifting away. Other mourners were coming forward to pay their last respects.

"Still, it is very open here." Sergei added. "And I don't like that building." He indicated the low-rise block of flats that overlooked the cemetery from the new estate. "Clear line of fire. Easy escape.

That's where I would be."

Cab glanced across to where the sun glinted off of windows. "I'll get it checked out." He called Turner up on the radio, then turned back to the Russian. "Is there anything else?"

"Shall we talk?"

"Yes, but not here. Let's meet at the Three Rabbits pub. Turn left out of the gate, it's just down the road. Big place on the corner, you can't miss it."

Calloway had heard that the family wake was being held at the Golden Fleece pub, opposite the main entrance. Closer, but he didn't want to intrude any more than he had to, and the Rabbits would be less busy.

Sergei nodded and disappeared and Calloway made his way to the exit. There was some commotion going on at the car park. Mrs Clark, Tricia's mother, was shouting and screaming. He pushed his way through the group to discover she was haranguing Taverner.

"This is your fault, you bastard! If it wasn't for you my Trish would still be alive! "

Taverner was as still and pallid as a statue. Pearce and his minders hovered uncertainly. Tears streaming down her face, Trisha's mother hurled herself at her brother, pounding at his chest with her fists. Her husband and two other men moved forward and, as gently as they could, helped her away and into the waiting car. They left a shaken Taverner, clutching at Pearce for support. Calloway's radio squawked.

"Turner here, skip. We're over at the flats now, just having a poke around. No sign of anything untoward."

"Alright, thanks. Give it another ten minutes then you can FO back to the station. I'll meet you there in a bit, we'll round everyone up for a briefing."

Laçis cursed under his breath and lowered the binoculars. The rifle remained in its case, it hadn't even been worth taking out. He was sat in the bedroom of the flats overlooking the cemetery - a girl's bedroom, judging from the My Pretty Pony toys and posters. The flat was owned by the Arikans, just one of many properties they had in the area. The tenant family had been "asked to go out for the day," apparently. One of Ismet's men had driven him here this morning, leaving him with the binos and the gun case. Laçis had rolled his eyes on checking out the rifle, it was like something his grandfather might have used. Besides, he had already told Ismet this was not the time or place for an assassination. Still, the man had been insistent and Laçis figured he could at least run some surveillance.

Even that had proven problematic, though. The central chapel blocked much of the view of the burial. The ornate archway concealed much of the entrance and car park. Even if he had planned a shot from here, opportunities would have been few and its source quite obvious. Which was why he had also taken a walk around the estate before setting up - it always paid to know escape routes.

Sitting back from the window, he raised the binos again. It looked as though the burial service had ended, people were moving around, some towards, some away from the grave. Taverner was there, briefly glimpsed in the midst of a group of men. There were a large number of young people, friends of the girl, he supposed. Then the usual family, supporting each other in their grief.

Another face caught his attention, a man in his early thirties. At the event but not part of it, judging by his body language. A reporter? No, they were all being held at the entrance. A policeman, then? That would make sense. As Laçis watched, another figure suddenly materialised at the policeman's side, making him start. Laçis leaned forward, frowning. This was interesting. This man, younger and shorter, had something odd about him, something almost familiar. The pair were talking, they obviously knew each other. Laçis gave a start himself when the younger man looked up and pointed directly at him. Well, the building, perhaps, but it felt like a direct contact.

Laçis jerked back, lowering the binos. He'd stayed here long enough, there was nothing to be gained by lingering. His driver would be waiting for him, round the corner, ready to drive him away. Gathering his gear, the hit-man wiped everything he'd touched and exited the flat. A quick trot down the concrete stairs and he was at the entrance. Cautious as ever, he took a quick glance out before exiting. There were two men in suits walking slowly in the street outside, looking up at the buildings. Police? If he stayed in place, they would be here in a moment. Back up to the flat? He didn't have the key, he had been locked in. *Brazen it out then.* He cursed the rifle case now, it was not obvious what it contained but neither was it inconspicuous.

Laçis took a breath, squared his shoulders and walked out into the sunlight. He whistled a tune, affecting a carefree swagger. A voice called out.

"Excuse me, sir. Police. Could I have a word?"

Damn! He turned, smiling. "Of course. How may I help?"

The one who had spoken was young, tall, his hair and suit rather untidy. He pointed to the case in Laçis' hand. "What's that you've got there, sir?"

"Ah, it is a snooker cue," Laçis replied, keeping the smile in place. The pair began walking towards him. He had no option. In one smooth movement, Laçis flicked the case open, flipped the rifle into his other hand, dropped the case and pointed the weapon at the two officers. It was not loaded but they would not know that. He put power into his voice, calling out sharply, "On the floor! Now!"

The pair did not drop but they did scatter, retreating quickly back the way they had come. One was already shouting into his radio. Laçis scooped up the case, turned and ran. Best not head direct to the car. His earlier exploration now paid off, the route was already clear in his mind. Within seconds he was out of view of the policemen, dodging down an alleyway, taking a running jump at the wall at its end. He threw the rifle over and followed, cursing at the barbed wire that cut his hand, scrambling over it and dropping into the vegetation beyond.

He was on the edge of the cemetery now and, without pause, headed north, keeping under cover of the foliage. From there, it was easy to cut across the riding school, the rifle now back in its case, following which he could disappear in the side streets. Despite adrenaline and the exertion, he was barely breathing hard. An important part of being pursued, he had been taught, is not to look like your are being pursued. Accordingly, he slowed his pace, nothing stood out more than someone running along a street. Two minutes later he stowed the rifle case in the boot, slipped into the waiting Escort, and was heading out of the area.

Chapter 19

At the Three Rabbits, Calloway ordered a double scotch and downed it. He then ordered a pint and carried it to a nearby table. The pub had just opened and was quiet. Besides, Calloway knew the landlord here, some of the Ilford mob used the back room for private do's. Sergei slipped quietly into the chair opposite, a coke in hand, placing the red crash helmet on the floor.

"All finished, then?"

Calloway nodded.

"Your services are quite short. A Russian service would be at least twice as long."

"You still have church services over there?"

Sergei looked uncomfortable. "Not so many. Most churches were closed in the bad times. Still, even the government cannot defy the soul of Russia."

Calloway took a sip of his beer and regarded his companion curiously.

"So you're a religious man then, Sergei? Seems quite odd, if you don't mind me saying. What with your line of business."

"I don't mind. And, to contrary. I believe you have saying? There are no atheists in foxholes? Seeing the worst in life sometimes means you have to search for the best. The alternatives are not so good."

"Alternatives?"

Sergei mimed drinking. "Vodka. Lots of it. I've seen some turn to it to dull their memories."

"Never thought I'd hear a Russian man speak out against vodka."

Sergei smiled. "Oh, in right amounts it is fine. But addiction? This does not end well."

Calloway's eyes glazed. His mind was cast back to his childhood. His father ranting and raging after coming home from the pub, reeking of booze. The man had died at the age of fifty. Calloway had not attended the funeral. He raised his pint glass and tipped it towards the man opposite.

"Aye," he said softly. "To absent friends."

They pair sat in silence for a few minutes. Sergei broke it.

"I had a reported sighting of Laçis in Seven Kings. In a sex house, close to the station. I checked but there was no sign. If he had been there, I don't think he is now."

"Seven Kings, eh? Well that would make sense. Close enough but not too close."

"You think he is after this uncle?"

"I don't know. If he were, why not take him out first? Why shoot the niece? Now, he has to face an alert enemy."

"I thought this too. And if it was just a warning, why would he still be here?"

"Exactly. Was the girl killed as a warning? A punishment? It doesnae really make sense for the Turks to have targeted her."

"The Turks?"

"Aye. Seems our man was hired by a Turkish-Cypriot gang from north London. The Arikans. They have been a growing problem in the area, looks like they are spreading out their operations."

"Which are?"

"Oh the usual. Girls, drugs, protection. Difference is, they seem to have major connections in the cocaine trade."

"Ah, yes. This is an increasing problem, no? Coming in from South America?"

"Aye, it is that. And it looks set to fuel a major gang war."

"This is causing trouble everywhere. Many of these drug gangs are so rich they can buy the authorities. It is causing some issues, especially for our people overseas. Our Mafia is growing stronger in those places."

"Your Mafia? I thought they were Italian."

"Ah, we have our own version. Some call them *Bratvá*, the Brotherhood. Whatever the name, the business is the same."

"Different name, same shit,then? So how are you getting around? You have a motorbike?"

Sergei nodded. "I do, it was supplied by a… friend. Easy way to get around and not be noticed. It is parked outside."

"My brother's into motorbikes. What is it?"

"A Yamaha. I believe it is a 250cc."

"Ah, is it one of the new SR's? Neat bikes."

Sergei shook his head. "No, it is not new. It is a few years old, I think."

"Oh." Calloway seemed surprised. "I thought given the backing and resources you have, you'd have chosen an up to date machine. Maybe a Suzuki Katana or something?"

"I do not know what that is. I put petrol in, it drives." Sergei shrugged. "Also I want to blend in, not stand out."

Calloway grinned. "Yet you chose a bright red crash helmet?"

"Given to me, not chosen. Also not new." He rolled his eyes. "Did you ever know a government department that liked spending money? No, just a plain motorbike. It is parked outside."

"I hope you locked it up. These cockneys will pinch anything."

"Cockneys?"

"Aye. It's what they call people born in this area. The East End. The place was known as a den of thieves in the old days. Tough area. The people didn't have much, they had to survive as best they could. Like most poor areas, I suppose. You must have the same?

"Officially, there is no crime in Moscow." Sergei gave a thin smile. "But of course, under surface, things go on. Not as bad as here. Our government cracks down hard on organised crime. There is change in the air, though. Many feel it, even if they do not talk. Afghanistan has not been the quick war we were promised. They are a tough people."

"I gather we found the same a hundred years ago. You served there?"

The Russian ignored the question. "But you. I think you also come from such a place? You have that feel about you."

Calloway shrugged. "I suppose so. Dundee was no paradise, that's for sure. I could have gone off the rails, but ended up in the police instead."

Sergei smiled. "It was similar for me. I was what you might call a hooligan in my younger days. Drove my dear mother crazy. So many problems." He sighed. " In the end, it was army or prison. I chose army and," he shrugged, "here I am."

Calloway was about to reply when his radio squawked. He answered then shot to his feet.

"Laçis has been sighted. He's here!"

They heard the sirens on their way back to the cemetery. By the time the pair reached the entrance, the area was swarming with police cars, there was a thrum of a helicopter overhead. A wan Turner rushed over to Calloway.

"Jones and I saw him, coming out of the flats. He pointed a gun at us!"

"You alright, Jon?" Calloway asked.

"Yeah, yeah, I'm fine. Anyway, he ran off northward. Units are out looking for him now. We're trying to seal the area but it's tough. If he cuts across into Wanstead Park he could go anywhere. Who's this?"

Turned indicated Sergei, stood quietly listening

"Never mind about him. Okay, so we have boots on the ground and the eye in the sky. Can we get a press release out?" He saw that the reporters, previously thinning out at the end of the funeral, had returned in force. "Full description, with a *do not approach, this man is armed and dangerous* on it."

Turner nodded and moved away. Calloway called to Jones. "Can you get over to the Golden Fleece, take a couple of uniform with you. If Taverner is there, let him know what is happening. But don't alarm the guests, the family have had enough to deal with today."

He waved away the approach of a pair of journalists and moved back into the cemetery.

"Sergei, what would you do in his shoes?"

"Get out of area as quickly and quietly as possible. Unless he has a hide already set up here."

Calloway rubbed the back of his neck. "There's thousands of houses and flats round here, so that is a possibility. But if he is working for the Arikans, they are likely ferrying him around. Still, it backs up your earlier sighting."

"And might confirm that his target is now your Mr Taverner?"

"Aye, true. Though he didn't take a pop."

"Not a good location. You see, in those flats, the sun at the time was here, behind us. So shining almost directly into windows. Plus his target is in a crowd, there is little chance of a clear shot."

"You don't think he has the skill?"

"Oh I am sure he has. But he would prefer, I think, to wait for a better opportunity. I am feeling he would rather be closer. This is a man who likes to be at short distance, he is a pistol or knife man as much as a sniper."

"Well, you're the expert. Tell you what, you want to have a scout round on your bike? I'll be here for a bit, then I'll be back at the station, barring any major incidents. Contact me there, or pop round to my flat later if you find anything."

Sergei smiled and gave a thumbs up. "Okay, boss."

The sweep of the area proved fruitless, with a total lack of sightings from members of the public. It was as though the hit-man had vanished. That was the main topic of conversation at the afternoon briefing. Still, as Calloway reiterated, at least they knew their man was still in the area. Further appeals would be going out on the news, all local stations were on full alert. Similarly, the young lad Webb had also vanished, though Calloway had less concerns about his safety following the conversation with Pearce. Still, he would have liked to talk to the dealer, he may have been able to fill in some of the missing parts of the puzzle. The briefing was drawing to a close when Calloway noticed Pavitt standing at the board, staring intently at a photo.

"Everything alright?" he asked.

"Sarge, you know something? The girl in the photo here."

"The photo found in the bin at the park?"

"Yeah. You know, I'm sure I saw another photo of her."

Now he had Calloway's interest. "Where?"

"At that guy's house. The one the guv asked me to survey. I'm sure this is the same girl. There was a photo on the mantelpiece. Her, a young lad, and an older couple. The guy's name is Birch."

"That rings a bell." Calloway thought for a second. "Signs. Outside houses. Big estate agents, right?"

"Yeah, that's him. But more besides. See, Julian Birch is the local MP. And sarge, I think this girl is his daughter."

Chapter 20

"Are you a hundred percent sure about this?" Calloway stubbed out his fag in the ashtray. Turner was eating a sandwich. Pavitt sat on the only other chair in the room, squeezed into the corner. They were in Calloway's office, he'd brought both men straight here after Pavitt's revelation in the briefing room.

"I am, skip. It's the red hair, it's quite striking."

Calloway swore. "Well, this gives us a dilemma. We know this Birch is in tight with the Chief Super. And Denham is away for another couple of days. So, question is, do we take this upstairs and risk getting told to mind our own? Or, do we wait for the guv to get back and let him make a decision? Or, given that this Laçis is still at large, do we pull Birch in for a chat?"

"Tough one," Turner mumbled though a mouthful of tuna and sweetcorn. "Why not go and see him, sarge? That way it'll be less official. If we pull him in and the press get hold of it…"

"That, and the fact we know the station is a bit leaky?" Pavitt ventured.

"Aye, you're both right, we need to keep this hush hush. Pavitt, did you get any sense of anything while you were at his place?"

"Didn't even see the geezer, sarge. It was his assistant or someone who let me in. Said they'd had trouble with the press, and there was also some hint of a threat. Nothing detailed, though."

"The press! Of course!" Calloway rustled through a pile of papers to his side. "She was at Snaresbrook last week. Same day I was there." He thought back to his chat with Sammy the reporter. "I think she was involved in a case. Hang on."

He flicked through the local paper. "Here it is. Michelle Birch, 23 , daughter of local MP Julian Birch, was called as witness for the defence today in a case involving her boyfriend. James Slater, 25, of Basildon, was arrested on a charge of Possession of Class A drugs outside Hollywoods night club in Romford."

"Fuck, a drugs case!" Turner snapped the lid shut on his tupperware lunch box.

"Well, that ties it in with our gangs, potentially." Pavitt observed.

"Doesn't it just," Calloway folded the paper. "And if that is her in the photo… makes me wonder if Michelle was actually the intended target? The girls look similar, at a glance." He thought for a moment and picked up the phone. "Smith? Calloway here, can you do me a favour? Check back through the statements in the Clark case. The vic's dog, I want to know what breed it was. You do? A Yorkshire Terrier? Ah, that's great. No, that was it, thanks."

He replaced the phone. "Do we know where this Michelle lives? I want one of you to pop round on some pretence. I don't know, neighbours complaining about barking, or something. Check if she has a dog."

"No need, sarge." Turner had flicked through another newspaper. He held it up, smiling. "There she is." It was the girl in the photo from the park bin, and she was holding a small dog in her arms. A Scottish Terrier.

Calloway gave a broad grin. "Well, now. Do me a favour, will you? Give Rick Douglas at Romford a call. Ask if he can fax over the papers for the Slater case."

"Righto, sarge."

"And following that, I think we need to have a wee chat with this Mr Birch."

Laçis paced the small front room of the safe-house. After yesterday's events at the funeral, the Turks had brought him to this terraced house in Bounds Green, insisting he stay here rather than in a bed and breakfast. To be fair, it made sense - it made him less visible and also meant he had a permanent driver. Balanced against that was the hit-man's concern that the situation was growing increasingly... *uncomfortable.* This level of involvement with an client was far more than he was accustomed to. It was against his standard operating procedure - *in, recce, job, out.* And now here he was, holed up in this house in North London, at the beck and call of Ismet. The place was comfortable and quiet enough. He had food, drink - they had even offered him drugs and girls. Laçis declined both.

His driver, a middle aged man who looked like a cab driver, was staying here too. That man now entered, bringing in a tray of coffee and biscuits which he placed on the low table in front of the sofa. He spoke little English, though Laçis had little enough to say, anyway. He sat, accepted the mug and nodded. He'd barely taken a sip when the garden gate creaked and a shadow fell across the window. The front door rattled open and Ismet came in.

"Ah, good, you are settling in, my friend," he smiled, taking the armchair opposite. He motioned to the driver and that man left the room, closing the door behind him. Ismet leant forward and helped himself to a Jammy Dodger. He sat back, munching. Laçis waited patiently, face impassive.

"A shame you could not take the shot at the funeral. Still, not the best circumstances. And I understand you were not happy with the weapon supplied?"

"It was a piece of shit." Laçis responded.

Ismet brushed crumbs from his suit. "Of course, of course. It was short notice, I apologise. Still, we have something much better coming through for you. Following your suggestion, we have a German rifle on the way. A Heckler & Koch, is that the one?"

"The PSG1? Good. Yes, that is good."

Ismet nodded. "It should be here in a day or so. I will bring it here."

"Excellent. I would also like the chance to test shoot it. Such a gun must be properly set up."

"Yes, of course, we shall arrange all of that for you. But after that, the question is, how do we get the opportunity to use it?"

"It seems difficult." Laçis placed the mug back on the coffee table. "According to your intel, this Taverner operates largely from a housing estate. There are some high rise buildings there, good platforms, but you have no access to them and new people are noticed very quickly. In effect, the king is in his castle, yes?"

Ismet nodded. "All true."

"Something else. There was a man at the funeral. He was talking to what looked like a policeman. I did not like the look of him."

"The policeman is Detective Sergeant Calloway. He is the officer in the case of the girl you shot. This other man…" he shrugged. "I do not know. Another policeman, perhaps?"

"No. He had the look of something else. And he spotted my position immediately."

"You think we should investigate?"

"Can you do that?"

Ismet smiled. "Money can buy you almost anything in this country. Ah, these English. Days of the Empire, tea and cricket *and all that*. Everything so proper and in its place, but beneath they are as greedy and as easily bought as the lowest rascal. Yet they look down on us." He sneered, leaning forward. "I tell you, my friend, they are in for a big shock, I think. Their tide is turning."

Laçis nodded politely. He was not this man's friend, neither did he care for the inference that he himself was easily bought - accurate though it may be. He steered the conversation back to the matter at hand.

"It would be useful to know who this other man is and, if necessary, to remove him."

Ismet's eyebrows raised. "If necessary. Still, best not turn a flea into a camel. Killing people brings a lot of attention in this country, and we are keen to avoid too much attention."

"Our problem remains, though. If I can not get close, then the rifle is good. But that needs preparation. We have to know exactly where Taverner will be, and at what time."

Ismet stared down at the worn carpet for a minute. "I have an idea. Something that might work. Let me talk to my boss. In the meantime, I will try and get this information for you."

"And the original target?"

"She is now staying with her father. They can both wait. This Taverner business has to take priority. We had not planned for events to move so quickly, but here we are. We must play the hand we are dealt, as I believe the English say. You sit here, my friend, take some time to relax. You will be busy soon enough."

Chapter 21

Calloway glanced at his watch for the third time and sighed. Next to him, Turner chewed his pen thoughtfully as he studied the crossword in his paper. Cab nudged him.

"Seven up is lemonade." He grinned at his own joke. Turner tutted and shook his head. They were in a chilly, institution-magnolia waiting room, on the second floor of the Norman Shaw Buildings on Victoria Embankment. It was actually a pair of buildings, constructed in Victorian times, when they were known as New Scotland Yard. That name had now passed to the modern office block on Victoria Broadway, home to the Met HQ since 1967. The north building now housed the offices of a number of MPs, easing the strain on a crowded Palace of Westminster. Julian Birch was one of those MPs. Following a call to his office yesterday, Calloway had called to arrange the appointment. Yesterday.

"It is quite unusual, at such short notice," the secretary had explained, but given that it was police business a space had been made. The appointment was scheduled for Tuesday at eleven, it was now twenty past. "He's on the phone to the Minister," the secretary had told them on arrival. "I'll let him know you are here."

Since then, they had sat waiting on a hard wooden bench. The decor didn't look like it had changed since Abbeline's day, Cab thought. He nudged Turner again.

"Did you know that during the building of this place, they found a woman's torso wrapped in a black petticoat in the basement?"

Turner grunted a response. Calloway, undeterred, continued. "Yes, it became know as the Whitehall Mystery. A couple of other bits were found nearby. This was 1888, so speculation was that she might be another Ripper victim. She was never ID'd, though."

Turner grunted again and excitedly filled in another clue.

"Ironic, eh? They build a police HQ on the site of an unsolved murder. You know -"

Turner was spared any further musings as the secretary appeared. "He will see you now."

They pair followed her through into a spacious office, behind which stood a sleek, coiffeured, man in his early fifties, dressed in a royal blue suit. Julian Birch, MP, leaned forward to shake both their hands and beckoned them to sit. He sat himself and smiled.

"Sorry to keep you waiting, gentlemen. Bit of a flap on with the Falklands situation, I'm sure you understand. Now, what can I do for you?"

"No problem, and thank you for seeing us, sir. I'm DS Calloway, this is DC Turner of Ilford CID. I'm sure you are aware of the shooting of Patricia Clark recently."

"Indeed." Birch frowned. "Terrible, terrible. I have passed my condolences on to the family, of course. Are you near to apprehending anyone?"

"We are following some strong leads, hopefully we will have an arrest soon."

"Good. Awful business. What is the world coming to?"

"Quite. Well, sir, as part of the enquiries we have unearthed some information directly relating to yourself."

"Oh?" Birch looked nonplussed. "How is that?"

"Your daughter, sir, Michelle? I understand she has been involved in a criminal case recently?"

Birch sat back in his chair, twiddling a fountain pen between his fingers. "Ah, yes. Michelle became involved with a bad sort."

"Slater?"

"Yes, that's him." Birch's lip curled. "Essex tearaway. New money. A flash harry, we used to call that type. But I fail to see…"

Calloway produced an evidence bag and slid it across the desk. "We found this in a bin at the murder scene. Can you identify the girl in the photo?"

Birch frowned. "That's Michelle. Not sure where it was taken. Looks like she's coming out of her office."

"Mr Birch, we believe your daughter was the intended target of the murderer. The young lady who was shot bears a marked resemblance to Michelle. She also has a very similar type of dog. We know that your daughter has a flat very close to the park, correct?"

The MP's face suddenly matched the colour of the walls. He coughed and poured a tumbler of water. "My God." He took a gulp and composed himself. "But… why on earth?"

"We were hoping you could tell us, sir. Is your daughter still at her flat?"

"No, she moved back in with us when all this business blew up in the press. Damned journalists, hounding her. We were able to shelter her more at home."

"Hence the request for a police visit?"

"Ah, yes. I believe one of your officers visited recently. Good chap, from what I hear."

"Aye, sir, he is that" Calloway paused for a moment. "I understand that as well as privacy concerns, there was also mention of a threat or threats?"

Birch waved a hand. "Nothing, really. Just the press nonsense."

Calloway leaned forward. "Mr Birch. Are you being personally threatened by anyone? Someone involved in crime, perhaps? Associates of your daughter, or of her friend, Slater?"

The MP took another swig of water. "No, of course not. Nothing of the sort. It's just all this business has me on edge, you understand? Has us all on edge. Poor Julia has not been sleeping well at all. Anyway, if that is all, gentlemen?" He stood abruptly, thrusting out a hand again, all smiles. "I have to be off, big vote in the Commons at twelve."

"Of course." Calloway retrieved the photo, stood and shook hands. "If you do think of anything else, I'll leave my number with your secretary. Thank you for your time today, sir."

"Oh don't mention it. Always happy our help our boys in blue!"

The pair left the office, pausing at reception. As they clacked down the long corridor to the main door, Calloway asked, "Well, what d'ye reckon?"

"I reckon," Turner replied, "That considering he's an MP, our man Birch is a shit liar."

Calloway had not been home long when the doorbell rang. He checked the peephole and let Sergei in.

"Good timing. I'm just back from the takeaway. Come through."

Five minutes later they were sat at the small dining table, scooping noodles out of foil containers. Sergei smiled. "I brought something." He reached into the carrier bag he'd brought in, and produced a bottle. "Wodka. The real stuff, not what you have in your supermarkets."

Cab rustled up a pair of tumblers, Sergei poured and they toasted. As they ate, they spoke.

"Any news, then?" Cab speared a prawn ball with his fork.

"Very little. I spent whole day driving round the area of the cemetery, working outwards. I found nothing. Laçis has vanished. I wonder if he is being hidden somewhere?"

"More than likely. The Arikans have properties all over, they could have him tucked away anywhere."

"You think he would stay in local area, though?"

"I guess so, if Taverner is still his target. I had that photo you gave me circulated, all our officers are on the look out for him."

"Until he makes a move he will be difficult to spot." Sergei nodded with approval at the lemon chicken. "And I imagine this Taverner is not a sort of man to be co-operating with the police?"

"Far from it. Aye, it's a tough one. I don't like the idea of waiting for this Laçis to pop up again. Puts him one step ahead of us all the time."

"And you prefer to be, what is the word? Pro-active? I like this, too. But how?"

"Well, the best I can do right now is speak to my colleagues at Wood Green, see if they can put some pressure on the Arikans. Maybe that will push them into showing their hand."

"The rushed shot often misses, we say. "

After the meal, Sergei admired Cab's stereo system and began browsing though his record collection. He looked puzzled. "These records. They are your fathers?"

"My father's?" Calloway carried the tumblers and bottle into the living room. "Nae, they are all mine. Why do you ask?"

"Oh, I am sorry. It's just that these records are all rather... old." He held up an old Al Bowly 78 by way of illustration.

Calloway smiled and sat, placing bottle and glasses on the coffee table. "I collect old records. And I'm into jazz mostly, and some old blues stuff. So, yes, most of my records there date back to the sixties, or even earlier. Do you listen to music much?"

"I do, but it can be difficult in my country. The Beatles, of course, were banned by our government."

"Banned?"

"Yes, they were not allowed to tour. And for many years you could only get their records on the black market. What we called *muzyka na robrakh*. You would say, music on the ribs." He smiled.

"On the ribs? What the hell does that mean?" Cab poured them each another drink.

"Vinyl was difficult to find and cost very much. But some clever soul found out that music could be put onto old x-ray films. They were cut into a circle, a hole made at middle, and music pressed onto them."

"My word! So you would be playing an actual x-ray, then?"

"Yes. It looked quite strange." Sergei lifted his glass in salute. "Ah, this is good wodka. So that way we could hear the Beatles, and other groups. Things have become a little easier, with cassette tapes, but it is still difficult to get new Western music. Slade, they were a group I always liked."

"Oh aye, they were good. I grew up with that."

"You still have family in Scotland? I noticed the picture of the lady and the baby in the hall."

Calloway drained his glass. "Aye, you might say that. You married? Have kids?"

Sergei chuckled. "This job is not so good for having relationship, but still, there is a girl. I write to her when I can." He gave a shrug. "Maybe one day."

The men sat in silence for a few minutes. Cab stood and returned with a London AtoZ. Flicking through the pages, he turned it towards Sergei.

"You may have this info already, but this is the main area of operations for the Arikan gang. Now, it's not for me to tell you what to do, but it may be worth having a nose around there. Your face isn't known, and you don't look like a copper. I'm sure you can come up with a decent cover story."

Sergei nodded. "Yes, I think this is a good idea. Laçis is more likely to be there than here."

"And I'll speak to Wood Green nick first thing tomorrow. I have a pal there, Ken. I'll let him know you are - "

"Actually I'd prefer you did not," Sergei raised a palm. Then, in response to Calloway's raised eyebrow. "Your stations here are not very *nadezhnyy*... secure. Information leaks from them."

Calloway bristled. "And how would you know that?"

"It is my business to know," Sergei shrugged. "This is always a problem when you are against people with money and resources, yes?"

Cab relaxed again. "Aye, you're probably right." He though back to his earlier chat with Denham. "Actually, you're definitely right. Okay, you go to Wood Green on the hush, and I'll do some nosing of my own." He glanced at the vodka bottle. "Now is that bottle half empty, or half full?"

Sergei grinned. "I should have known never to get into a drinking match with a Scotsman." Still, he reached out to pour them both another shot.

Chapter 22

Calloway ordered his head to be quiet and rummaged through his drawer for the pack of aspirin. He swore - stapler, pens, wine gums, no aspirin. Salvation came in the form of WPC Smith, coming into the office and placing a glass of fizzing water on his desk.

"Alka-Seltzer, sarge, Thought you looked a bit rough," she smiled.

"You're a star. Thanks." He took a sip of the drink, grimacing.

"Good night, was it?"

"Not really. I stayed in."

Smith shook her head in mock disapproval. "Drinking at home? It's a slippery slope, sarge."

Calloway laughed and winced. "Aye, that it is. Anything new in?"

Smith's smile faded. "Nothing. A few sightings of our suspect, but they all turned out to be false. Oh, the papers came in from Romford on the Slater case, I popped them in your tray. And a DS Bradshaw returned your call, his number's there."

"Thanks. Oh, and can you give everyone a shout. Wednesday briefing in -" he checked his watch, "half an hour. Do you know where Turner is?"

"He's out taking a statement on a GBH case, came in last night. He should be back soon. I'll round up the troops."

Calloway drained the glass and winced again. Next, he picked up he phone and punched in the numbers on the Post-it note. "Ken? It's Cab over at Ilford, thanks for calling back."

"Alright, mate, how's it going. Gather you had some interest in our friends the Arikans?"

"Aye. They're webbed in with a case we've got running here. The shooting of a young woman."

"Ah, yeah, I read about that. What can I do for ya?"

"Nothing specific. Just after some general intel really."

"Tell you what. I'm tied up in court tomorrow, but how about you pop over on Friday and I'll give you a guided tour?"

"Wood Green's cultural highlights, eh? That shouldn't take long."

Bradshaw laughed. "Here, I went to Dundee once. It was shut. Give me a bell tomorrow morning, we'll sort out a meet."

Calloway returned the laugh. "Cheers, pal. See you then."

That sorted, he turned his attention to the Slater papers. Nothing stood out. The man had been found guilty of possession of Class A drugs, cocaine, to be precise. But the amount was not large, and it was a first offence. Slater picked up a fine and a suspended sentence. Smith had been diligent, adding some press cuttings in with the papers. They showed a smiling Slater, arm around Michelle Birch, on the steps of Snaresbrook Court.

Calloway glanced up as Turner came in.

"Morning, sarge. Alright?"

"Morning. All done?"

"Yep. Poor lad got battered outside the Valentine last night. What you got there?"

"The Slater case."

"Oh right, our MP's daughter. Anything?"

"Not really. I'm wondering where he got his marching powder from, though. Wonder if our friend Webb was involved?"

Turner sat at his desk and shrugged. "Could be. He's not been seen for a while. Shall I get him pulled in if spotted?"

"Aye. I've called a briefing in ten minutes, let's go over it there."

The briefing was almost done when the Chief Inspector strolled in. Houlihan came to a halt mid report, everyone in the room stood up.

"Carry on, don't mind me," he took up position in the corner. Houlihan coughed and continued "Er, so the door to door of the flats directly overlooking the cemetery didn't turn anything up. Two were occupied at the time - a retired couple and a young mother. The third was more interesting. A young couple live there, they appeared nervous under questioning. A Mr and Mrs Osman, who claimed to be out for the day, saw nothing and know nothing."

"Did you get a look round inside?" Calloway asked.

"No, they wouldn't let us in. Want me to get a warrant, sarge?"

"Probably not worth it. If our man was there he'd have tidied up, and I wouldn't want to put a young couple at risk. Might be worth finding out who their landlord is, though?"

Houlihan made a note and nodded. Calloway cast his gaze

around the room. "Anyone else? Anything else?"

"Just one thing, sarge." It was Pavitt. "I know we identified the dog breed, but I popped round to Miss Birch's flat anyway. Had a chat with her flatmate, Amanda. She confirmed that Michelle's dog was a terrier, and also told me that on the day of the shooting, Michelle had taken it to the vet. Early morning appointment, the thing had been throwing up all night, apparently."

"Good, good work. Well that explains why she wasn't in the park as usual, I suppose. Saved by a sick pooch. Alright, let's crack on."

The team filed out and Chief Inspector Malcolm Woodville moved to study the whiteboard. With his swept back white hair and sunbed tan, he put Calloway more in mind of a morning TV host than a copper. He was known, behind his back, as Woody, both for his surname and his passion for golf - though some old-hands said it also referred to his personality. "Any closer to an arrest, Calloway?" he asked without turning.

"Not really, sir." Calloway gathered up his papers and put them in the folder. "There's still a few leads we're following up."

"I see. You know the press are having a field day with this?"

"Aye, sir, I know. We're doing as much as we can."

Woodville turned and stared up into Calloway's eyes. "And this *doing* includes harassing Members of Parliament, does it?"

Calloway had a sinking feeling. "Sir?"

"You visited Mr Birch yesterday. Why would you do that?"

"Just an informal chat, sir. We think his daughter -"

"Let me make it clear, Detective Sergeant. It's not your place to go tramping around Westminster bothering MPs. Got it?"

"But sir -"

"Got it?"

"Aye, sir. Got it."

"Good." Woodville placed his hands behind his back and gave a little bounce on his toes. "Now, Detective Inspector Denham is back tomorrow. I except you to brief him so that he can give me a full report. Jolly good. Carry on, then." With that, he breezed out of the room, leaving Calloway to mutter "And up yours too," at his back.

Sergei made his way out of the The Salisbury, back into the fresh night air. This was the fourth pub he'd been in on Green Lanes, the long street that ran the length of Wood Green. It had been the most friendly place, if not useful, with a lively crowd singing along to a trio of Irish musicians. For cover he'd adopted the role of a Polish builder, just moved into the area. No-one was likely to distinguish the accent, besides which he could speak enough Polish to get by, if pressed. In each place he chatted to people, trying to get a general sense of the area. In some cases he dropped hints about wanting to buy drugs, but no offers had been forthcoming. In fact, most of the people in these pubs had been local officers people having a drink after work.

As he stood on the corner, he spotted a burger place just along the side road. His stomach grumbled to remind him he hadn't eaten since midday, he followed its advice. The place was typical of its kind, a large board above the counter displaying lush photos of food items that bore little relation to what was served in a styrofoam box. As Sergei was ordering, three youths came in behind him. He paid for his burger and left, pausing on the corner of a nearby alleyway to take a bite.

He'd barely swallowed the first mouthful when he was conscious of a presence. The youths had followed him out and now cornered him, blocking the entrance of the alleyway. Sergei shut the lid on the food container.

"Nice wallet you have there, man," one of the group said. Two of them were white, one was black, maybe around twenty years old. Two were eyeing him, the third keeping lookout behind them. Sergei shrugged.

"English not good. What you say?" As he spoke he stepped slightly forward, leaning in a little, lining the closest youth up for a left hook.

"He said, arsehole, give us your fucking wallet!" The second youth snarled, pulling something out of his denim jacket pocket. It was a craft knife, Sergei noticed, the sort of thing used to cut carpets. Very popular with English hooligans, he understood. He raised his hands, shrugging in mock ignorance, then exploded into action.

The burger was thrown into the face of the knife-man. The nearest mugger got a clip to the jaw that sent him staggering back into the lookout. The knife-man was quick to recover, but Sergei had already anticipated his next move. He walked straight into a kick to the knee, there was a sickening crunch, a squeal of pain, and the man was down. Without pause, Sergei kicked out again, knocking the blade clattering into the wall.

The lookout ran off, his friend close behind. Like a lion dragging its kill, Sergei grabbed the shoulders of the downed youth's jacket and pulled him deeper into the shadows of the alleyway. He sat the bewildered attacker up against the brickwork and squatted before him. The man's face was pale with fear and pain. He sobbed, clutching at his knee, as Sergei expertly checked his pockets. He smiled at what he found - a small ziplock bag containing white powder.

"Where did you get this?" he waved it in front of the young man's face.

"My knee! You've broken my fucking knee, you cunt!"

Sergei sighed, "Is not broken. Just tendon damage. Now, where did you get this?"

"Fuck you!"

The sob turned to a scream again as Sergei pressed his hand onto the injured knee.

"Alright, alright! The snooker club. Just up the road. Bloke called Ferret."

"Ferret? I hope you are not lying to me." He raised a hand.

"No, no, I swear it. Ask for him, he'll sort you out."

"I see." Sergei stood. "You should get to hospital, have knee checked. And stop robbing people. It's not nice." He walked back up to the street, swearing at seeing his burger spread across the pavement. Food would have to wait.

The snooker club was only a block north of the pub. He wrote a fake address in the book on reception, paid the fee and went upstairs. Brushing through a plastic-curtained doorway took him into a darkened room filled with around ten snooker tables. Cigarette smoke hung suspended in the lights over the baize. The only noise was the muted buzz of conversation and the click of snooker balls. Sergei approached the nearest pair of players. A young ginger man stood chalking his cue.

"I'm looking for Ferret?" Sergei asked. The man merely gestured, in reply, to the rear of the hall where a group of men were gathered round a table. One of them, puffing on a large cigar, was just taking a shot as Sergei approached. He noticed that all of the group looked Turkish in origin.

"Ferret?" Sergei asked. The cue- man straightened.

"You mean Ferrit? Who's asking?"

Sergei took the ziplock from his pocket and discretely flashed it. "Friend of mine said you could get me more of this."

"Did he now?" Ferrit passed his cue to another and beckoned Sergei forward into the light. He was a stockily built man in his thirties. His eyes were the most piercing blue Sergei had ever seen. "And who are you?"

"My name is Pavel. I am from Latvia." He spoke the next in Turkish. "I am in the market for supplying a good quantity of your product to some friends of mine. It could be a big order."

Ferrit's eyebrows raised. "You speak Turkish?"

Sergei smiled "A little. I spent some time working there a couple of years ago." He didn't mention that it had been as part of an undercover team tracking arms dealers.

Ferrit returned the smile. "Welcome then, welcome. You arrive at a good time. There is new stock arriving very soon. But come, let us talk in my office, we can have a drink there." He ushered Sergei forward, placing an arm across his shoulders. Sergei fought down the urge to break it and followed his new friend's lead.

Chapter 23

Calloway's bum had barely touched the seat of his chair on Thursday morning when the call came through from Denham.

"Wish me luck," he muttered as Turner smiled. Two minutes later he was in Denham's office. His boss look tired, drawn. He motioned for Calloway to sit and lit a cigarette. Calloway noticed the ashtray was brimming.

"Alright, guv?" he ventured.

"No, I'm sodding well not. I get back from a conference that was so boring I considered suicide, only to get a bollocking from the Chief, earache from the press, news that there's an armed hit-man running round the streets of Manor Park and still no signs of a fucking arrest! God's sake, Cab, what's going on!"

"Sorry, guv. We're still following up leads, but it looks like our man has gone to ground. We're working on some ideas to flush him out. I'm going over to Wood Green tomorrow, see if I can pick up any intel there."

There was pause as Denham seemed to zone out for a second.

Calloway had never seen him like this. Then it hit him. The news this morning, talk of an operation in the Falklands.

"They're going in, then?" he said softly.

Denham nodded. "Yes. South Georgia. And the BBC are fucking announcing it in advance, to all and sundry!" He took a furious drag on his cigarette. Calloway slid a folder across the desk.

"All the latest case updates are here, guv."

Denham nodded and waved his hand. "What is it with this MP, then? Why is he of interest?"

"We believe his daughter was the intended target of the assassin. Poor Tricia, who looked like her, was in the wrong place at the wrong time. Turner and I went to have a chat with him. Nothing official."

"And?"

"He knows more than he's telling us. But…" he shrugged.

"But he's golfing buddies with the Chief."

"Aye, exactly."

"Gut feeling, Cab, what do you think?"

"I think I'd like to have him in for proper questioning. But I'm guessing that's not an option?"

"Short of him being caught red-handed over a corpse, yes, it is. But, if that's your gut feeling…" Denham stubbed the cigarette out. "You never heard it from me, I don't know anything about it, you were acting off your own back, but I agree. And as long as you are discrete - and I mean discrete - then have a poke about, dig up what you can. Try the daughter, friends of the daughter, anyone who knows the daughter. Someone must have an idea."

"Aye, guv."

"And what was it you weren't telling me before? No, I didn't forget. Don't hold out on me, Cab."

"It's all in my report, guv. Our man is called Andrejs Laçis. He's Latvian, former special forces, now a gun for hire, it seems. But that's for your eyes only."

"Still think we have a mole?"

"Aye, that I do. Besides, releasing that info to the public won't help us. His photo is out, that's enough."

"You found this out how?"

Calloway pressed his lips together. "Can't say right now, guv. Let's just say we have someone out there working to the same ends as us. Exposure would mean shutting him down."

Denham rubbed his temples. "Christ. Alright. You've got a few more days, then all this goes upstairs. Clear?"

"Clear. Thanks, guv."

On his way downstairs, Cab bumped into Gemma coming up. She looked strained. They had spoken on the phone a couple of times since their date but this was the first time he'd seen her.

"You alright?" He gently touched her arm.

"Not really. Case came in last night. Well, early this morning, actually." She glanced at her watch. "I've got five minutes. Want to buy a girl a drink?"

Calloway carried two large mugs of coffee over to the table in the corner of the small canteen. It was quiet at this time of day, before the lunch-time rush.

"Here you go."

Gemma smiled and took a sip. She sat back and closed her eyes. "Ah, I needed that."

"Rough one?"

She nodded. "Fire in a flat. Elderly vic. Poor old dear, never stood a chance."

Calloway reached over and placed his hand on hers.

"Not an accident then, if you were there?"

"No. Well, it's not official yet but all the signs point to arson."

"Bloody hell! Who'd do that to an old lady?"

"No idea. Some sicko, perhaps? Kids mucking about and it went wrong? We've not had the ID through yet, perhaps that will shed some light." She shuddered and placed her mug back on the stained table. "The smell…"

Calloway squeezed her hand. "Aye, I can imagine."

Gemma glanced at her watch again. "Damn. Sorry Cab, I have to get this report in."

He smiled. "Aye, no worries." They both stood. "Listen. Not the best time to ask, I know. But would you fancy coming over to mine for a bite to eat? Saturday night, perhaps?"

She smiled. "Yes, yes, that would be nice. I'll speak to you later, alright?" She gave him a peck on the cheek and turned to leave, halting at the appearance of a PC at the canteen door.

"Oh, Miss Bellotti, just thought you'd like to know." The young officer glanced at his notebook. "The landlord identified the lady in that fire last night. Her name was Webb. Emily Webb."

Spider first heard the news on the radio. It didn't really register. Not until he saw the TV news did he know for sure. The reporter was outside a burnt out flat… his mum's flat. Frantically, he rang her number. The line was dead. He phoned Mrs Marks, his mum's friend

who lived in the same block. A young woman answered, Mrs Marks'
daughter she told him. Mrs Marks couldn't come to the phone, she
was too upset. Yes, it had been Mrs Webb in the fire. Apparently the
police had been round all the flats that morning, asking if anyone
had seen anything. No-one knew for sure, but the gossip going round
said it looked as though petrol had been poured through the
letterbox. The whole block was in shock.

Spider put the phone down, sinking to the floor, placing his
head in his hands. *Mum* was all he could utter as the tears flooded
out. After a few minutes he stood, grief turning to white hot anger.
The Arikans. There was no-one else it could have been. They'd pulled
him in for questioning, so he knew torture was not beyond them.
And hadn't that arsehole Yousuf said his people would stop at
nothing? *Well, if they wanted a war, they could have a fucking war.*

He quickly gathered a few things together. He wondered if
Danny would be making an appearance, no doubt to tell him to stay
put. Sure enough, as he zipped up a holdall, Danny's car pulled up
outside the front. By the time Danny reached the front door, Spider
was out the back, over the garden fence, and away.

Chapter 24

Calloway swore again in frustration, tapping his hands on the steering wheel. The Friday morning traffic on the North Circular was heavy, made worse by roadworks at the A10 junction. The long promised Barking extension to the North Circular was still not underway. He'd also made the mistake of nipping into the station first, adding even more time to the journey. He span the dial on the car stereo, trying to find some music he liked. After a couple of turns, he gave up and switched it off. Forty-five minutes later, he finally turned into the car park at Wood Green nick, where DS Ken Bradshaw beckoned him over to park next to a yellow Ford Escort. Both had seen better days. Bradshaw threw a half smoked ciggie to the ground and got into the Escort, Cab jumped into the passenger side, wincing at the harsh squeal of the door.

"Sorry I'm late," Cab muttered, "Bloody traffic."

"No worries, mate. I got held up myself. Big row outside Manhattan's last night. Three stabbings."

"Only three? Quiet night, then?"

"Quiet for a Thursday," Bradshaw laughed.

"You sure this rust bucket will make it?" Cab winced again as Bradshaw crunched the gears, reversing them out of the main gate.

"It's what's under the hood that counts," Bradshaw grinned. "So, what's your interest in the Arikans?"

Calloway filled him in on the basics as they turned onto the High Road, heading south. "I've also got a source working on the ground," he explained.

"Undercover, or a snout?"

"Let's just call him a freelancer. He rang me last night. Says he's made a connection with one of their dealers. Guy called Ferrit, working out of the snooker centre on Green Lanes."

"I know the place. We've had it under obs for months. It's a difficult one to crack, though. They tend only to employ family and friends, so any of our guys stand out like the proverbial spare prick."

"Never raided it?"

"Waste of time. Limited access. Narrow stairway up to the main room. Plenty of time to get rid of any hooky gear, or get it out the back. Besides, we don't think that's where they're storing it."

"My man said something about new stock coming in soon."

"Did he, now? That's interesting. That would be the time to hit them. Hang on, I'll radio that in."

He slowed down, ignoring the blare of horns from behind, calling back to the station before resuming the drive.

"So, where are we off to today?" Can asked.

"There's a few places down here they tend to hang out. A restaurant, but that got turned over last week."

"Courtesy of Taverner's mob, we think."

"Ah, Terry Taverner. Been a few years since I had dealings with him. Back in the days when I was at Barking, working under old Tommy March, remember him?"

Calloway chuckled. "Aye, I do. They called him the Genie. Every time someone opened a bottle, he'd appear."

"That's the feller." Bradshaw smiled, then indicated a building on the left. "There's the snooker hall." They passed a large, Victorian pub on a corner, then Bradshaw pointed again. "That's the restaurant."

"They were quick getting the window fixed." Cab noted.

"That's the way it works round here. It's a tight knit community and the Arikans run it with a firm hand. Classic gang tactics, really. Hello..."

"What's that?"

A young man had come out of the restaurant and was walking briskly down the street.

"That's Demit. Old man Arikan's youngest boy. Rare to see him out and about." Bradshaw slowed down, prompting a V-sign from a passing motorcyclist. Demit walked the next block, passing the post office before stopping outside another restaurant. "Yep, that's another one of their places. But who's this?"

Demit was waving to the driver of a white transit. That man rolled the van forward and pulled up directly outside the restaurant.

"Food delivery?" Cab ventured. The driver got out and looked around.

"Maybe. But an unmarked van? Most traders would have livery. And the driver doesn't look local."

"Tell you what, drop me off at the corner there. I'll take a walk back past them, have a wee gander. They won't know me, right?"

Bradshaw rubbed his chin. "You're not supposed to be here, really, mate."

"Aw, I'll just have a look, that's all. I'll be right back, I promise."

"Alright. Make sure you are. I'll call this in, in case it's more than peas and carrots."

Calloway nodded and slid from the car as it came to a halt. As he walked, he took out a cigarette and lit it, using the smoking hand to conceal his face. Within a couple of minutes he was approaching the van, both men were at the rear open door. Trying his best to look uninterested, Calloway paused and made to cross the road directly behind the transit. A quick glimpse as he went past showed a number of large cardboard boxes. He lingered as long as he could as Demit opened one up to pull out a kid's teddy bear. Not wishing to push his luck any further, Calloway crossed, headed quickly back down the road, crossing again to the Escort. Bradshaw had the window half down.

"Looks like boxes full of teddy bears." Cab told him.

"Teddy bears? To a restaurant? Fuck." Bradshaw already had the radio in his hands. "All available units, this is DS Bradshaw. Suspected major drug deal on Green Lanes, outside number 41. Two suspects, unloading white Ford transit van. Immediate response, repeat immediate response!" He motioned to Cab. "Nice once. Back in the car, Cab, we'll take it from here."

Calloway obeyed as Bradshaw jumped out. He watched in the rear view mirror as the DS made his way back up towards the van, but on the other side of the road. Calloway didn't want to risk turning to look, so he adjusted the mirror. He could just make out the driver starting to heft boxes out of the back as the restaurant door opened. Suddenly all hell broke loose. There was a shout, and Bradshaw came sprinting across the road, dodging traffic. The driver made for his cab as the DS flew into him, the pair disappearing from view. The restaurant door was slammed shut, and Demit ran, heading south.

"Shite!" Calloway made a snap decision. He was out of his area, but there was potentially a major crime in progress. As Demit flew past the car, Cab hurled the protesting door open. It caught the young man on his hip, sending him careering across the pavement, bumping into an elderly man laden with two bulging carrier bags. Apples and potatoes rolled across the pavement, the man swore, Calloway was out of the car. Demit recovered quickly though, and with a short glance behind him, was off again.

Cab pounded after him as he swerved two more shoppers, then cut off the main road. Calloway followed into the side turning, just in time to see his quarry duck into an alleyway that ran back up behind the shops and restaurant. With a surge that brought fire to his lungs, Calloway sped around the corner, only to run almost smack bang into Demit. A large van was parked in the alleyway, blocking most of it. Cab shouted out "Stop, police!" and made to grab, but Demit was quick off the mark again, wheeling to punch Calloway in the face, knocking him back. Demit took advantage of the space created to run back out onto the road, across it and into the alley on the far side.

Cab muttered "Christ!" bringing a hand up to his bleeding lip, as he turned and gave chase again. The far alley was empty, which gave him a clear view of his prey. The fences on one side were too high to easily climb and the back doors of the shops on the other side were all shut. Demit had no choice but to go straight ahead, following a glance behind, laughing at his bleeding, wheezing pursuer. He put on a spurt and sprinted out of the far end of the alley and into the road beyond. Calloway heard the squeal of brakes and sickening crunch, the sound urging him forward. By the time he got there, a small crowd was already gathering around the crumpled figure in the middle of the road, the ashen faced driver of the builder's truck that had hit him sat motionless behind his wheel.

"Police!" Cab shouted as he approached. "Someone call an ambulance! Now!" He knelt, grimacing at the blood pooling under Demit's head. The man was twitching. Calloway did his best to soothe him and make him comfortable, anything other than that was beyond his meagre first-aid skills. Sirens were already sounding, a jam sandwich screeching to a halt as it came round the corner, lights flashing. Within seconds uniform were taking control of the scene, so Calloway took a few steps back. Bradshaw suddenly appeared at his elbow.

"Quick, Cab, with me. Let's get you out of here."

Spider took a brief look round, then clambered over the fence into the overgrown rear garden. Fumbling in his pocket, he pulled out the keys and unlocked the back door, sliding quickly inside. The house was one of the places he used, renting an upstairs room. It was damp, dingy and run down but the landlord took cash and asked no questions. Once in the room, he peeled back the stained carpet in the corner and, using the tip of the old army bayonet from the bedside cabinet, pried up a floorboard. He reached in, smiling as his hand closed around the plastic bag within. He withdrew it, replaced the board and carpet and checked. Yep, there were three bags of pills inside, stored away for a rainy day. That day was now, he figured. If he was going up against the Arikans, he needed some fire power; he needed a gun. He knew where to get one, but even something basic would cost.

Spider stuffed the stash into his holdall, thought for a second, then dropped the bayonet in as well. He plugged in the cooking ring in the corner, heating up the battered old kettle to make himself a pot noodle. As he spooned the tasteless mulch into his mouth, he thought about the best place to sell a bunch of pills in one go. Tossing the empty pot aside, he rummaged through the papers and fliers on the scratched dresser. Lifting up one, he smiled. *Ilford Mod Alldayer,* it read. *Sunday April 25th.*

He'd been to one before, a few months back, held at the Ilford Palais. Some enterprising DJ had rented the place out for the whole day and night, put on a bunch of bands and had four of five DJ's doing sets. Spider guessed the idea had come from the old Northern Soul clubs like Wigan Casino, where dances would go on all night.

Still, it had been great for him. Hundreds of mods all in one place, many of them looking for a little lift, and the Palais had a huge car park at the back that was ideal for dealing.

All he had to do was hide up for a day, then get back down to Ilford on Sunday. He wasn't sure just how much the Turks knew about him, or his hideaways. Would they come after him again? Did he need protection? For a second he thought about calling Pearce. No, that was best avoided, he'd rather keep a good distance from that psycho. The screams he'd heard as he left the garage flashed back in his mind; the screams and the chilling laughter that followed them. No, he'd call his cousin Gavin, he'd put him up for a couple of nights. Shoving a few more bits and pieces into his bag, Spider locked the door and headed for the nearest phone box.

Chapter 25

"Sarge, the press conference is at nine-thirty," Smith called to Calloway as he walked to his office the next morning. "The guv said he wanted you there."

"Thanks, Smithy. Anything new in?"

"Not really. Houlihan and Jonesy visited our Mr Slater, I've left their report on your desk."

Calloway nodded to Turner, who was busy on the phone, sat down and flicked through the papers in front of him. Just like Smith said, nothing of any great use there. As expected, Slater had refused to divulge any information about his coke supplier, well, he had no reason too now that his trial was over. A call came through from Bradshaw at Wood Green letting him know the latest. Demit was still in intensive care, on life support. He hadn't regained consciousness since the collision. Calloway's role in events had been downplayed in the official report - not that he'd done anything wrong in chasing a suspect, it would just streamline things if Bradshaw was the man on the spot.

Still, the transit van and driver had been grabbed and, as expected, the teddy bears had been stuffed with coke. A sizeable amount, Bradshaw told him. The fact it was being transported so openly showing just how confident the Arikans were getting.

Thanking the DS, Calloway hung up and glanced at his watch. *Just time to grab a coffee before the press meeting.* He bumped into Kit Kat in the canteen. The big man beckoned him over.

"What's new, sarge?" Cab knew that, in any station, Desk Sergeants were the font of all wisdom.

"Chief's not happy, Cab. He's heard all about your shenanigans in Wood Green."

Calloway shook his head. "Shite. Is nothing secret in this place?"

"You should know not. I gather Wood Green kept you out of all their reports, but you know how it is. Walls have ears. And sausages."

"Aye. Oh well. I'm sure I'll be hearing from him later on. Now I have to entertain the gentlemen of the press. At least they won't have heard of it."

Calloway's optimism was misplaced. The fifth question in came from the local press, with the journo from the Ilford Recorder asking. "We've heard you were involved in an incident yesterday where a young man was severely injured in an accident. Can you tell us what happened?"

Christ. How did the bugger know about that? Calloway did his best to keep a poker face. "I'd ignore any gossip you hear, if I were you. Our sole focus here is to apprehend the killer of Patricia Clark."

"Which you haven't yet done." the reporter fired back, with a sneer.

"True. But we are following a number of substantial leads."

"You said that last week," came another voice.

Calloway clenched his fists behind his back. "Aye, we did. But investigations take time. This is real life, not Starsky and Hutch."

Denham stepped in. "Well, ladies and gents, we'll wrap up there if there's no more questions? Thank you all for coming, of course we will keep you up to date with all major developments as they occur." Then he growled into Calloway's ear. "My office. Now!"

Cab followed, appreciating the sympathetic glances from Turner and Smith. Denham said nothing until they were in his office.

"This is turning into a major shit-storm. First Taverner, then this MP, now I find out you were involved in a Wood Green op without any prior authorisation!"

"It wasn't an op, guv. I just happened to be on the spot when it all kicked off. A mate over there was showing me round the manor. I was looking to get info on the Arikans, that's all."

"And they just happened to be unloading a van full of coke as you drove past?" Denham fumbled in his desk drawer for a lighter.

"Aye, that's it, guv, straight up." Cab shrugged and raised his palms. "That's how blatant these people are getting. They think they're untouchable."

"Until the lad yesterday got touched by a truck, eh?"

"Granted, that was unfortunate. He did give me this, mind." Calloway indicated his still swollen lip.

"And in return he has severe head injuries, three cracked ribs and a broken arm, apparently. Not a good look is it, Cab?"

"No, guv, it isnae. But how comes the press got on it?"

"Who knows? Lots of witnesses? Someone's talked at Wood Green? Could be any number of things."

Denham sat back in his chair and looked up at the ceiling. "I can't tell you how close upstairs is to side-lining you on this. I've been going to bat for you, but I need a result soon. Straight answer

- how close are you?"

Calloway whistled through his teeth. "Straight answer? It's hard to say. I'm sure Birch knows more than he's letting on but seems he's untouchable. We have the dealer Webb still floating around, the murder of his mother might prompt him to be more talkative, if we can find him."

"And the Arikans?"

"Well, given the score yesterday, Wood Green now have good reason to go in on them. That might turn up something. They may still be hiding the hit-man somewhere, or could be he's out of the country. We planned to stir things up, draw them out, but I'm worried now this might have the opposite approach, they could go to ground."

"And you still think they are behind the murder?"

"Oh, I'm sure of it. But she wasn't the intended target, Birch's daughter was. But without talking to him…" He let the statement trail away.

Denham closed his eyes and exhaled smoke. "You're a good copper, Cab. If you weren't I wouldn't be sticking my neck out. I can buy you a few more days, that's it. In the meantime I'll do some digging on Birch. If we can isolate the daughter she may prove more amenable. You track down this Webb and keep an eye on Taverner and co. And stay away from Wood Green, for fuck's sake. I can cover yesterday, but no more cock ups. Clear?"

"As a bell, guv."

Sergei knew that something was wrong as soon as he entered the snooker hall. He was on time, Ferrit had told him to be here at noon and here he was. The place was very quiet, considering it was a Saturday - empty, in fact, apart from the same group at the back of the room. Sergei walked across, alert on every step. He had a small cosh inside his jacket, but was unarmed other than that. Not that there was an shortage of weapons to hand in a snooker hall. On his first visit, he'd been sure to familiarise himself with the layout of the place. He went through a mental check-list again; the door to the toilets, the small bar at the side, the short corridor leading to an office (one small window) and the fire escape (possibly locked?). Keeping a neutral face he approached Ferrit and his men.

"Well, well, well," the bulky man turned at his approach. "If it isn't our friend Pavel."

Sergei stopped a few paces away and smiled. "Hello." He shrugged. "I am here. There is some problem?"

"Problem is," Ferret pushed out his chest, "you turn up asking to buy, I mention new stock coming in, two days later we're hit by the police. Forty grand's worth of merchandise gone. So we ask ourselves, *who knew about this?* And the answer is - *you.*"

Sergei noted how the men flanking Ferrit angled forward slightly, fists closing. He steadied his breathing and subtly put a foot out, angling his body to the best position. One hand hovered close to his inside pocket. His smile vanished, his features hardened. There was only one chance at this.

"First off," he spoke quiet and low now, "I came here to buy. I am not a, what is the word, grass? Second, I knew no details of your consignment, where and when it was arriving. Perhaps you have some leak in your organisation?" That drew a murmur from the group. A good tactic, Sergei thought, as he had always been taught.

Off-balance your enemy physically and psychologically. "Third," he continued," Had I been the person who informed police, would I really be so stupid as to return here? Like this? Alone?" He drew back his shoulders and splayed his hands out to the sides. It was simultaneously a gesture of vulnerability and threat. Being fluent in body language went a long way in situations like this. To back down was to invite attack. He held the position and locked eyes with Ferrit. The Turk held for a couple of seconds then mumbled and turned away.

"Okay. Perhaps you are right. You did not know. And I told Demit it was stupid to deliver in the front door. Still, he as paid a high price. His father has been at his bedside all night."

The tension eased and Sergei allowed himself to relax - slightly. These people were dangerous, it would not do to be too comfortable around them. Ferrit was speaking again.

"But it does mean that we do not have the quantity of product that you asked for. I can get it, but it will take a few more days."

Sergei nodded and looked disappointed. Given the slightly conciliatory tone, he decided to push his luck. "There is something else you might help me with." He stepped forward now, laying a hand on Ferrit's shoulder, bringing him in close, talking conspiratorially. "My associates are having a problem with a particular person. This person is very… careful. We are looking for some way to eliminate them. It is not an easy job, or we would do it ourselves. It calls for a more professional approach. Do you know of anyone who could do this?"

Ferrit shrugged sympathetically. "We may do. Let me speak to my uncle and I will see if we can help you with this problem. If we are to do long term business this will be something nice we can do for you, no?"

Sergei smiled and patted the man on the shoulder. "Excellent. You are a good man, my friend. Now, I shall leave, I see this is a difficult time." He took out a card and scribbled a number on it. "When you have anything for me, just call this number. I will call you back."

With that he walked slowly from the hall, back down the stairs and into the busy street. As he walked back to his motorbike, he took some short, sharp breaths to dispel the adrenaline running through his system. *He should let Calloway know about this.*

Laçis had just finished eating lunch when the men came for him. A tense looking Ismet, the hulking Serkan in tow as usual, called out to him as soon as he came in the front door.

"We have to go. I am to take you to meet the boss."

Laçis stood, wiped his mouth with a napkin and placed the dish in the sink. "Very well. I will get my jacket."

As he moved to the hall and put the jacket on, Ismet spoke again.

"We have to ask that once in the car you are blindfolded. Mr Arikan is very particular about his personal security."

Laçis swore inside, but maintained a clam exterior. "Very well. I shall listen to my music." As they walked to the waiting car, he pulled the Walkman from his pocket and slipped on the headphones. By the time the car pulled away, Laçis, sat in darkness, was relaxing to Purcell. He chuckled to himself as the journey progressed. Certainly, not being able to see provided a measure of security, but

Laçis was easily able to count left and right turns, and the music provided him with a convenient way to measure the time. By the time the car drew to a halt, he was confident that he could retrace the route, should it be necessary to do so.

The blindfold was removed, Laçis left the car and was escorted into the lift at a corner of a small, underground car park. A block of flats, he thought, an expensive one, judging from the high end vehicles parked there. With four men plus himself, the lift was cramped, the mood was tense, silent until the ping denoted they had reached the top floor. Another large man was there as the lift opened, to lead them along a short corridor and into an expensively decorated penthouse flat. Only Ismet followed Laçis in, the pair being ushered towards a large sofa at the end of the room. Laçis barely had time to appreciate the panoramic London view before the man on the sofa spoke.

"You are the killer?" The elderly, white-haired man leaned forward, hands resting on an ornate walking stick. He wore a tailored shirt, formal trousers and a pair of basket-weave slip on shoes. His eyes were hidden behind a pair of tinted Ray-bans.

"I am," Laçis responded.

"Sit, sit," the man gestured. "I am Nasir Arikan. You have been working for me, I gather." He indicated the nearby armchair and Laçis sat. Another man placed a tray on the coffee table between them, pouring two glasses of water and two small cups of coffee before leaving the room. Arikan leant forward, drank some water, then sipped the coffee. As he drank, Laçis spoke.

"I have. And I must apologise again for my error. It was most unfortunate."

Arikan waved a hand. "Think no more of it. As events transpired, it worked to our advantage. Perhaps it was fated."

Laçis, following the lead, also sipped water and then the coffee. It was dark and bitter, he had to force himself to drink it without pulling a face.

"And now," Arikan sat back," We have our own tragedy. My own son. My youngest." The man paused for a moment, controlling his emotions. Laçis did not like where this was going. He had a feeling he was to be dragged even further into the affairs of these people. Arikan removed the Ray-bans and wiped his eyes with a liver-spotted hand. "All night we have been at his bedside."

Laçis was at a loss. "Something has happened to your son? Someone hurt him?"

Arikan dropped his hand and fixed Laçis with a stare. The hit-man started despite himself - these were the coldest eyes he had ever seen. In his time, Laçis had worked with and against many dangerous people. He had even once been in close proximity to Smirnov, the Gatchina Psychopath but even that had not elicited the same primal response as from this seemingly innocuous elderly man sat before him. Arikan thankfully looked away and spoke again, his voice thick with emotion.

"My boy lies at death's door because to the actions of the police. Of one police in particular." He clicked his fingers and the man who had brought the coffee returned with a folder. He handed it to Laçis.

"All the details we have are in there."

Laçis opened the folder and flicked through. "Detective Sergeant Calloway." He recognised the photo as the man who had been at the funeral. "I see. And the original target?"

"Her too. And her father. Kill them all!"

Chapter 26

Saturday evening, and Calloway was stirring the sauce when the doorbell rang. *Bugger, she's early*, was his immediate thought. Yet opening the door revealed a smiling Sergei, a bottle of scotch in hand. He followed Cab through to the kitchen.

"Smells nice."

"Oh, aye. Just a wee pasta sauce. I have a friend coming for dinner," Cab explained.

Sergei raised an eyebrow and grinned. "A *friend*? I see." Then the smile vanished. "What happened to your face?"

"Oh, a run in with a tearaway. He came off worse."

"You gave him a beating?"

"No, he got hit by a truck."

"Interesting. And effective, I imagine?"

"It was an accident, mind!"

Sergei thought back to the snooker hall. "Ah. The Arikan boy?"

"Yes, how did you know that?"

Sergei filled him in on the Wood Green visit. Calloway poured them both a tumbler as he did so. "That was brave of you." He raised the drink in a toast.

"Not really. There were only four of them," he smiled and drained the glass. "Oh, something else."

"Go on."

"I have some information on your politician. Birch? You may be interested to know that some months back he took part in a trade visit, to Cyprus."

"Did he, now? " Calloway drained his own glass. "Now, that is very interesting. Any more details?"

"We think he may have had contact with certain criminal elements there. There is nothing more than that."

"And how on earth does a Russian operative find out about the doings of a British Member of Parliament?"

Sergei just shrugged. "We have many people in Cyprus."

Cab shook his head. "What the fuck am I doing?" he smiled. "Well, okay, that gives us a potential connection to the Arikans. Still doesn't explain why they'd want his daughter dead, though?"

"Deal gone wrong? Some type of blackmail? Could be many things."

"Aye, I suppose. Alright, thanks for that. I'll pass it on to my boss, he'll be able to follow that one up."

He moved to pour them both another shot when the doorbell rang again.

"Shite, it's Gemma. She can't see you here." Calloway was flustered.

Sergei laughed and pointed to the balcony. "Is not a problem. I'll go out this way."

Calloway stared at him as though he were mad. "But we're on

the third floor!"

Sergei was already halfway out the balcony door. "Is fine. See you soon. And oh - " he pointed to the whisky bottle in Cab's hand. "Don't drink too much of that. It is not good for a man's... performance." He laughed, clambered over the balcony and was gone.

Calloway put the glasses in the sink and stowed the bottle in the living room as he moved to the hall.   Smoothing down his hair in the mirror he opened the door to a smiling Gemma.

"Sorry," he explained, "I was, er, cooking in the kitchen."

She held up a bottle of wine in response and Calloway led her into the flat.

"What happened to your face?" she asked, voice full of concern.

"Oh it was a - it was nothing, just a work thing. Here, let me take your coat and pour you a drink." He examined the bottle. "*Valoplicella*," he read from the rather plain label.

"Yes. It's from my cousin's vineyard in Verona," Gemma explained, sliding out of her jacket. She sat in an armchair as Cab retreated to the kitchen, turning down the sauce and checking the pasta before returning with a glass for them both.

"Well now" he said, clinking glasses. "Cheers!"

Spider thanked his cousin for the lift as he got our of the car. "I'm taking Angie out for Sunday lunch, I can pick you up again about three?" Gavin responded.

Spider nodded. Scooters were turning up in their droves, the queue out at the front of the Palais was already round the corner. The event went on into the night, but Spider reckoned he could offload all his stash within a couple of hours. Then, cash in hand, he could nip down to Barking and see the gun guy. He'd already made a call and set up a meet. Two hundred quid would get him a decent piece and ammo. That should be easy to raise, given the size of the crowd already here.

Ilford Palais sat on the High Road, at the edge of the shopping centre proper. It had been the main local dance hall for generations - a ballroom in the twenties and thirties, a dance hall in the post war years, a disco since the sixties. All the big local bands had played here, even Bobby Moore and Geoff Hurst were regulars at one time. The huge car park at the back was tailor made for dealing. Not overlooked, hedges down one side, if you set up in one corner you could see any car coming into the entrance a mile off. Spider began circulating immediately, spotting most of his regular punters.

"Put the word out, " he told them. "Anyone wants gear, send 'em my way."

He walked round the front of the building to work the queue, but ducked back out of site. A pair of tuxedo-clad bouncers were on the main door, and one of them was Danny. *Figured*, Spider thought, Taverner's firm ran all the door crews in East London. Anyway, he didn't want to be disturbed, so he quickly returned to the car park.

By one o clock he was well on target. Punters were able to go in and out of the Palais, once their hand had been stamped. Those looking for a little boost for the coming hours wandered over in twos or threes to the corner of the car park. Spider only had one bag left when the Old Bill turned up, a plod car with two in pulling into the entrance. The pair got out, to the jeers of those hanging around, sat on scooters, chatting, comparing chrome jobs. Spider didn't panic, it looked routine. These events rarely attracted any trouble, all the mod crews inside - the Hornchurch, the East London, the Tottenham crew, even those from further afield - were cool with each other. Everyone was there for the music, to pose and to dance.

Still, as the pair of cops strolled around the car park, he grew nervous. That was probably what attracted their attention. One glanced over as Spider dodged into the shade of the hedge. He nudged his colleague and they both walked forward. Spider didn't know whether to stay or go. Running was always a sign of guilt, perhaps he could bluff it out. He got ready to ditch the last bag of blues.

As it turned out, the coppers didn't need to get that close. One raised his radio when they were about thirty feet away. Spider swore, they'd obviously made him and were calling it in. Again, *hide or run*? No, there was a better option. The surface of the car park was rough tarmac in places, with lots of loose gravel and stones. Spider bent and scooped up a handful. Straightening, he yelled at the top of his voice "Do the Bill! Do the Bill!" and hurled the stones at the advancing pair. It had the desired effect. There was laughter and a roar from the forty or so youths in the car park. Someone else took up the shout. "Do the Bill!" and ran up to the police car, smashing the back windscreen with their crash helmet.

The cops beat a sudden retreat, one shouting again into his radio, as a hail of stones flew their way. The pair were chased round to the front of the building, though there was little relief there. Still, they might have got away with it had not the youngest copper pulled out his truncheon and whacked the nearest person - who happened to be a young lad stood there minding his own business. There was a shout as more mods came running out of the front door.

Within a minute came the sound of sirens as two cars and a van screeched to a halt outside the Palais. Uniforms poured out as the situation deteriorated. They attempted to form a line across the High Road but were met with a torrent of stones from the car park and cans and glasses from inside. More sirens, more vehicles, and the police soon had a fully fledged riot on their hands. Spider, still a few bob short of his target, desperately grabbed a few stragglers, making a couple more sales before deciding to cut his losses. Gavin's place was about a half hour walk away, luckily in almost the opposite direction to the Old Bill station. With a last glance round at the chaos he'd caused, he took off at a brisk pace.

Chapter 27

Calloway shaded his eyes against the low morning sun coming in through the office window, picked up the plastic cup of lukewarm coffee, grimaced and put it down again. Denham appeared in the doorway. "Feeling rough?"

"Like a parrot took a shite in my mouth."

"Must've been a good night?"

Calloway shrugged. Truth be told, he couldn't remember much about it. He and Gemma had enjoyed a nice meal, then sat in the front room drinking and chatting - well, he was drinking, she had to drive home. One part stood out. They had been talking for a while when Gemma asked about the photo on his phone table in the hall.

"The woman and the baby. Your wife and son? Daughter?"

"Daughter. Aye. Maisie." He lapsed into silence. Gemma moved closer to him on the sofa and laid a hand on his arm.

"Cab, what happened?"

Perhaps it was the wine, perhaps it was the company, perhaps it was the stress of the last couple of weeks. Regardless, it was still so hard to talk about. The familiar pain surged through him. He looked away, unable to meet Gemma's eyes. "I was working a late shift. Glasgow, this was back in the seventies. March 15th, 1977… A call came through to the nick. Mary, my wife, had phoned, she was in bits. By the time I got home the ambulance was already there. Maisie… my wee Maisie was dead."

"Oh Cab, that's awful!" Gemma took his hand in hers.

"She was three months old. Cot death, they called it. No-one could explain or say why it happened, what it even meant, it was just a phrase they used. *Just one of those things*, as they say. Mary blamed herself, I blamed myself, what else could we do? You can't hate a disease or an accident. But when a wee bairn dies of nothing… that's hard to take." He swallowed hard and closed his eyes. "We struggled on after that but it was difficult between us. We were divorced within the year, and that was that."

He lifted and tilted the wine bottle on the table. Empty. Sergei's whisky bottle was almost full, though. He stood to get it, poured from that and downed it in one. He felt Gemma's hand on his shoulder and turned towards her.

After that, everything was a blur. He'd woken up alone, naked, in bed, with a pounding headache. There'd been no sign of Gemma, though the dinner things had been tidied away. With nothing else to do on a Sunday, he'd showered, dressed and come into the station. He wanted to research more into Birch, find out if there was any more info on his Cyprus trip.

"Cab? Cab?"

Calloway snapped back into the present. Denham was talking to him. "Sorry, guv, miles away." He slid the folder over the desk.

"Here, take a look at this. I got some intel on Birch last night and followed it up this morning. Seems that our Right Honourable friend had a little jaunt a while back. A trade trip to Cyprus."

Denham sat, slipped on his glasses and scanned the papers. "Well, now. That is interesting. A visit to Cyprus and, some months later, a threat from Turkish Cypriot criminals. What are you thinking?"

Calloway rubbed his face. "An existing connection? Perhaps they've been into him for a while? Or something new. Blackmail? He hardly seems the sort to become a drugs mule. Though who's going to check an official trade delegation for contraband? Especially Class A drugs."

"Class A…" Denham drummed his fingers on the file. "That's got to be it. We know cocaine is the next big thing in street drugs. But it's already the drug of choice for celebs, for the rich, the jet-setters, the movers and shakers."

"As in our glorious rulers? Our members of parliament, say?"

Denham nodded and thought for moment. "Let me talk to a mate of mine at Westminster. In the meantime, keep this under your hat. If Birch is involved, we don't know how deep this goes." He stood and turned to leave. "Nothing until you hear from me, right?"

"Aye, guv,"

As Denham left, a PC from downstairs poked his head round the door.

"Just had a call through, sarge. Your mate Webb has just been spotted in Ilford. At the Palais."

By the time Calloway was down the stairs, uniform were running all over the place. He spotted Houlihan chatting to a WPC by the snack machine. "Micky, with me, now," he called, rushing out the back to his car. Houlihan jumped in.

"Where's the fire, skip?"

"Buckle up. Webb's been spotted at the Palais. According to uniform it's all kicked off down there."

They followed two squad cars and a van out of the gate and for the short drive down the High Road. Sure enough, there was a major affray in progress as the Rover screeched to a halt on the corner before the Palais. A large crowd of youths stretched across the street, yelling, hurling abuse and cans and glasses at the thin police line. New shields and helmets were being handed out from the back of one of the vans, kit that had been introduced after the riots that had blazed across the country last year. Calloway pushed his way forward, ducking a beer can that narrowly missed his head. He scanned the crowd of angry faces ahead, no sign of Webb. In his concentration he moved forward out of the police line, attracting the attention of some of the crowd.

"Pig!" someone shouted and a fist flashed before his face as something else hit him on the shoulder. Calloway cursed and threw out a punch, slipping as someone grabbed the collar of his jacket, pulling him off balance. As he fought to keep on his feet, a large shape loomed on the edge of his vision. Houlihan, growling "Get back, you cunts," before laying about him with a truncheon. The big man grabbed Calloway by the scruff of his neck and pulled him back to the safety of the police line.

Calloway nodded his thanks and hurried back to the car, closely followed by the DC.

"If Webb saw police, he'll likely have run," Cab reasoned. "He won't have come this way, that's through the police and towards the station. He won't have gone north, right?"

"Yep," Houlihan agreed. "Only way over the rail line is the Plessey footbridge, and that's behind us."

"So, east, but then he's on the High Road, in full view all the way to Seven Kings. No, he'll have gone south, through the back streets. Hold on. We're going through."

"Shall I turn the music on, skip?"

Calloway laughed. "Just for now." He switched the headlights on full and blared the horn as Houlihan hit the blues and twos. Tyres spinning, the Rover shot forward, uniform jumping aside as it headed east along the High Road. Calloway gambled on the crowd being hyped-up youths rather than serious rioters and his hunch paid off. They parted like butter and, save for one or two hits to the bodywork, the car made it through unscathed.

"Down here, skip, by the big church" Houlihan indicated the right ahead and Calloway span into the turn. Luckily the traffic here on a Sunday was light. Beyond lay another large thirties estate, much like that surrounding Valentines Park, long, straight rows of terraced houses.

"He'll likely stay off the main road. We'll quarter these side streets." Calloway span the wheel again, ignoring the angry gestures of an on-coming bus driver. He sped up and down the side roads, as fast as he dared, ignoring the dull throb in his temples. As they worked deeper into the estate, Houlihan pointed.

"There. That's him."

Calloway gunned the engine, surging forward. Although the siren was off now, Webb still heard them. He turned, spotted the oncoming car, span around and ran. Houlihan was already on the radio.

"This is Juliet India Six, heading south on Littlemoor Road, Ilford, in pursuit of suspect. Request assistance, any available units."

With a crackle the call came back in from HQ. "Acknowledged Juliet India Six. Please be advised, no units available due to on-going incident on Ilford High Road. In fact, we've get extra bodies being bussed in from Barkingside."

"Shite!" Calloway slammed on the brakes as a kid, one of a group kicking a ball around, ran into the road in front of him. The pause gave Webb the chance to dart around a corner.

"He's heading for South Park," Houlihan said. "If he makes that we've got no chance of catching him."

Calloway sped off again, swinging a left at the bottom of the road, flipping the blues and twos back on. They just spotted Webb disappearing around another corner as they came into the turning. Calloway cursed as a large van began backing out of a driveway halfway along, blocking the way completely. Blaring the horn only got a gesture from the driver. Still swearing, Cab jumped out of the car and sped off on foot, pounding the pavement in his haste to get to the next junction. There, he turned left into South Park Drive; too late. Ahead, he could see Webb was already at the park. There was no entrance here, but Webb began a desperate scramble up the railings. Breathing hard, Calloway made a supreme effort and managed to grab Webb's ankle as the youth was almost over the metal rails. He yanked hard and both he and Webb tumbled to the pavement.

Webb lashed out with a kick but it glanced off Calloway's leg. Still, he was up and on his feet again, leaving Cab clutching thin air.

He was about to rise and give chase again when something happened - the sound of that awful crunch when the truck hit Demit flashed into Cab's brain, overwhelming him for an instant. He reeled back against the railings, black spots dancing on the edge of his vision. There was a screech of brakes as Houlihan pulled the Rover up to the kerb and jumped out.

"You okay, skip?" He glanced about, in vain, for any sign of Webb.

"Shite!" Calloway retched and spat on the pavement. "Shite!"

Chapter 28

Laçis sat back in the rear seat and closed his eyes. After yesterday's meeting with Arikan, he had been driven back to the safe house. There, he'd studied all the files had had been given on his targets: the MP, the daughter and the policeman, and still with Taverner on the reserve list. This situation was a rapidly spiraling out of control. Still, if he managed carry out the hits quickly, he could be out of this mess and back to his secluded Auvergne retreat in days. To this end, he had asked to be driven to the area where the MP lived. He would carry out a preliminary reconnaissance today, make his plans overnight, then, with luck, have the job completed in the next day or so. The policeman might be trickier, a police station was not a good place to arrange a hit. Still, he had some of Arikan's people checking out Calloway's home address. An early morning doorstep hit might be the best approach there.

The driver grunted and Laçis opened his eyes. This part of London was different to anything had seen so far. As they crossed from Woodford into Chigwell, the streets became wider, the houses larger. Rather than fast food joints and pubs, here there were bistros and wine bars. Serkan had been assigned as his driver today. "He will look after you," Ismet had said. Laçis didn't doubt it. He even wondered if the hulking brute had orders to finish off Laçis once the job had been done. Well, that was something to worry about in the future. For now, Serkan slowed as they came to a junction on Manor Road. He waved a huge, hairy hand ahead.

"There. The second house past the junction. The MP's home."

"Slow down as much as you can, but do not stop," Laçis ordered. To the right stood a large, curved white wall, with a heavy black iron gate at its centre. Behind it stood a bored looking security guard, all covered by a wall mounted camera. Beyond, the top half a large white house was visible, with balconied French windows across its front aspect.

"Take the next right." Going in through the front was clearly not an option, perhaps there would be easier access at the rear. But these were not regular city blocks, the next turn was not for some distance. Turning right and right again brought them into a smaller road, lined with large, if not as large, houses. Halfway down, a sign read Private Road, No Admittance. *So no access through the back then*. Laçis had Serkan three point turn and take them back to the small green at the top of the road. He sat and thought for a moment. As he did so, he spied the top of a large structure over the trees, what appeared to be some sort of tower. He tapped his driver on the shoulder.

"What is that place?"

Serkan glanced up from his newspaper. "Huh? That? Oh, it's Claybury."

"Claybury? What is this?"

"it's a hospital. Well, not really a hospital, more a looney bin."

"Looney bin? What does this mean?"

The man twirled a finger at his temple. "A place where they send the loonies. The mad people."

"I see. I would like to go and take a look. If we may?" He raised an eyebrow.

Serkan sighed, folded his newspaper, tucked it down the side of his seat and swung the car back onto the main road.

Claybury Hospital had opened in 1893, one of the many new purpose built asylums of the late Victorian era. Sat atop Tomswood Hill, its large water tower was a prominent local landmark. The hospital itself, a vast, sprawling red brick edifice, had once housed over two thousand patients. It's construction marked a considerable change in standards of care, in it's day being widely recognised for its pioneering work in the treatment of mental illness. More recently, the term asylum had been changed to psychiatric facility, and, with the shift to care in the community, the number of patients living at the hospital had drastically fallen. Indeed, there were some local rumours that developers had their eye on the place as a site for potential upmarket flats.

For now, however, it was a simple enough thing to drive in through the ornate gates, past the entrance lodge and right up to the main buildings themselves. As Serkan busied himself with his newspaper once more, Laçis got out for a look around. Closer, the tower loomed even larger. He shaded his eyes against the bright sunshine and looked up.

"Marvellous, ain't it?" A voice spoke beside him.

Laçis brought his gaze back down. An elderly man in a rather worn grey suit stood smiling next to him. He wore a battered old cap with a large hole in it.

"Yes. What is its purpose?" Laçis asked.

"Water tower, see? Water for the hospital." The man pointed up to the multi-spired top. "An 'undred and seventy feet tall. From the top you can look out across the whole of London."

"You can get up to the top?"

"Oh yes. I did once. Over a hundred steps. I was younger then. Got in trouble." The man grinned.

"Arthur? Arthur!" A young, white jacketed Asian orderly approached the pair. "Come on, Arthur. It's time for your cup of tea."

"Ooh, tup of tea, yes. Right oh." The old man shuffled off, cheerfully chatting to himself.

Laçis waited for the pair to leave, then moved to the base of the tower. One door, locked. A matter of seconds to pick the heavy, old lock, then he was into the cool interior. Taking the steps two at a time, he was soon at the top, breathing barely affected. Any water tank had been removed at some point, leaving a large, dusty space under the eaves. The old man had been right. Through the tall, narrow windows to the south west, London spread out before him; the Post Office Tower, the office blocks, the white walls of the Tower of London. But of more interest, to the north east, across one road and that narrow lane, he could see the rear of the MP's house. Laçis took out a scope from his inside jacket pocket.

Peering through it, he smiled. At least half the garden was in clear view from here, particularly the rear terrace. In fact, as he watched, a middle aged woman came out of the open French doors and sat at an outside table. Laçis tucked the scope away and trotted back down the steps, feeling the happiest he had for several days.

Calloway was back behind his desk nursing a strong coffee and a bacon sandwich. There had been a steady stream of youngsters being brought in and booked following the Ilford Riot, as it was now being called. So many, in fact, that other stations were dealing with the overflow. He had been going over and over what had happened with Webb, eventually deciding it had been a combination of exertion, hangover and general stress. Still, there was nothing to be done now, Webb was off and away.

Denham popped in, shut the door behind him, and sat on the corner of Turner's desk.

"Well, then. I had a word with my Westminster pal. Turns out coke is growing in popularity there just as fast as everywhere else. He's making more enquiries for me, but word is that half the toilets in Parliament have traces of coke in them, especially round the bars."

"Explains a lot, given how things are going," Calloway offered his boss a ciggie. It was accepted. "So. We have a Turkish group running coke into London. We have an MP who's recently been to Cyprus. His daughter has been targeted by an international hit-man, who may have been recommended by a major drug cartel."

"And his daughter is hanging out with a convicted drug user." Denham added. "And Taverner?"

"I'm wondering about that. Maybe it was just a coincidence? Similar looking girl, same time, same place?"

"Bit of a stretch, isn't it, Cab?"

"Aye, maybe. But stranger things have happened at sea. Remember that murder case in Epping forest last year? We only got the guy on pure chance, that woman on the bus coming forward, remember?"

"True." Denham took another puff on the Marlboro and exhaled slowly. "Bugger. We're going to have to question Birch again. I'll have to clear it with the with the Chief."

"How about we offer to visit him rather than pull him in, guv? Might sweeten the pill a bit?"

"Good idea. And I'll do the talking this time. You can come with. I'll get it sorted tomorrow. Now, Cab?"

"Yes, guv?"

Denham stood and stubbed out the fag. " You look like shit. Get home, will you. I'll give you a call if anything urgent comes in."

On his way out, Cab bumped into Gemma. She was talking with a senior officer, but held a hand up on seeing Calloway, walking over to him.

"Hello, sleeping beauty," she smiled.

"Hi, I, er… listen, about last night. I'm sorry if I er, if…"

"Got drunk and passed out?"

"Aye. That." He thought for a moment "Hang on. I woke up in bed… naked."

"DS Calloway, are you blushing?" she laughed.

"Did we, er, I mean… I don't really…. did we…"

She moved close and whispered in his ear. "Perhaps. You might never know." Then, moving back. "Got to go. Will call you later. *Big boy.*"

Calloway didn't know whether to laugh or cry, so he settled for shuffling off quickly to his car. Some Count Basie improved his mood on the drive home where, after parking up, he decided to visit the takeaway to grab some dinner. His usual fan club were on the corner, swearing, spitting, smoking. One of the older ones called him over.

"'Ere, Mr Calloway, little Stevie here reckons he saw some blokes hanging round your flat earlier. Ain't that right, Stevie?"

A kid of about twelve, one finger up his nostril, came over. "Yeah. Two geezers. They was in the flats, then was walking round outside, looking up at your balcony."

"Is that right?" Calloway bent down towards the boy. "What did they look like, son?"

The boy scratched his head. "Not seen 'em round here before. They had black hair and moustaches. They looked like that bloke in the film. Wassisname? Omar Sheriff."

"I see." Calloway straightened. "Alright. Thanks for letting me know. That's good of you."

"Good enough for a bottle of cider?" the boy grinned.

Calloway rolled his eyes. "No. You'll get me sacked."

The group groaned.

"Tell you what, though." He rummaged in his jacket pocket for his cigs. "Here you go, there's half a dozen left in there. You shouldn't smoke, though, it will stunt your growth."

"Stunt!" Stevie cried joyfully. "Rhymes with c-"

"Alright, alright," Calloway interrupted. He handed the packet of Marlboro to the grinning kids and decided to head straight back to the flat, the takeaway could wait.

A search around the area found no sign of the strangers, though, and the flat was still locked, safe and sound. Still, he made sure to lock all his doors and windows that night.

Chapter 29

Taverner moved to hand the stall-holder a fiver, but the man waved it away.

"On the house, Mr Taverner," the man explained, expertly twisting close the paper bag of apples before handing it over. "And pass on my regards to your mother."

"Thanks, Joe," Taverner accepted the bag and handed it to his minder. Pearce loomed suddenly at his shoulder, making even the crime boss jump.

"Fuck me, Eddie! You trying to give me an heart attack?"

"Sorry, T. Wanted a word. Heard I'd find you here."

They were in Stratford Market, the ever-suited Taverner and his minder Les standing out amongst the usual Monday morning shopping crowd. Taverner continued.

"Just picking up some fruit. Going over to see Mum a bit later, she likes her fruit."

"Do you think it's wise, T, being out and about with this shooter on the loose?"

Taverner sneered. "Fuck him. If he gets close enough to shoot, he's close enough to be shot. Besides, there's more than Les keeping an eye on me."

Pearce glanced around, clocking the familiar faces of two other firm heavies mingling in the crowd. He smiled. "Should've known. Anyway, thought you might like to know. The Webb boy has done a runner."

"Terrible what happened to his mother." Taverner's eyes flashed. "Animals! No news of him?"

"Well, someone that sounds a lot like him bought a gun last night, off Ronnie the Leg in Barking. He rang me this morning to let me know. Want me to go looking for him?"

Taverner motioned to his minder and moved off up the street. "No, let's leave him be. With any luck, he might do our job for us. Swine. I tell you, Eddie, this is going beyond the pale. Bad enough that they're flooding the streets with their Class A muck. And all this heroin too, it's diabolical. The thought of my grandkids growing up with all that filth around turns my guts."

"Yes T, it's horrible stuff."

"Like I've been saying, it's time to get out. Mark my words, Eddie, I'm lining up deals that will have us out of all this bollocks soon enough. I'll see you do alright, don't worry. Maybe you could get a nice little place by the seaside, eh? Retire and have a bit of peace and quiet for a change. So, anything else?"

"Well, the Arikans say they want a face to face. Bloody liberty if you ask me. Besides which it will be a set-up."

"Course it will, course it will. Still," Taverner had by now reached his Bentley, parked on a double yellow line. "I think we should do it. A set-up can go both ways. Tell them we set the time and place, they'll only know just beforehand. Call everyone in on it, I want the whole firm ready."

He paused halfway into the rear door of the car. "Whoever we don't have at the meeting will pay a visit to Wood Green. We hit them at both ends, the same time."

Pearce grinned. "Right, boss. I'm on it."

Spider span the cylinder and pointed the gun at his reflection in the bedroom mirror again. The revolver was heavy, but felt good in his hand. Something of a museum piece, perhaps, but it went bang and fired bullets, that's all he needed to know. He'd got it from Ronnie the Leg in Barking just last night. Even with his Palais drug deals, Spider had been fifty quid short of the asking price, but Ronnie let him have the gun regardless. One revolver and six bullets, enough to do the job.

His next problem was getting close enough to do it. To that end, he'd been asking around. He knew the Arikans were based at Wood Green, knew they had some cafés and a snooker all there. Still, he couldn't just go bowling in tooled up on the off-chance Ismet and his goon would be around. No, he had to play this smart. Sneak around. Follow them. Find out what their routine was. Then, at the right time... *bam! Yeah, like some sort of spy, or a proper gangster!*.

He'd had the chance to pick up some clothes from another of his bedsits. Checking had revealed that, yes, there'd been a couple of "foreign looking blokes" nosing round asking questions about him. Now, he packed everything he needed in a travel case Gav had leant him and, saying goodbye to Angie, slipped out the door and headed for the bus stop.

An hour later he was in Wood Green, wearing shades, a baseball cap tilted low over his face, looking for a cheap bed and breakfast close to Green Lanes. He found one not far from the restaurant he'd picked up the drugs from.

Once settled in, Spider took a walk around the area. It was a Monday lunchtime, the place was busy, it was easy enough to blend into the crowds. He hung around for as long as he dared opposite the restaurant. He was just about to move on when a bloke came out who he recognised as one of those who'd been at the garage. The memory brought a shudder. Repressing it, he stayed on the opposite side of the road and followed the man.

He noticed, with some satisfaction, that the guy's faced was bruised and he wore a cast on his right wrist. It wasn't a long walk, the man disappearing into the doorway of snooker hall a block away. Spider waited a few minutes, then crossed the road, slipping into the dark entrance. Inside, an old geezer poked his head through a hatchway, asking to see a membership card. Without pause, Spider did a one-eighty back out onto the street.

He realised this might take a little more planning than he had first thought. *Surveillance, that was what the old bill called it.* Yeah, he'd *surveill* this place first off. There was a café directly opposite, he could sit at a window table, have something to eat, drink tea. Ideal. Dodging traffic, he crossed the road.

Calloway was up early that morning, reviewing his options. He first called Smith at the station. She confirmed that Denham had arranged a meeting with Birch at his Chigwell home for tomorrow morning. She gave him the address and mentioned he was to pick up Denham en route.

Cab thought long and hard before making the next call. Checking the card, he began dialling the number Sergei had given him. Even though he was calling from home, he still wondered if the line was secure. *Christ, I'm getting paranoid*, he thought, then immediately dismissed the idea. He was phoning a Russian safe-house, to pass a message to a Soviet agent working deep undercover in the UK. He had every reason to feel paranoid. Nonetheless, he put the call in. Sergei rang back within five minutes. Calloway filled him in about Webb, and about the interest in his flat. Sergei sounded concerned.

"Do you have other place to stay?" he asked. When Calloway said not, there was a pause. "I can be with you in thirty minutes?"

"No need, Sergei, I'll be fine. Oh, my guv and I will be visiting the MP tomorrow, see if we can dig a little deeper on what happened in Cyprus."

"I see. Maybe I can be there?"

"Uh, I don't think that's a good idea."

There was a laugh down the line. "No, I did not mean at meeting, I meant in area. Laçis is still at large, and it now sounds like these criminals have a personal interest in you. You might require assistance."

"Well, I suppose I can't stop you. And thanks." He gave Sergei the address, rang off and turned his mind to breakfast.

Chapter 30

Calloway pulled the Rover up to the wrought iron gate and wound down the window. He reached to press the intercom buzzer but the security guard beyond was already opening the gate, waving the car forward.

"Nice place," he murmured to Denham. His passenger merely grunted in response. The car crunched to a halt on the driveway, the front door to the large house was already opening. The figure of Birch, dressed in casual slacks and a cashmere sweater, welcomed them as they took the steps up and into the spacious hallway.

"Morning, sir. I'm DI Denham, I believe you've already met DS Calloway?"

Birch ushered them through the cavernous interior and into a kitchen with a floor-space larger than Cab's entire flat. Denham was talking on the move.

"Thank you very much for agreeing to talk to us today, sir. We'll try not to take up too much of your time."

A middle aged blonde woman nodded at them nervously in the kitchen. "My wife, Julia." Birch waved a hand. "I thought we'd sit out in the garden as it's such a pleasant morning. Could you bring us out some coffee, darling?"

They followed the MP out through French doors and onto a terrace overlooking an immaculate striped lawn. Colourful flower beds bordered each side, the lawn ran down to a small grove of trees at the far end of the garden. The trio sat at a wrought iron table. Birch waited for his wife to emerge and deposit a tray of coffee and biscuits before talking again.

"Well, I hope I can help. Is it this murder again? Such a terrible affair." He poured coffee.

"In a way, it is," Denham began. "Though recent information has led us to follow some new lines of enquiry. We understand that you visited Cyprus last year, as part of a trade delegation?"

Birch looked pensive. "Yes, that's correct, I did. Part of an initiative to export British tech, I seem to remember."

"I see, sir. And while you were in Cyprus, did anything unusual happen?"

The MP took a sip of coffee and placed the china cup back down on the table. "No, I don't think so. Such as?"

"Were you approached by any unfamiliar people? Locals perhaps?"

Birch pushed out his bottom lip and shook his head. "No, nothing like that. It was all rather dull, as such delegations usually are. Why do you ask?"

Denham fixed Birch with a stare for a moment. "I noticed you have private security on your gate?"

"Yes. Well, after all that fuss with my daughter. The press, you know, it caused an awful kerfuffle."

"And where is your daughter now, sir?"

"She is back here living with us. We insisted she move back in during the trial. We felt it was better."

"And has she seen Mr Slater since the trial?"

"Not as far as I know. We certainly didn't approve of him, did we darling?"

Mrs Birch was hovering in the doorway. "No dear," she replied, fingers fluttering. She appeared to be about to say something else when Birch glared at her. Denham caught Calloway's glance and raised an eyebrow. He turned to Birch again.

"Sir, can you think of any reason why someone may wish to harm your daughter?"

"Didn't your colleague ask me all this before, Inspector? I have to say, I can see no relevance in this line of questioning. Yes, Michelle fell in with a bad sort but that is all behind us now. She has learned her lesson, we plan to move on as a family and - "

He was brought up short as a large, dark shape bounded out of the house towards them. The black Labrador made directly for Calloway, attracted, perhaps, by the biscuit he was lifting towards his mouth.

"Toby! Toby!" Mrs Birch re-appeared at the doorway again. "Bad boy!"

But it was Toby that saved Calloway's life. The dog lurched up, going for the biscuit, spraying drool as it came. Calloway tilted back in the chair, which overbalanced and fell. As he went back, Cab felt, more than, heard something whistle past him. There was a loud smack of impact into the brickwork behind them. Denham, the old soldier, instantly recognised the sound.

"Sniper!" he shouted. "Down!" He fell to the floor, reaching out to grab and drag Birch with him. Calloway was already off, crawling for the cover of the borders. Mrs Birch ducked back inside the house. The oblivious Toby was enthusiastically hoovering up the remaining biscuits from the plate on the table. Denham, now atop the prone and obviously terrified Birch, shouted out.

"Call the police! Mrs Birch? Call the police! Tell them officers under attack, firearms involved! *Now!*"

Another bullet whined overhead, shattering a plant pot on the patio.

"Cab! Cab!" Denham called. "Are you hit?"

"I'm fine, guv," came a voice from the shrubbery. "I'm going after him."

Before Denham could say anything to stop him, Calloway was off. Crouched over, he stayed in the lee of the garden wall, heading for the trees. The shot must have come from the rear of the house, the shooter had to be up high to have the elevation to fire over the wall. Cab was more angry than scared, and that anger pushed him forward. Still keeping low, he wound through the grove, then into the cover of the large shed beyond it. A six foot fence ran behind it, Calloway ran to the door at its centre. Lifting the latch, he peered out cautiously. Beyond was a narrow lane, lined by similar houses.

There was no-one around, no vehicles parked. He looked left and right, then quickly scanned the windows of the houses opposite. *No sign of life there, all windows closed.* The ground sloped up, so perhaps those windows were high enough? Then he saw it. Peeking through the trees beyond the house to his right, at the crest of the hill, the corner of a tower. *Claybury*, he thought. *Of course!* Without further pause, he was off.

Sergei's head swivelled at the flat crack of the shot. He'd been in the area for an hour or so, slowly driving round on the motorbike. The MP's house was obviously well guarded at the front, but the rear was less secure, just a tall fence with a gate in it. Still, it was in a private lane, overlook by the houses opposite. Any stranger hanging around would very obviously stand out. So he began scouting the immediate neighbourhood; a busy road at the front, the side streets were quieter but had no obvious hiding places.

He widened the circle. To the east, the houses were clearly larger and more expensive. *Millionaires Row*, Cab had called this place, the streets lined with the homes of football players and television celebrities. *Very different from the flats and prospekts of childhood*, Sergei thought. To the north, a golf club and the M11 motorway. To the west and south, he was back into the usual looking streets for this part of London, not far, as it happened, from Calloway's flat. But still nothing that looked suitable for an observation post.

Pausing for a rest, he'd looked up, and laughed at his own stupidity. In some ways, he had been too close to see it - the huge tower that nestled among some old looking buildings at the top of the hill. Sergei revved the bike and set off again, keeping the tower always to his right. Eventually, he was back on Manor Road. Opposite a line of bungalows to his left, stood an ornate entrance, its gates open.

There was no guard or barrier, so he simply rode up the long driveway to the red brick buildings ahead. The site was much larger than he'd first thought, a hospital of some kind, it seemed. He smiled briefly to himself as he pulled up before the main entrance. Hospitals were always busy, lots of people coming and going. And the tower did not appear used, he wondered what its purpose may have been.

There were people walking around, in and out of various doorways. Most were clearly staff, others were mostly elderly, with one or two younger ones. As one of the younger men slowly approached, staring transfixed at the motorbike, Sergei understood what the function of this place was. He nodded to the young man, who gingerly patted the bike before wandering off. There was a car park to one side, half full. Sergei put the bike on its stand there and removed his crash helmet, looking up again.

The tower must have been thirty-forty metres high, with tall windows in the construction at its top. He glanced north east. Not visible here, through buildings and trees, but he imagined that the MP's house would be in direct line of site from anyone at that elevation. With a quick glance around, Sergei moved to the heavy, black-painted wooden door at the tower base. *Locked.* There was no window to look into. He crouched down to examine the lock when a voice called out.

"'Ere! What d'you think you're doing?"

Sergei straightened and turned, a smile already on his face. A middle-aged man approached, wearing a brown coat, a large ring of keys at his belt. A janitor, perhaps?

"Sorry. I am a little lost. I came to see a friend."

"Well you won't find him in the here. Which ward is he in?"

Sergei ignored the question. "What is this tower for?"

The janitor regarded him with suspicion. "It was built as a water tower for the 'ospital. Empty now, They took the tanks out years ago."

"Okay. Thank you." Sergei smiled again and walked briskly off, glancing back quickly as he reached the corner. The man was still by the door, almost as though he were guarding it now.

Back at the bike, Sergei considered his options. Incapacitating the janitor and breaking into the tower would not be difficult but it would attract attention. On the other hand, what if Laçis were there, what if he were armed and in place? This might be the closest that Sergei had come to his target so far. A risk, then. Too much risk. *Attention might mean capture, exposure.* No, better instead to get down to the house and somehow warn Calloway. Not through the front, though.

Sergei set off at a brisk jog to the eastern perimeter of the hospital grounds, soon reaching a basic wire fence that he was over in seconds. He lowered himself into the road beyond, just the other side of which lay the private lane. He was about to cross the road when he heard the crack. Exhaling, he span and went over the fence again, cursing as he snagged his jacket on the top. Dropping to the grass and rolling, he was up on his feet and sprinting towards the tower as the second shot rang out overhead.

Chapter 31

Laçis swore and moved back from the window. He'd removed one of the small panes in the old leading, the wind whistled through the gap. The first shot had been good, how it had missed he couldn't say. The second had been in anger, a rare lapse on his part; this situation was obviously getting to him. In seconds, he had the rifle packed and was hurrying down the stairs.

It had been simple enough to find the caretaker on the last visit. A combination of bribery and the intimidating presence of Serkan had resulted in the acquisition of the spare key for the tower. The pair had returned early yesterday morning before the main hospital shift started, and let themselves in. Laçis left Serkan in the dusty entrance hall, perched on a folding chair, thumbing through a copy of *Fiesta* magazine and climbed the hundred-odd steps once more. Setting out his gear, Laçis had sat in wait until the light faded, binos trained on the rear of Birch's house almost the whole time. There had been no movement apart from two women popping in and out. One presumably the wife, the other a cleaner, judging from the pinafore and bright yellow gloves.

Today had been better. There had been three brief glimpses of Birch himself. Not enough to get a shot, but enough to put Laçis on full alert. So when Birch reappeared with Calloway and another man, Laçis smiled, relaxed into his firing position and focused fully on his targets. One to each head was the plan. Rapid fire was the main reason he had chosen the PSG1, a semi-automatic, designed specifically for counter-terrorism use. Steadying his breathing, Laçis peered through the telescopic site… *Calloway to the left, then a slight movement right to takeout Birch sat opposite.* But something had gone wrong. Calloway had disappeared on the first shot, his place taken by a large, black dog. In frustration, Laçis snapped off another shot towards Birch, but he was already moving. Following that, it was clear that everyone had gone to ground. No sense in remaining in place. A golden rule of sniping was *shoot and move.*

Serkan must have heard the shots, he was already on his feet when Laçis reached the ground floor, peering out the door. He turned with an questioning glance, to which Laçis merely shook his head. The big man checked outside again and exited the tower, Laçis close behind, rifle case slung over his shoulder. They were at the car within seconds. Other people may have heard the shots but, way up above as they were, would most likely discount them as a car backfiring or similar. Serkan gunned the engine and span the car. Laçis hissed at him "Slowly. Always escape slowly, draw no attention."

The driver grumbled but took them out onto the driveway at a slower speed. Something moved in the edge of Laçis' vision and he twisted in the seat. A man was sprinting across the grass towards the tower. It was the short man from the funeral, the one who had been speaking to the policeman. Laçis was torn. The identity of this man was a mystery. Yet to stop and confront him now would be foolish - police would be swarming these streets very soon. No, best escape. Quietly. *Slip away*, as he had been taught. He turned to face front again, sliding down in the seat.

Sergei was going so fast he almost bounced off the tower door. He rattled the handle. *Locked again!* Without pause, he raced back round to the front of the tower. A pale blue car, a Volvo, was heading down the drive. Sergei raced to his motorbike, slammed his helmet on, and sped off in pursuit. He just had time to see the car turn left out of the gate before it disappeared from view. There were already the sound of sirens fast approaching, he wanted to miss those, too. Revving the engine, he shot through the gates, swerved away from a blaring car that almost hit him, and began weaving his way through the traffic.

By the time Calloway reached the tower, both Laçis and Sergei were long gone. Cab was breathing hard, had torn his trousers on the fence and was pissed off. A man in a brown coat appeared, and Calloway shouted at him, flashing his warrant card.

"Get this fucking door open now!"

The caretaker grumbled but complied, Cab pushing past him into the interior. An empty ground floor, nothing apart from a couple of old chairs and small table. Mars Bar wrappers on the floor. The lingering smell of fag smoke. And something worse. In the corner, under some newspaper, a large turd. Calloway gagged and moved back, looking up the stairs. Swearing, he began the ascent. He moved carefully into the space at the top - not because he thought the shooter might still be in place, but for forensics. In contrast to downstairs, the large space here was tidy, the only signs of occupation being a broken window and some marks in the dust. Still swearing, Cab retraced his steps. By the time he was back at ground level, a police helicopter was buzzing overhead, and sirens sounded from all around. Denham appeared, closely followed by a firearms officer.

"Anything?" he asked, glancing up.

"No, guv. He was definitely up there, I'd say. But he's fled the nest." He pointed into the room. "I'd say there were two of them, though. One sat down here as look-out."

"Anything for forensics?"

"Not much. Might be some prints down here but I doubt you'll find anything upstairs. Oh, there is a turd in the corner." He grinned. "Shall you bag it up or shall I?"

Denham rolled his eyes. "Fucking great. A sniper taking pot-shots in leafy Essex and he's off away, scot free."

"At least he didn't hit Birch, guv."

"True. But here's the thing, Cab. That first shot wasn't aimed at Birch… it was aimed at you."

Sergei crouched low over the handlebars as he cut in front of another car. More horns blared but he could waste no time, the Volvo was not far ahead. He had no clear idea who was in it, having barely caught no more than a quick glimpse of the driver, he needed to make an ID as quick as possible. Once he had eyes on, then he could make a decision as to his next step. He was also aware, though, that disturbance and noise from behind might alert the people in the car.

Accordingly, he hung back a little, The Suzuki handled well, the weather was dry and sunny. If not spotted he should be able to follow Laçis, if that was who was in the Volvo, all the way back to whatever place he was using as a base. Peering ahead, Sergei risked overtaking one more car, putting him two behind his target.

They were soon passing under the M11 motorway. From his remembered local geography, Sergei guessed they were heading for the A406 North Circular, most likely then following it back to north London. That made his job easier. However, coming out of the short tunnel brought something that would make his job harder - the thrum of a helicopter overhead. Sergei took a quick glance up, catching sight of a police helicopter some fifteen metres directly above. *Had they spotted the Volvo?* Sergei scowled. *No, they had spotted him!* A motorbike seen leaving the scene of an attempted shooting at high speed... Laçis had followed the rules to the letter, in and out, unseen. Sergei had attracted attention all the way through.

The sound of sirens drifted to him again. Getting off the main road, dumping the bike, slipping away on foot, all easy enough to do... but then he would lose Laçis. No, he had to keep going and deal with the police as and when he needed too. The Russian made a decision - speed was of the essence now. He accelerated round the car in front getting as close as he dared to the Volvo. Yes, there was definitely a passenger in the rear seat.

Both Serkan and his passenger glanced up at the whirring from overhead.

"Police!" the driver spat.

"Onto us? But how? No, too quick." Laçis thought for a

moment, then turned to look out of the rear window. They were just approaching a large roundabout, readying to take the main road back to Bounds Green. The car behind he dismissed immediately; an elderly couple out on a lunchtime drive. A motorcyclist behind them, then a white van. He turned to Serkan.

"Do not take the exit first time. Go round the whole roundabout, then take it the second time."

The big man shrugged but complied. Laçis took a quick glance again. As they came off the roundabout, the motorbike was still with them. He gave a tight smile. The face was not visible but the build was right. *That man again.* He shifted the rifle case in the footwell and reached inside his jacket for his pistol.

"Serkan, we have a tail," he called, drawing the Beretta out from its shoulder holster. "Keep driving as normal. The police, I think, are interested in our friend, not us. Let us keep it so."

Serkan made no reply but the car slowed a little, keeping it just within the speed limit. The motorbike maintained distance. It was a a straight drive all the way across to North London now, all on this main road until close to home. Would the biker make his move before the police moved in on him? Or would he attempt to escape? Laçis made a decision.

"Take the next exit from this road. Find us somewhere quiet. Then, when I tell you, break hard."

Chapter 32

Sergei dropped back but it was too late. A face had bobbed up in the rear seat of the Volvo and turned - he'd been spotted. Nothing to do now but hang in and see how things developed. Of more immediate concern were the helicopter and approaching sirens. Ahead, the Volvo accelerated up an exit ramp. Sergei revved and followed, bearing right at the roundabout at the top, coming off the North Circular, straight across a mini roundabout and suddenly back into residential streets; Sergei trailing the car, the police helicopter trailing him. A few more turns brought them into a narrow, rough surfaced lane, houses on one side, trees on the other. *Smart*, Sergei thought. The trees overhung the road.

The sign at the top of the lane said Forest Glade, this was obviously the edge of some large wooded area. Sergei was surprised again by just how many green spaces London had. Sunlight flashed through the green canopy overhead, the helicopter sound faded slightly. The face showed white in the rear window of the Volvo again. There could be no doubt that Sergei was following them now, question is, if it was Laçis, what would his course of action be? He couldn't shoot without knocking out the rear window, and a sniper rifle was hardly the best weapon in the circumstances. Still, this was a dangerous man, a professional. Sergei eased off the throttle. *Best keep a respectful distance.*

Serkan gripped the steering wheel tight as the car bucked in the ruts.

"Still want me to brake?" he asked.

Laçis glanced at their pursuer again. "No, not yet. There! Left, left!"

Just ahead he had spotted a turning. Serkan span the wheel, spraying dirt, through a set of open gates and into an industrial estate. The place looked run down and largely empty, only a grease-stained mechanic looking up from a car engine as they barrelled in.

"Keep close to the buildings, be ready to stop," Laçis ordered, flashing a look behind again. The motorcyclist was still there. He slipped the rifle case over his shoulder and flicked the safety off the Beretta. Part of him still burned to confront the pursuer, to discover who he was and why he was here. He had a notion already, that his former government employers had sent him, most likely. They never took kindly to people... *leaving...* especially in such circumstances as had prompted Laçis' flight. That would certainly explain the man's dogged pursuit and nerve. KGB, or one their numerous off-shoot agencies. He would be well-trained, committed, a dangerous adversary. And he was here to kill Laçis, there could be little doubt of that. To test himself against such a foe? What a glorious thing that might be. *But no. Not here. Not now. Now was the time to escape.* Let the large idiot driving the car deal with the pursuer.

The car swung round another corner, into the lea of a large warehouse.

"Stop here," Laçis called. He was rolling out of the door before the car had come to a halt, pausing only to snarl,"The man on the motorbike. Kill him," before vanishing up a loading ramp and through the open shutter beyond. A figure in a brown overcoat called to him, Laçis ignored the man and pushed on into the dark interior.

Stacks of boxes, packing material strewn around, a spotty youth staring at him, then he was through and out the other side. Still the persistent whirr of the helicopter overheard, and the nerve-jarring wail of approaching sirens. Keeping close to the wall of the building, the assassin edged back towards the estate entrance. *Damn!* A grey saloon car had just appeared there, blue light flashing on its dashboard. It sat in the entrance, the driver speaking into a radio. Laçis came to a halt. From the volume of the other sirens he estimated he had little more than a minute to escape.

Without pause, he strode quickly towards the car. The driver looked up, eyes widening in recognition. In an instant he was out of the car, a young man with unkempt blond hair, wearing a baggy suit. He held up a card of some kind, shouting "Police, stop there!"

Laçis in turn recognised him as one of the policemen who'd challenged him outside the cemetery. But this time, the gun he carried was loaded. Without any pause or thought, Laçis raised and fired the Beretta in one easy motion. Two shots to the body, and the gun was holstered again, Laçis stepping over the man and into the driving seat of the police vehicle. He crunched the gears into reverse, shot back out into the lane, span the wheel and was away.

Sergei slid the motorbike to a halt, kicked out the stand, and was off in an instant. He placed the crash helmet on the saddle and moved up tight against the wall to his left. The car had turned the corner ahead, brakes screeching. Sergei dropped to his hand and knees in a sprawl, peering around the corner at ankle height. The Volvo sat there, rear door open, engine ticking over. As Sergei watched, a hulk of a man heaved his bulk out of the driver seat and turned to look his way. Sergei took in the wide shoulders that strained the seams of the man's sport jacket, the large, hairy hands, the heavily featured face that radiated aggression. He slipped a hand to his hip, drawing the knife - a simple kitchen knife he had bought from a supermarket a few days ago. Easy to obtain, unremarkable, but sharp. Sergei slowly stood, cupping the handle in his palm, blade concealed behind his forearm. With a short in and out breath, he stepped out of cover and walked towards the car.

The huge man responded immediately. With a snarl, he raised both hands and charged, fingers flexing. *A wrestler then*, thought Sergei. He continued walking forwards calmly, a smile playing across his lips. Then the man was on him, lunging forward to grab. Sergei angled right, moving his left shoulder away from the hand, simultaneously whipping his own right hand up. The concealed blade sliced through the sleeve of the sports jacket and into the flesh beneath. Instantly, Sergei sent a quick backhand stab towards his attackers abdomen. But the man, despite his size, was quick. With a yell he sprang back, leaving empty air between his belly and the knife point. He grinned, teeth white beneath the blackness of his thick moustache, left hand reaching into a pocket. The fist came out gleaming with the shine of a heavy knuckleduster.

Sergei, knife once more concealed, shifted his weight, moving to the man's right. He knew that one hit from that fist would knock him to the floor. Movement was his friend now, no sense going toe to toe with a monster. Blood dripped from the right arm to the gravel. Sergei nodded.

"That must hurt," he taunted, wanting to goad his opponent forward. But the thug was too experienced for that. Instead, he feinted right, then shot forward left, his speed almost catching Sergei out. The blade flashed up again, this time it was expected. The knuckleduster smashed into Sergei's forearm, the jarring impact sending the knife flying. But Sergei was also fast. He fired out jabs with his left, once, twice, into that big, ugly face, following up with a kick to the balls. The man twisted, deflecting the kick with his thigh, throwing out that brass-clad left fist again. It caught Sergei on the shoulder, but he rolled it back, absorbing the force. Now he was inside the big man's guard. A brutal chop into the carotid sinus sent the brute stumbling back, a stamp to the ankle took him screaming to the floor.

Approaching sirens diverted Sergei's attention. As he turned to look, the man on the ground, despite his agony, reached out to snatch up the fallen knife. In a bloodied grip, he thrust up, aiming at the inside of Sergei's thigh. With a curse, Sergei knocked the stab aside with his knee, reached down with both hands and twisted the blade out of the attacker's grip. In one smooth movement, he reversed the point and plunged it deep into the man's chest.

As the giant fell back, Sergei glanced about. An open doorway atop a ramp was the obvious escape choice for Laçis, but he was likely long gone by now. And those sirens were loud. Retrieving the knife, he sprinted back to the Yamaha. Two kicks and it burst into life. As workers came shouting out of the building, Sergei was already accelerating through the gate. A crumpled form lay to one side, a man in a suit. With no time to investigate further, Sergei burst out into the lane beyond. The helicopter was low, and he could hear the screech of tyres away to the right. Sergei immediately took the bike directly across the lane, over the small bump beyond, and away into the trees.

Fortunately, the woodland was sparse enough to navigate, albeit slowly, but thick enough to give some cover from the eyes above. Still, there would be no escape by road. His prayers were answered when the bike edged out onto a narrow tow-path beside a canal. These still dotted the area, relics of the days of Georgian trade and commerce, before the days of steam and rail freight. The water looked distinctly green and uninviting, but Sergei was out of options. Jumping off the bike, he grabbed the handlebars and saddle and heaved it into the canal with a splash. The crash helmet and knife followed. Then, as the hum of blades closed in overhead, he crouched at the bank, lowered his legs over the side and slid into the chill waters.

He made two sharp exhales then took a deep inhale and submerged. Using the bank to his left as a guide, he swam quickly as possible northwards. Three minutes later, he came up for air, careful to lift only his face above water, keeping close to the bank. Back the way he'd came, the helicopter sounded to be at treetop height, the blare of sirens still continuing. With another deep breath, he sank again, leaving barely a ripple on the dark surface, and was gone.

Chapter 33

The mood in the briefing room was intense. The news of Turner's shooting had hit everyone hard; the young DC was still in intensive care, lucky to be alive according to the doctors. Furthermore, Woodville was back and was currently berating the whole team, his usual urbane manner gone as his eyes blazed with anger.

"What the actual fuck? I've got an MP getting shot at in his own home, in the presence of two officers. I've got an officer in intensive care, shot in broad daylight. I've got one, perhaps two suspects who just..." he waved his hands dramatically, "disappeared into thin air, despite the most intensive local manhunt in living memory. There's a police car been stolen, we've had a riot in Ilford, and I've got the body of a mystery man in the morgue. What the actual fuck?"

Denham tried his best to smooth things over. "We're following up numerous leads, sir. And we do have an ID on the dead man, now. Smith?"

Smith read from her notes. "We believe the deceased to be one Serkan Yalçın, sir. A known associate of the Arikan family. Had previous for ABH and Demanding Money with Menaces."

"Ties in with our earlier intel, sir." Calloway piped in now, "that this hit man was hired by the Arikans in order to take out either Mr Birch or his daughter. We're still a little vague on the details."

"Vague? Vague? We've got World War Three going on in Woodford, and all you can give me is vague?"

"Technically, it was Highams Park, sir," Calloway responded, earning him a glare from Woodville. Smith came to his rescue.

"The deceased matches the description given to us by the caretaker at Claybury Hospital. He and another man, matching the photo of our original killer, persuaded him to give them a spare key. He claims they threatened him, though perhaps money changed hands. Either way, the pair got access to the water tower."

"And that's where the shots came from?"

Denham stepped in. "We've not had the full report back from ballistics yet, but yes, realistically, that's the only place they could have been fired from."

Woodville removed his glasses and pinched the bridge of his nose. "Alright. I know you are all concerned for you colleague. DC Turner is a fine young man. An outstanding officer." *You barely ever spoke to him*, Calloway kept the thought to himself. "But if anything, this should spur you all on to increased efforts to close this case. Calloway, I understand the first shot was aimed at you. Any ideas why?"

Cab shrugged. "I can only guess it was because of what happened to the young Arikan laddie, sir" he offered. "Perhaps they blame me for it. It's become a personal thing for them, they thought they'd take me out of the picture, too."

Woodville didn't exactly radiate sympathy but moved on. "Julian, er Mr Birch, will be coming in shortly to give his statement. Denham, Calloway, I'll expect yours by the end of the day."

"Any chance we could question him, sir?" Calloway persisted.

"About what, exactly?" Woodville hissed.

"Sir, I'm sure the key to this whole situation lies in Mr Birch's visit to Cyprus. Date-wise, it all seems to tie in. I think if -"

"You *think*? And where has that thinking got us so far, *Detective Sergeant*?" the words were icy cold. "I already told you to think before accusing an upstanding member of the local community, a person committed to public duty. A Member of Parliament, no less. I *think* that you should take a step back and *think* some more, don't you? Denham, all statements to me by three this afternoon, clear?"

With that he departed, leaving the team muttering amongst themselves. Denham called them to order.

"Alright, alright. The boss is on point, we need to get our shit together and get this sorted. It's the best thing we can do for Turner, now. I want the bastard who did this and I want him nailed to the wall, got it?"

The team began filing out, Denham stopped Calloway.

"Turner. What happened, Cab?"

Calloway sighed and sat on the table edge. "He was on the way to Claybury after the first shout when the call came in about the alleged gunman being spotted. He was close by, so he was first into the estate. He was shot twice at point blank range, his car taken. To be honest, he's lucky to still be with us, guv."

"Same guy?"

"Bullets not confirmed yet, but the descriptions from workers on the estate all match."

"I gather there was another man too, on a motorbike. It was actually him that the eye in the sky was tracking. Again, according to locals, it was the motorcyclist who killed the Turkish guy. Yamaha motorbike -"

"Red crash helmet? Fuck." Calloway proffered a fag to Denham and lit one himself.

"Your mystery man?"

"Yep. But he's not a bad guy, guv, he's, he's...."

Denham held up a palm. "I don't want to know. If he's your source, that's your business. I wouldn't want to hear something that I have to report upstairs."

"Got it. Thanks, guv."

"Not to say that gives you *carte blanche*. And you're right about one thing. After Turner, this is personal. If your... friend... can get us to this heartless bastard, so be it. Any other leads? Webb?"

"He's still hanging in the breeze. His mother's death was definitely arson, though." He flicked through his folder. "At around three in the morning. Traces of an accelerant poured through the letterbox, most likely petrol. The fire spread fast, Mrs Webb most likely would have been dead from fumes before the flames reached her. Those flats weren't built with fire safety in mind."

"You think it was the Arikans?"

"Seems most likely. There was only one witness. A, er..." he checked the notes again. "A Mrs Cane, the neighbour. She was up, couldn't sleep. Says she saw someone out front, a large man, but it was dark and she didn't have her glasses on. That's it, guv."

"Well, *large man* fits our dead guy. Sounds like the Arikans think Webb set them up for the Taverner hit."

"Guess so. This lot don't play by the old rules. Nothing's off limits any more."

"God help us. And where's Webb junior now?"

"Could be anywhere."

"You think he'll go after the Arikans?"

"Who knows, guv. He's a dealer, not a gangster. But something like this could tip anyone over the edge, right?"

Denham nodded thoughtfully.

"Is your lad alright?" Calloway asked. "I saw they re-took Georgia the other day."

"Yes, he is, thanks, as far as we know. But it's all on top, now. This is just the start. And you? It's not every day a man gets shot at. At least not in Woodford."

"Oh aye, I'm okay. Nothing a quiet night in won't fix."

"With some company?" Denham arched an eyebrow.

Cab rolled his eyes. "Again, there's no fucking secrets round here, is there?"

Denham gave a tight grin. "No. Not many. Keep an eye on the team, will you Cab. I understand everyone will be on edge right now. I'm just off to the hospital now, meeting Turner's family there.

Calloway exhaled smoke. "Good luck with that, guv. And yes, I will."

Before he left, Denham had one other question. "You alright going back home, Cab? I mean given this hit-man might be after you? If you need a place to stay I have some old army buddies who can help."

"I'll be fine, guv. You know what they say, an Englishman's

home is his castle. And that goes twice for the Scots. We built the best ones, after all."

Spider was growing impatient. He thought this surveillance lark would have been easy, it was proving to be both dull and unproductive - a couple of days now, and nothing. He'd thought maybe one of the Arikans would show his face, then he could run across the street, pop him and be off. But there'd been no sign of them, apart from one time a big car pulled up outside the snooker hall. By the time Spider, sat in the café opposite, had noticed, the inhabitants were in through the door, and the car had driven off. He paid at the counter and sloped back to the B&B, the gun heavy in his pocket, shoulders raised against the drizzle.

Once there, he packed his case, settled up with the owner and headed up to the tube station. As he walked he reviewed his options. If he could find out where the top man lived, he could break into his house and do the job. But who would have that info? Pearce might, he thought, but did he really want to be in debt to that nutter? Then again, he already was… the guy had saved his life, after all. Though, he reminded himself, it was Pearce who put him in that chair in the first place. *Shit.*

There was always the filth, surely they would know, but there was no way to access that information. Sure, that copper wanted to speak to him - not that the Scottish prick had been fast enough to catch him. But he was hardly likely to give out the info that Spider needed, especially given the reasons. Still, others at the nick might have access to the info. Word was that Taverner had someone on the inside at Ilford, but again, that would again mean going through Pearce.

Sat on the tube, Spider racked his brains for any other contacts who might be useful. He had a decent network of dealers and customers, most of them on the dodgy side of the law, it might be worth putting some feelers out. Time to get round some of the clubs again, then, make a few phone calls, call in a few favours. The Tottenham crew would be a good start, they had more links in this area. One guy sprang straight to mind - Wrighty, one of the Tottenham faces. He was also tied in with the local Yardies, they'd have no love for the Arikans. The thought came just in time; Spider hopped off the tube at Finsbury Park, nipped across the platform and was soon heading for Seven Sisters.

Chapter 34

The Arikans were not happy. *Why would they be?* Laçis thought. A missed opportunity, a failed hit and one of their top enforcers dead. Not to mention a son still on life support in hospital, and a hornet's nest stirred up, with police flooding the whole of north-east London. Still, it was not as if he was totally to blame - it was a slim shot from that angle, and the policeman had been lucky to survive. The pursuer was of more concern to Laçis; the police could be predicted, the Arikans less so, but they presented no immediate threat. No, the man on the motorbike, that was something that need dealing with as a matter of urgency.

He was sat in the front room of the safe house, a collection of baroque music playing on the Walkman, as the argument raged above him. Ismet he knew, the two other men he had seen at the old man's flat. One was the middle son, name of Mehmet, the other was a cousin, or something. They were gesticulating, talking loudly in Turkish. Every now and then one would point at Laçis, sat impassive on the velour sofa.

Eventually, the arguing stopped, the two men stomped out of the house. Ismet, muttering to himself, flopped into an armchair.

"Mr Arikan is not happy, as you might expect. Still, he recognises the difficulty of the situation and has decided to give you another chance."

Laçis, removing his headphones, merely nodded. *How good of him*, he thought. Ismet continued. "The loss of Serkan was... unfortunate. We are sill not clear as to who killed him. Surely not a police officer?"

Laçis decided to keep his cards close to his chest. "There was another man following me. The same one I saw at the funeral, with the a policeman. I believe he may be a private detective of some sort. Or perhaps he works for your rivals?"

Ismet took the bait. "Taverner... yes, that would make sense. And now they have killed one of our best men!" His face fell, his voice thickened. Quickly, Ismet recovered himself. "So, we have one more reason for vengeance! Here is what has been decided. We shall meet with Taverner and his people, and you will kill them."

Simple as that. But Laçis maintained the calm facade, merely asking. "Where will this meeting take place?"

"The details are to be decided. But Mr Arikan welcomes your input - what is the best type of vantage point for you, somewhere outside, or a building? What is the optimum range? These type of things. Once we have an idea of the meet location, we will work to place you in the best position."

"Who chooses the location?"

"We expect they will, so we will have very little notice. However, we shall endeavour to narrow down the options beforehand. It is likely to be somewhere open but not too public."

"And if they also decide to spring a trap at this meeting?"

"Ah, we fully expect them too. They are not so clever as they imagine! You will not be the only, what is the saying, ace in our sleeve?"

Laçis slowly nodded. "I see. Then I shall wait for your word. In the meantime, I have a little personal business to attend to. Might I have use of a car and driver once again?"

"Yes, of course my friend, but please do not wander too far."

"I shall not." Laçis gave a cold smile. "Just back across to the neighbourhood of the hospital. And while there, I may well be able to eliminate one of Mr Arikan's targets, too."

Calloway leaned on the horn, swearing at the black cab that had just cut him up. The heavy showers had reduced the evening rush hour traffic to a crawl, something he always found both baffling and frustrating. Back home nothing short of a blizzard slowed things down. In London, even leaves falling at autumn could create gridlock. His mood was dark, not only because of what happened to Turner and the subsequent fall out, but because of Birch, too. Earlier that afternoon, he'd been on the upper floor, walking past Woodville's office. The door had opened as he'd approached and Woodville and Birch emerged, along with another suited man, a solicitor, from the look of him.

"Thank you, Nigel, I'll give you a call tomorrow," Birch was saying to the suit. Then he turned back to Woodville, who leaned in close to whisper something in Birch's ear. The whisper was accompanied by a handshake, one hand covering the other. Woodville disappeared back into his lair. Birch glanced round, catching sight of Calloway. There was not the merest flicker of acknowledgement or recognition on the MPs face, he simply turned and walked away towards the stairs.

"Charming," Cab muttered. "I almost took a bullet for you."

The blanking had been one thing, what annoyed Calloway even more was the growing certainty that, whatever his involvement in this matter, Birch was not taking any blame at all. Nothing would stick, he was part of a group and class that looked after their own. And meanwhile, a local family of decent, hard-working people were still mourning their murdered daughter. Still, there was nothing to be done about the situation. Or was there? Calloway resolved to talk to Denham about it tomorrow. He knew his guv hated cover ups and shady dealings as much as he did, perhaps he'd have some ideas.

Placing his battered briefcase over his head, Calloway dashed from the car to the entrance of the flat. At his front door, wiping his face, he fumbled for the keys. He had just put the key in the lock when something hard prodded into his lower back. An accented voice spoke calmly and softly into his ear.

"Open the door slowly and go inside. If you move too quickly, I will kill you."

Calloway sat back into the sofa and relaxed as best he could. In the light of a single lamp, he could just make out the features of the man sat opposite. Laçis. There was no mistaking the shape of the pistol pointed steadily at Calloway's chest, either.

"So you're the one who shoots teenage girls, then?" Cab hissed.

Laçis didn't so much as blink. "it is my job. But it is unfortunate that I hit the wrong girl. For what it is worth, I regret it."

"And do you regret trying to blow my head off yesterday?"

A ghost of a smile. "I always regret a missed shot. Every professional does."

"Professional? Jesus, what sort of profession is murdering people in cold blood?"

It seemed Laçis was not in the mood for small talk. "The man who followed me yesterday. The man who was with you at the funeral. Who is he?"

Calloway saw no reason to lie. "He's here for you. From Moscow, I believe. KGB, or something, I'm a wee bit hazy on the details. His name is Sergei."

Laçis' eyes narrowed. "And how do you make contact with him?"

Calloway suddenly understood his use here. If Laçis wanted him dead, he would have shot him in the foyer. No, the man wanted information. And then? "If I tell you, what happens to me?"

"I am under contract to kill you. But if you co-operate, I will make sure that your death is instant and painless."

"That's awful big of you. Not much of an incentive, though. And you may be a killer but I don't have you pegged as the torture type."

"I was trained to perform whatever task is required to get the job done," Laçis responded.

"Funnily enough, your pal told me the same. Were you trained at the same place?" Calloway's only strategy now was to play for time. For what, he didn't know.

"Different time and place, similar training, I imagine. Answer the question."

"Oh, I was just wondering, see, what with you being-"

Laçis leaned forward menacingly, the barrel lowering slightly.

"Have you ever been shot in the kneecap, Mr Calloway? It is not a fatal wound, by any means, but it is most unpleasant."

"Alright. I don't contact him, he contacts me. He usually just turns up out of nowhere. Exactly like you did earlier."

The barrel rose back up. "He will have given you a contact number. And probably some code word to speak when it is answered. Tell me."

Calloway was out of options. "The number is on a card in my wallet. It's in my inside jacket pocket. Can I reach for it?"

"Very slowly."

Calloway inched a hand up the front of his damp jacket and into the pocket. He lifted the wallet out with two fingers, then flicked it forward to land on the carpet between them. Laçis slowly stood. The pistol didn't waver.

"Place your hands behind your head and stand." As Calloway complied, Laçis motioned with the gun. "Move to the wall there, turn and face it. Keep your hands behind your head."

Calloway was almost at the wall when the doorbell rang.

Chapter 35

Calloway turned, sensing Laçis' hesitation. The man was scowling, glancing into the hall as the doorbell rang again. He motioned with the barrel.

"Walk to the door. See who it is. Very slowly."

Calloway complied. Through the peep-hole came the fish-eye view of Sergei's face. He looked thoughtful.

"It's Sergei," he softly informed Laçis. A slow grin spread across the hit-man's face.

"Call to him. Tell him you will be one second."

Calloway clenched his fists but had no choice, the pistol remained levelled at his chest. He turned to the door and called out. "I'll just be a second, Mr Sergei. Bide a wee while, will you?"

He moved back at Laçis' prompt, that man now taking his place, bringing the pistol up level to the peephole. He inhaled slowly. As his finger tightened on the trigger, Calloway yelled "Duck!" and barged into the killer, shoulder to hips, crashing the man into the front door. The barrel spat out a bullet that slapped into the wall high up in the corner. In the tumble, Cab reached out, grabbing at the door handle. He fell to his knees, dragging the latch down as he went, taking the butt of the pistol in the side of the head for his trouble.

Laçis cursed and jumped clear, stumbling into the telephone table. Sergei was shouting from outside, trying to shove the door open, banging it into Calloway's side.

Cab lunged for Laçis again, trying to bring him down in a rugby tackle, but the man was prepared this time. He hurled himself back, colliding with the door frame of the living room. The front door exploded open as Sergei kicked it, dropping into a kneeling position, the gun in his hand pointing into the hall. But Laçis did not pause, he span and disappeared through the doorway. By the time Sergei made the living room, the killer was through the kitchen door and over the balcony. He returned to the hall and helped Calloway to his feet.

"You're not chasing him?" Calloway asked, hand coming up to rub the swelling forming by his eye.

"Not in the dark when he has a gun, no. It would be suicide. Come, let's get you sat down."

He led Calloway to an armchair, disappeared into the kitchen and returned with a tea-towel soaked in cold water. He scrunched it up and placed it on Calloway's face.

"Hold this in place, it will help with the swelling."

His pistol had disappeared, Calloway noticed. He thought it best not to mention it.

"Well, thanks for visiting," he quipped. "I'm glad you came when you did. Your pal was just about to execute me."

Sergei shrugged and smiled. "Thanks for the warning. So what did he want? I take it he took you by surprise?"

"That he did. He seemed very keen to know about you. He asked for your contact details. I'm sorry, I had no choice."

Sergei waved it away. "Do not worry. The number will be changed very quickly. Anything else?"

"No, not really." Calloway removed the towel, grimacing at the blood stain on it. "He didn't seem happy that you were tracking him. He did seem happy enough to kill me, though. Pour a drink while you're up, will you, there's a new bottle of scotch in the cupboard. I should call this in," he added as Sergei returned to the kitchen.

"No point," came the reply. He will have organised his getaway route already. Probably has driver waiting nearby.

"But a shot was fired," Calloway replied.

"But no-one was hit," Sergei came back in with the bottle and two tumblers. He poured a measure for them each. "Perhaps no-one even heard it"

Calloway took a swig and sat back, eyes closed. "That's as maybe, but I can't let this go unreported. I'll keep you out of it. As far as anyone's concerned, I overpowered Laçis and he ran off, we'll leave it at that. Besides, you were almost killed. And so was I." The realisation and shock of the event was beginning to kick in. He knew the signs of old; hands trembling, breath short, vision blurring.

"Breathe!" Sergei knelt in front of him, staring him in the eye. "Inhale nose, exhale mouth. Short bursts, not deep. Slowly, don't rush. You are okay."

Calloway followed the directions and felt his heart rate slow. Within a few minutes he was back to normal. Another thought occurred to him "How did he find out where I live?"

"I told you before, your institutions are not exactly watertight.

Those hooligans found out easily enough, yes? Did Laçis mention who'd employed him?"

"No. Damn, that's twice now we've had him up close and twice he's got away. I take it that was you chasing him on the motorbike at Woodford?"

Sergei nodded. "Yes. He escaped, though his friend stayed behind to stop me."

"I heard. And did you hear that Laçis shot DC Turner? He's still in intensive care."

Sergei's eyes flashed, his face twisted. He hissed something in Russian. "For this I am truly sorry. Thanks to my errors, your friend suffered this injury." His fingers whitened on the tumbler. "Curse this *sukin syn*, who shoots innocents."

"I doubt you could have done anything to prevent it. Poor Jon was just in the wrong place at the wrong time. Shite, what a mess. But how did you get away?"

"I swam," Sergei leaned forward in the sofa and poured them each another nip. " I dumped motorbike in canal, then swam away. Called my people from a phone box, they picked me up."

"You dumped the motorbike in the canal?" Cab raised his eyebrows.

Sergei laughed. "Yes. My people were not so happy. Always complaining about budgets. Still they gave me another. Well, more moped than motorbike, but it works."

That's where you got your gun from too, I suppose."

"Yes. A Walther, like your James Bond," he laughed. "Well, after yesterday…" he shrugged.

"Ah, Yalçin. The man who tried to stop you, no doubt. Jesus, where will this end?"

Sergei's eyes narrowed. "Not until Laçis is dead." Then his face softened. "Is there somewhere else you can stay? He may return."

"You think so? I don't know. Maybe. I mean yes, my boss offered." He raised a hand to his forehead. "MP's, spies, assassins, gangsters. And poor Turner. So young."

"You should get that bump checked. You may have concussion. If you let me use your car I could drive you to a hospital?"

"No, no, I'll be fine. When I call it in I'll tell them to send a medic out to check me over. And I'll stay here for the night. But why did you come round, you have some news?"

"Yes. Your politician, Birch. We hear that he is to be investigated by your security services. It seems that something did happen on his visit to Cyprus. You want my guess?"

"Aye, go on."

"Probably the classic sex trap. Attractive young woman, or man, approaches when him in bar or restaurant. They get talking, have some drinks. Go back to hotel room and..."

"And everything is filmed on a hidden camera, right? Does that really still happen?"

"More than you might think. There I things I could tell you about some very famous people."

Calloway waved a hand. "Don't. I know too much already. But why Birch? He's a small fish in political terms."

"Influence is influence, no matter how small, and who knows what he might become. Anyway, I doubt you will see him again. He has been passed up the - what is your expression- food chain?"

"Aye, that's it. And good riddance, too. So. Now what?"

"We need to flush Laçis out again in some way. We have missed him twice. Third time is the charm?"

"Let's hope so. Well, you'd best be off. I'll call this in, then have a chat with my boss. See what we can come up with." He rose, following Sergei to the door. The Russian scanned outside before he left, then paused, a puzzled look on his face. "One thing."

"Yes?"

"When you called out to me, the second time. Why did you call out the name of a bird?"

"A what?" Calloway mirrored the puzzled expression.

"A bird," Sergei reiterated, waving his hands. " A bird. I clearly heard you shout *duck*!"

Chapter 36

"Time to level with me, Cab. I've given you all the rope I can, I just hope you haven't bloody well hung yourself." Denham sat back expectantly in his chair. The guv had called him in immediately on arrival at the station that morning. Word had got round quickly that Calloway had faced the hit-man and fought him off. Even Kit Kat had been impressed when Calloway, sporting an impressive black eye, had come through the desk. Now, in Denham's office, Calloway patted his pockets for cigarettes and swore when he found none.

"Alright, guv. And I appreciate what you've done so far. But part of the reason I've not been totally open is I didn't want you to get dragged into any shite. I still don't. Can I speak off the record?"

"Christ, Cab, you survive two attempted assassination attempts and you're still holding out on me? Okay. Out of the office it is then." He glanced at his watch. "Thirteen hundred hours, somewhere quiet. Not the Red Lion or the Papermakers, too many familiar faces. We'll meet at the Red Cow in Ley Street, that'll be quiet at lunchtime."

"Aye, okay."

"Right. Get off to your briefing then, don't keep your team waiting."

On his way to the briefing room Calloway was stopped by a worried looking Gemma.

"Cab, are you okay? I heard you saw the hit-man, that he came after you? Are you okay? What happened?"

He took her hands in his. "Yes, yes. I'm alright it's fine. Just got a bump or two." He grinned despite the dull throb behind his eyes. Then the grin faded. "Gem, listen. This guy knew where I live. He knew where I was, on two occasions now. I think… I think…"

"Cab, are you dumping me?" she asked, face falling.

"Yes, no, I mean just for now. If this guy has eyes on me, things will be dangerous. I don't want you dragged into that. Or your father."

"My god you think he would?"

"Well, you saw yourself what happened to Mrs Webb. Just until all this is over, I promise. These are heavy people. Taverner and his mob are bad enough, but this lot…"

She sighed. "You're right, I suppose. But I'm tougher than I look, Mr Calloway, I don't need looking after."

He smiled again. "I know. And I wasn't suggesting that you did. Besides, I think Denham is slapping a police guard on me, which might curtail any… extra-curricular activities."

They gripped hands for a second, about to move into a hug when a smirking PC walked past. Calloway coughed and straightened, dropping his hands. "Yes, well that is excellent, Miss Bellotti, thank you. We'll speak soon."

Gemma laughed, rolled her eyes and walked away.

Laçis opened his eyes as Ismet tapped his arm. He had been summoned to see the old man again, apparently, there has been news from Taverner's people. He switched off the Walkman and followed

Ismet out to the car, accepting the blindfold with a curt smile. At the flat, old man Arikan was still in a dour mood. His son remained on life support, Laçis was informed, the prognosis remained poor, it was still touch and go whether the young man would even survive. Forestalling his next question, this changed nothing, Laçis was told, they still wanted Calloway dead.

As he sat sipping tea, he took this information in, declining to mention his visit to Calloway the previous evening. No point in letting these people know he had failed again. Besides, he was beginning to wonder if Calloway had divine protection, having been under Laçis' gun twice, yet still he lived and breathed. He zoned out slightly as various members of the family and entourage expounded, in detail, what they would do to Taverner, to Pearce, to Calloway. Finally, the old man raised a slightly tremulous hand and silenced them all.

"The English want to meet on Sunday," he told them. "We will not know the location until a very short time beforehand."

"You trust them?" asked Mehmet. "This could be a trap, Poppa."

"Of course it's a trap!" the old man wheezed, before coughing violently. His son moved forward but was waved away. Once recovered, Arikan continued. "The instant, and I mean the instant we know, we have our friend here taken directly to the site."

He motioned to one of his minders, who spread a large map across the tabletop. "Now, this meeting place could be anywhere. But let us apply our intelligence. Where would Taverner choose? What do we know about him? Tamir?"

He motioned to a middle-aged man in a sharp suit, who placed an open folder next to the map, adjusted his glasses and began reading. "We know he watches his grand-son playing football every other weekend. He plays golf regularly, one of the few time he ventures out of East London. Most of the time he is in one of his pubs, or at one of his businesses. He has several, including a scrap metal yard in Rotherhithe, a property company and a pig farm in Essex."

Laçis chuckled at the last, drawing a hard stare from the man. He continued. "His property company has been buying up old dockland sites."

"Why would he do this?" asked Mehmet. "I thought the docks were all closing?"

"They are," Tamir replied. "So the land there is cheap. However, there is a plan to set up an enterprise zone in the area. This means exemption from property taxes and simplified planning. The whole place is earmarked for luxury flats, office blocks and more, so Taverner stands to make a fortune from selling the land to developers. He already owns the Grapes pub in Limehouse, and just recently purchased the dockside area behind it, Dunbar Wharf."

Arikan nodded. "Show me on the map."

As the group huddled around the table, Laçis sipped the rest of his tea and reflected on last night's events. He was annoyed with himself, though no-one looking at him would guess. He should have shot the policeman straight away, it was very unlikely he would know the exact whereabouts of the man called Sergei. And his own luck in Sergei arriving had turned to misfortune when he'd failed to kill even one of his targets. His ruminations were interrupted by the old man talking to him. He asked Arikan to repeat the question.

"What does our professional have to say? What would your

choice be if you wanted to meet and attack an enemy?"

Laçis glanced over the map and the locations marked in red marker pen. "Not in a pub. Too busy. Too many eyes. The football field, too public. It is in a large park, no?"

"You shot a girl in a park in broad daylight, " hissed Mehmet.

Laçis regarded him with a cool stare. "I did. But she was not expecting me and I was working alone."

"Be quiet, Mehmet," the old man chided. "Continue."

"The pig farm?" He smiled. "To obvious. Practical, though. So the scrapyard, the docks or the golf course. The first seems also obvious, but the other two are also public places, no?"

"They are" Tamir agreed. "But the docklands site will be deserted. When the docks were closed, they were all fenced off. Health and safety. Demolition has already started in some places, but on a weekend you could meet there without any risk of interruption. And it is home ground for Taverner."

Laçis examined the map. "There are many empty buildings here?"

"Yes," David confirmed. "So plenty of vantage points that would overlook the open areas."

"And many ways to exit, I imagine. Including the river itself."

"We could easily have a boat on stand-by, or a car parked in any of the local streets. Could you shoot from the far bank of the river?" Arikan asked.

"What is the scale? Do you have a rule and a pen?" Equipped with both, Laçis made measurements. "Maximum range is 600 metres, so it is possible, given a suitable vantage point on the opposite bank. But closer would be better, especially if there are high buildings. What about the golf club?"

Tamir spoke again. "It is a little way out into the country. Secluded. Look." He traced a finger on the map. "The course lays on the edge of Epping Forest, here. One road in and out. No buildings around it. And, according to our information, Taverner is a major shareholder in the club. I wonder if he could call for it to be closed for a couple of hours? Time enough for a meeting."

Mehmet jabbed the map with the marker pen. "He could easily have men concealed in the woods, perhaps holes are already dug."

Laçis could only agree. "This also is a possibility."

Arikan smiled and Laçis was again put in mind of a shark. "The question is then, are either of these places in which you can work? Targets in the open is good, yes?"

"They are, given platforms from which to shoot. And also if I can avoid any perimeter guard." He bent in for a closer look at the map. "Though as you say, there are no buildings at this golf course, except for this, the club house I imagine?"

"Couldn't you hide in a tree?" Mehmet sneered.

Annoyance flashed across Laçis' face. "People did in the past, you know? In the Great Patriotic War, Soviet snipers would sometimes tie themselves in up high in a tree and shoot as many fascists as they could before inevitably being killed themselves. Brave people. I would not expect *you* to understand."

Mehmet flushed and stepped back. The old man gave a throaty chuckle. "Ah, yes, such fighters, such heroes. And today we have…" he glanced at Mehmet and Tamir, "boys and lawyers. Continue, my friend."

Laçis turned his attention back to the golf club. Taking the pen, he drew two large straight lines centred on the club house, then joined them with a rough circle. "This is the effective range, given normal conditions. So let us see." He was silent for a couple of minutes, tapping his teeth with the pen. He stabbed a finger on the map. "What is this?"

Mehmet leaned in, checking the list of symbols at the side of the map. "It says *water tower*."

Laçis raised his eyebrows. "Another one?" before lining up the ruler again, checking the distance. "That might be possible, if there is access to this tower." He sat back and looked at the old man. "I would like to visit both sites if possible?"

Arikan nodded. "We shall arrange that."

"And which do you think Taverner will choose, Mr Arikan?"

"I agree with your assessment. Out of these choices, the club and the dock are the most likely. The question is, what sort of man is this Taverner? A creature of habit? Then likely the golf club, where he spends his Sundays. Or is he a man eager to impress, to show us how important he is? Then the docklands site."

"Either way, we have look to have a suitable platform in each." Laçis gave the briefest of smiles. "Should he choose either of these sites, Taverner is as good as dead."

Chapter 37

Calloway got to the Red Cow just after one, Denham was already at the bar, just ordering as he walked in.

"Make that two pints, Frank. And a couple of packs of crisps, too. Prawn cocktail."

The pair settled at a table in the corner, as predicted the pub was quiet, even at lunchtime. It was a somewhat seedy, dilapidated place, home to a few hardened old drinkers rather than the young office crowd.

"Alright," Denham took a sip of beer and placed his glass back on the soggy beermat. "Spill the beans."

Calloway sighed. "Okay. Well, this contact I have, who's been feeding me the info? He's a Russian agent, name of Sergei."

"A Russian what? Fuck, Cab, you don't muck about do you?" Denham was wide-eyed. He glanced around then leant in closer, whispering. "What sort of agent? What are we talking about here, exactly?"

"I don't know exactly, I guess he's KGB, or something. But basically he's here to stop, apprehend or kill Laçis. Our hit-man is former Soviet Spetsnaz but decided on a career change. Now he touts himself out to the highest bidder, particularly some of the big drug cartels. The way I see it, the Arikans are now dealing with the cartels, makes sense they'd use a recommended hit-man when they needed one. And, I guess, using Laçis shows the cartels that they are serious operators, not some cowboy outfit."

Denham rubbed his temples. "And just how closely have you been working with him?"

"Well…" Calloway hesitated. "Last night, when Laçis was at my flat Sergei turned up. He saved my life."

"He's been to your flat?"

"A couple of times."

"You've had a Soviet agent at your flat? Fuck, Cab did you have tea and biscuits? Did you make him a nice dinner? Jesus!"

Cab said nothing, just took a swig of the flat lager.

Denham was shaking his head. "Cab, if this gets out you know what would happen?"

"I don't suppose it would boost my promotion prospects, guv."

"Promotion? You'd be lucky to stay out of jail. And not some cosy little open prison, where you can take an Open University degree in basket weaving. I'm talking military jails, Cab. I've seen some of those, believe me, holiday camps they are not!" He sat back and took another mouthful of beer. "Who else knows?"

"No-one, guv. Scouts honour. All the team know is that I have a source. You know how it is, no names, no pack drill."

"Well thank God for that, at least. How does he contact you?"

"He mostly just turns up. He was at the Clark funeral, he's also popped up a couple of other times. He's very well informed. As you'd expect, I suppose."

"And can you contact him?"

"Aye, well he did give me a number and a sot of code word."

"Code word!" Denham rolled his eyes again.

"I know, I know. Believe me, guv, this has been on my mind all the way through. But here's the thing. This guy has a real handle on Laçis. He knows his methods, he knows his likely moves. He's already been onto him twice, closer than we've got. To my mind, having Sergei on-board is our best bet at flushing our man out."

"What do you want me to do, give him a fucking sheriff's badge? Cab, he's a Soviet agent!" Denham glanced around and lowered his voice to a whisper. "Can you imagine what upstairs will say about this?"

Calloway fidgeted. "Aye, well, I was wondering if we could just nae tell them. For a bit at least. I've a feeling we're close to bagging Laçis."

"No, Cab, I can't *nae tell them*. When you said off the record, I thought, oh maybe it's some old lag, or someone's wife you're knocking off, not something out of a James Bond film. Fuck!" he repeated, before sitting back in his chair, sighing and closing his eyes. Calloway remained silent for a minute or two, quietly sipping his beer. Denham's eyes snapped open and he leant forward again.

"Here's what we do. I have to report this. More than my job's worth as they saying goes. But we'll play it down. This guy approached you, dropped a bit of info, that's it. You didn't report it at the time because you got wrapped up in the case. This, this Sergei, was it? He never visited your flat, you never had cosy chats, you don't have any contact details for him. Clear?"

"Crystal, guv. And thanks."

"Don't thank me yet, Cab. There's no way of knowing how Woodville will respond to this. You're hardly his favourite copper at the moment, anyway. As it is, I stand to get a bollocking myself. I am the OIC, after all."

"Aye, well, thanks anyway."

"You owe me for this, Cab. Big time."

"Oh, there's something else, guv."

Denham glared at him. "There's more? What is it, a nuclear bomb in a briefcase? Do you have Dr No on speed dial?"

Calloway shook his head. "It's about Birch. Sergei told me his people have intel that Birch was somehow compromised in Cyprus."

"He denied anything when we asked him."

"That he did. But according to Sergei, the big boys are getting involved. Special Branch, MI5, whoever, the spooks are taking an interest."

"Well, that puts him out of our hands. Could be a good thing, at least the boss can't blame us. Well, not for that, at least. I still don't see why they'd put a hit out on his daughter, though?"

"Maybe he tried to stiff them? Or perhaps he just failed to play ball and this was them showing how serious they are?"

"Maybe. Either way, whatever Birch has been up to is no longer our problem from the sounds of it. Our issue is bringing in Laçis. Any ideas?"

"Sergei's suggestion was to flush him out. We almost had him at Claybury, and that was without planning. I reckon if we could entice him in with some bait, we could get him next time."

Denham shrugged. "Great, but what's the bait?"

Calloway drained his pint and placed it back on the table. He remained silent. Denham swore again.

"Oh no, Cab. No. There's no way I could allow that. No way. It's not going to happen!"

"Thanks," said Spider, accepting the cup of tea from his cousin. They were sat in Gavin's kitchen, Spider having returned there last night after his trip to Tottenham. He'd tracked down Wrighty to his usual drinking den and the pair had had a good chat. The buzz on the street was all about the beef between Taverner and the Arikans. Whenever the lions fought, the jackals gathered, Wrighty had laughed, explaining there could be rich pickings to be had in the fallout. Still, there had been little concrete information. The Tottenham crews were largely at odds with the Arikans, though lacked the muscle to directly oppose them. Still, Wrighty agreed to put the word out and filter any information back to Spider.

"So what now?" asked Gavin.

Spider took a gulp of tea, winced and added in two teaspoons of sugar. "Dunno, really. Can't see any way of getting to this Arikan geezer, he's never seen in public."

"Even then, have you really though about this? Tony, you're talking about shooting someone. Dead! It ain't like the movies."

"How would you know?" Spider instantly regretted the remark. Gavin was a former Para with tours of Northern Ireland under his belt. "Sorry," he added.

Gavin waved the remark away and rested his tattooed forearms on the table. "I could call up a few old mates, if you like. They'd have no love for scum like Arikan."

"And what do they think about drug dealers?"

"Ah, that's different," Gavin laughed. "You're family. Listen, what happened to Aunt Anne was a disgrace. When's the funeral, by the way?"

Spider swallowed hard. "Still waiting to hear from the old bill. Autopsy, investigation, all that."

"Right. And this shooter. You know how it works?"

"Point it, pull the trigger, bang, innit?"

Gavin rolled his eyes. "Basically. It's an easy physical action but the brain sometimes freezes. That's why soldiers undergo so much training. That and because sadistic instructors enjoy it," he laughed. "Listen, I still don't think you should do this, but I understand why you feel you should. If you like, I'll run you through some training. I'd rather you had some idea what you're doing than going in blind. And I'll give you support. If, and I stress *if*, you do this, you'll be in a proper two and eight after. At least let me be your back up?"

Spider sighed. Yeah. Okay. Thanks, Gav."

"No worries, cuz." Gavin lifted his mug in salute. "That's what family's for, right?"

Chapter 38

Calloway was eating his lunch in the canteen when he got the nod that Denham wanted to see him. Since yesterday's meeting he hadn't seen the guv at all. That morning's briefing had been short, Denham had not been in attendance. Ballistics had confirmed that the shots fired at Claybury were 7.62×51mm rounds, in common use throughout the NATO countries. Angles of impact confirmed the tower at the hospital as the point of origin, though there had been little doubt about that. The two pieces of information had been combined to produce a list of likely firearms involved.

More welcome news was that Turner was off the danger list and being moved out of intensive care. "Serious but stable," Smith had read from the hospital report. That had lifted the tension somewhat, though the attack on Calloway at his home had increased it again. Talked turned next to a plan to flush Laçis out, though there was little enthusiasm for hanging Cab out as bait. *At least they think something of me*, Calloway thought with a smile.

He finished his apple pie and custard, placed his tray on the rack, waved to Sandra behind the counter and strolled down to Denham's office. From the look on the guv's face it wasn't good news.

"Sorry, Cab," Denham gestured him to sit. "You're off the case. Not my decision, but there you are."

Calloway sighed. "To be expected, I suppose. How much did you tell Woodville?"

"The bare minimum. Just what I needed too, but even that was more than enough. You'll likely be getting a visit from Special Branch soon, so I hope you weren't planning any holidays?"

"Shite. No, you're alright, guv, you did what you had to. Hope none of it comes back on you."

Denham waved the thought away. "Anyway. I want you to take a couple of days off. Have a rest. You could do with one anyway after getting knocked about so much."

Calloway's hand went to his still swollen eye. "Fair enough, guv. And then what?"

"There's always something else going on. Right now, we've a series of aggravated burglaries, an attempted rape, and a missing teenager on the books. We'll keep you busy enough. Alright, be off with you. I want you to tidy your files up and hand them to DS Parkes, he'll be taking over."

"Aye, no worries." Calloway stood to leave, pausing in the door as Denham spoke again.

"And Cab… off the case means off the case, right? No heroics. Got me?"

"Got you, guv."

Half an hour later, he'd just finished sorting his files when Smith came in to collect them.

"I'm here for the files, sarge. Sorry."

"Don't be, Smithy. These things happen. Important thing is the investigation goes ahead and we nail this guy."

"Yes. Well, anyway the team just asked me to let you know that we're sorry."

Calloway flushed. "Aye, well, aye that's nice. It's, er - I've enjoyed working with you all, I'm sure we will again. Let them know, will you? Anyway, I'm off to visit Turner now, then I'll be back in a few days, so you've not totally got rid of me yet."

Smith smiled and left with the files. Calloway took a moment to sit back, taking in the uncharacteristically clear desk before him, and the vacant desk opposite. For a moment the events of the last couple of weeks flooded over him, particularly the confrontation with Laçis. His hands began trembling, his pulse racing. With an effort of will he suppressed the panic. Perhaps coming off the case would a good thing. It rarely ended well when cases got too personal, and there was nothing more personal than having a gun pointed at you. Aye, a few days off would do him good. On Sunday he might nip back to that record fair again, he could give Gemma a call, go out for a meal. Yes, a nice quiet weekend, that's what he needed…

As Pearce's Jag came through the corrugated iron gates and pulled up, Taverner was shaking hands with two young men in suits. By the time he was out of the the car and walking across the open space to the riverside, the men were leaving, heading back to the Porsche parked by the entrance. Taverner was grinning like Cheshire cat.

"Good meeting, T?" Pearce asked, joining his boss, looking out over the glittering Thames beyond.

"Good? Fucking marvellous. Mark my words, Eddie, this is it. We're moving into Division One. Times are changing. All that Ronnie and Reggie stuff, it's gone. This is where the money is now." He waved a hand around the empty and quiet docks. "Dunbar Wharf. He was one of the richest men in Britain, you know, old Duncan Dunbar? His old man was a sweaty sock, came down to London and set up a brewery. Dunbar junior used the money from that to get into shipping. He was born here actually, in one of the old houses on Narrow Street. Trading, shifting goods, investing, he tripled his money in as many years, made millions. We can do the same now, with the potential of this place. We don't need the old ways any more."

"To be honest, I quite like the old ways, T." Pearce looked around at the derelict site. All he could see was concrete and old buildings. "You know where you are. You know what's what, none of this fannying about with shares and portfolios." He indicated the departing Porsche. "That lot would shit 'emselves at the first sniff of trouble. Pricks."

"Ah, Eddie, Eddie. You've got to move with the times, go with the flow. The sort of dosh these people are talking would take years of graft to make, even with the drug trade. Now, with all this," he waved a hand around, "we sign a few bits of paper, make a few bungs in the right direction and stand to make millions. *Millions*, Eddie. No argie-bargie, no shootings or beatings. And, best of all, no risk of getting your collar felt. It's like I've been telling you these last few months, there's no need for none of that old nonsense any more."

"No need." Pearce repeated blankly.

"Anyway, what did you have to tell me?"

"The Arikans, T. They're up for a meeting, this Sunday. Gives us a couple of days to put everything in place."

"Ah right, those bastards. Well I suppose it needs doing, for the family if nothing else. But that's it. After this we're out. This deal will buy a lovely place in Florida. They have smashing golf courses there."

"Righto, T. Well, you just leave all the arrangements to me. I'll have our guys in place, we'll get the Turks here early Sunday morning while there's no-one about. Everything will be sorted."

"Sweet, Eddie, sweet." Taverner turned and looked up and around again, as though imagining the luxury apartments that would soon be built here. "Florida," he smiled.

Chapter 39

For what felt like the first time in weeks, Calloway hadn't set the alarm and slept in. Getting up just after ten, he made a quick breakfast then spent the morning on all the household chores he'd been putting aside. The newest item on the list was getting some filler for the bullet hole in the wall. The front door was undamaged, just a scuff mark that he could sand and polish out. After poking round in the cupboards, he decided on a trip to Romford. There were closer DIY stores, but he fancied spending the day wandering round the shops and market - there was a second-hand record stall there he'd not been to for a while. Mindful of the fact his vision was still a bit fuzzy round the edges, he jumped on the bus. For once, it was nice to go somewhere without rushing, without wondering what the hell might be waiting at the other end.

Gavin tapped on the bedroom door and peered round it. Spider looked up from the magazine he was reading.

"There's a phone call. Some geezer, asked for you."

"Did he say who it was?"

"No. But he said he has some information for you."

Spider flicked the magazine aside and stood up. "Weird. No-one's supposed to know I'm here. Best take it I suppose."

A few minutes later he walked into the kitchen, where Gavin and Angie were stood chatting over a cup of tea.

"Alright?" Gavin asked.

"Yeah, I suppose." He rubbed the back of his neck. "Geezer told me where Arikan is going to be tomorrow. Time and place."

"Blimey!" Gavin raised his eyebrows. "So how did he know where to find you? And did he say who he was?"

"I asked him both. He said I wasn't that hard to find, which is a bit worrying. And he said he was a friend of Mum's. Wanted to see things put right. Said he knew I wanted the same."

"So what you gonna do? Is this kosher you think? Could be a trap from this north London lot?"

Spider narrowed his eyes. " Could be I suppose. But what if it ain't? I mean there's plenty of people want him out the way, I imagine. He's hardly ever seen in public, this might be my only chance to do what I said I was gonna do."

Gavin glanced at his wife. "Are you sure about this, Spider?" Angie asked. "I know you've been wrapped up in some bad stuff, but this is another level. Remember what happened to your Uncle Vic."

"Yeah, I know. A twenty year stretch for going over the pavement."

"Exactly," Angie pointed out. "And he didn't even shoot anyone. Apart from that copper. And that was only in the leg."

Spider pulled out a chair and sat, resting his elbows on the table. "I know. But look, with this info I can be in and out. The bloke said he might only have one or two people with him, they ain't gonna get involved once they see I'm tooled up."

"Or they might shoot you," Gavin rinsed his mug in the sink. "They're gangsters, cuz, they'll be tooled up too. Where will he be, anyway?"

"Limehouse. Place called Dunbar Wharf. Apparently the old man will be there tomorrow morning. He'll be driven up in his car, then he'll be out for a while, then back to the car. All I have to do is hide nearby and pop him as he comes back."

"Easy as that, eh?" Gavin shook his head. "Alright. Listen, if you've really made your mind up to do this, I'll drive you over there. I ain't getting more involved than that. I can't, can I love?" He patted Angie's stomach.

Spider's eyes widened. "Really? Shit, when did you find out about that?"

"Just a couple of days ago," Angie smiled. "We've not let anyone know yet, you're the first. We wanted to keep it quiet for a bit, you know?"

"Well that's smashing," Spider grinned, then turned serious again. "And do you mean it? You'll back me up?"

"Driving only," Gavin replied. "I know that area well enough. Dad worked the docks, remember? I'll tuck away somewhere and wait for you. Can't imagine there'll be anyone about that time on a Sunday, the whole place is derelict now. But the first sign of any trouble or the plod, and we're out. Clear?"

"Yeah, clear."

"Good. Now, listen, the Hammers are at Highbury this afternoon. Fancy going?"

"What, shout at a few Gooners?" Spider laughed. "Sounds good. Let's go."

Calloway got back later than he'd planned. After packing away his DIY bits and pieces and putting the newly acquired Art Tatum album on the turntable, he looked in the fridge for food. The contents were not promising. A carton of milk, a pack of ham, some tomatoes and a lump of cheese with bluey-green spots on it. He shook his head, berating himself for not checking before he went out to the shops. Despite what he'd told her the other day, he wondered if Gemma would fancy going out for a meal. He rang her, but only got the answerphone, so left a brief message. A takeaway it was, then.

It was cloudy and starting to spit with rain again as he walked down to the shops. He cut through the back alley, unusually there was no sign of the kids hanging around at the far end. The rain, he thought, they were probably down at the arcade. Halfway along, a sound brought him up short. The squeal of brakes as a large car came to a halt at the mouth of the alleyway ahead. Hurrying footsteps behind brought Cab spinning round. Too late. Someone grabbed his arms, a cloth was pressed across his face. A punch to the gut took any fight out of him and the ground and sky tilted as he was dragged towards the car. The last thing he heard was a voice growl, "Get him in the back," then the world went dark.

Chapter 40

Taverner straightened his tie in the mirror and nodded in approval at his reflection. He might be pushing sixty, but he still looked good. And sixty was no age these days. Not like his old man, worked liked a pit horse and dead a year after retirement. No, Terence had been smart, he'd sussed early on what a mug's game the straight life was. No-one gave you anything, least of all the bastards in charge - best to take it. He had, with both hands, and now look where he was, sitting on a million pound deal, with the prospect of a sun-filled retirement ahead. His wife poked her head around the bedroom door.

"Eddie's here, love." She smiled as she turned, patting the collars of his jacket. "Looking smart as always."

"And you, Mrs Elizabeth Taverner, look as beautiful as the day I married you." He kissed her. "I should be back in an hour or so. Let's go out for Sunday lunch. Up west somewhere?"

"Sounds lovely."

Minutes later, he was in the back seat of Pearce's Jag, nodding to him and the two lumps in the front. At 8.30 on a Sunday morning the traffic was light. Cutting down Burdett Road and onto the A13, they were soon driving through the narrow streets of Limehouse.

"Arikan's getting here at 9.15," Pearce explained. "I told him to park by the gate, then walk across to meet us at the dockside."

"Who's he bringing?"

"Well he was never going to come on his own, so I said he could bring two men. It's been agreed everyone will be clean, he's said we can search him."

Taverner grunted. "And what about this sniper geezer? It's a bit out in the open here, isn't it?"

"No need to worry about that." Pearce grinned. "We've got people all round the place, besides which, word is they've fucked the guy off."

"Alright. And what's the plan? When do we hit them?"

"Not at the docks," Pearce took out a silver cigarette case and offered one, Taverner waved it away. "We've got teams going in on the Arikan places at 9.30. We hit the old man in his car on the way back. Simple job. Van behind, van in front, block him in, bang. That way, you're well out of the picture."

"Good." Taverner settled back into the plush leather. "Shame I can't be there to see it, but at last my Tricia will be able to rest in peace."

The rest of the journey passed in silence, and the tyres soon crunched loose stone underneath as two more of Pearce's crew directed them through the squeaking gate and into the dock site beyond. The weather had brightened up, just a few puddles left from last night's rain. The breeze was fresh off the river, gulls cried in the bright morning air. The Jag pulled up next to a couple of transit vans and emptied. Taverner strode over to the dockside, accompanied by Pearce and his two men - names of Danny and Sean, he remembered. Then it was a matter of waiting.

At 9.20 there was a squeal of metal and another crunch of tyres as a tan S-Class Mercedes swung in through the entrance. Three men got out and were promptly frisked by the guards at the gate. One looked over to Pearce and nodded, then motioned the three across the open space to the waiting group.

"Alright, lads, off you go," Pearce spoke to Danny and Sean, the pair of them walking back towards the gate. Taverner squared his shoulders, and fixed a steely glare on the central figure of the three approaching. He was old, perhaps a decade older than himself, but straight backed, a proud looking man, turned out as immaculately as Taverner, in a camel-hair coat over a dark blue mohair suit. As he drew closer, Taverner could see that although the hair and beard were white, the eyes glittered with intense life. He was flanked by two younger men, one a son, judging from the resemblance. They stopped a couple of yards away.

"Mr Taverner," the old man nodded.

"Mr Arikan," Taverner returned the nod. "Thank you for coming. I gather we have some business to untangle."

"Indeed, we do. Such a tangle. And can I first begin by extending my deepest regrets and condolences on the loss of your niece. It was a most unfortunate error and one that, were it in my power to do so, I would go back and change."

Taverner took a breath and pressed his lips together. For a moment he said nothing. "I understand. And the man responsible?"

"No longer in our employment."

"I see. That is a shame, I would like to have... met him." Taverner hissed.

"I understand. I would feel the same way in your position. I do feel the same way…"

"Ah yes, your son. I heard. Has there been any news?"

"No. He has not regained consciousness and the doctor tells me that even if he does, he may have suffered considerable brain damage." The eyes flashed with an inner rage.

"I see. I am sorry. And the man responsible?"

"The policeman? Ah yes, well that brings us to our first matter?" Arikan glanced at Pearce who waved across to Danny and Sean. The pair disappeared into the doorway of one of the few remaining buildings and emerged with a figure in-between them. It was a man, a burlap bag over his head. As Taverner watched with growing confusion, they half-led, half-dragged their prisoner across the concrete to the dockside. The man was pushed towards Pearce, who, with a flourish, removed the bag, revealing a bruised and blinking Calloway. Arikan smiled.

Laçis was settled into his spot. Over the last two days he had recced both the golf course and the dock site. When the call came through, he was glad it was to be the docks. There were numerous platforms here to choose from, what with most of buildings being vacant. He had chosen the flat roof of what might have once been a warehouse as the best option. The place was derelict, but all the staircases were in good order. A metal ladder on the upper floor led to the flat roof area. There were three exits on the ground floor, not including the many, largely smashed, windows. Ismet waited in a car two minutes jog away, they could be up on the main road and out of the area within five minutes. The weather was clear, there was little wind. He'd had another chance to work with the rifle, it was ready and so was he. At last he could finish this damn job and return home.

At the sight of the first car arriving, Laçis switched of the Walkman, removed his headphones and took a prone position. There was a slight lip around the edge of the roof, so no need for a tripod. He rested the barrel on the brickwork, put an eye to the sight and slowed his breathing. He remained so still that a gull landed within arms reach, eyeing him curiously. Laçis ignored it, intent only on the scene playing out below. After some twenty minutes, a second car pulled up. Arikan's, he recognised it from the car park under the flats. He tracked the old man as he walked across the space to the men at the dockside. As another man was dragged out from a nearby building, Laçis slowed his breathing even further, curling his finger around the trigger. The bag was removed from the man's head, revealing the battered and bruised policeman. Laçis took careful aim. Arikan removed a white handkerchief from his breast pocket and wiped his forehead. Laçis took the shot.

Calloway stumbled and blinked in the bright sunshine. He'd woken up tied to a chair inside what looked to be a shipping container. He had no clue where he was, or what time it was. The room was bare, apart from a single light bulb, a stained mattress on the floor and a bucket. Over the intervening hours, a man in a balaclava had come in a couple of times, with a bowl of food and some water. He cut Calloway's bonds and left without a word. With nothing else to do, Calloway had fought down his rising panic and tried to get some sleep. He had been asleep when the door had screeched open again, three men this time. He was dragged onto his feet, tied, and a bag placed over his head. From there he was led out into the open air and bundled in the back of a van. Diesel, judging from the sound of the engine. He tried his best to count turns and listen for sounds, as he was sure Sergei would have done, but was soon hopelessly confused. Instead, he fell into an almost trance-like state, the icy feeling of dread increasing as the van slowed at its destination. Dragged out, he was walked into a building, pushed onto a chair and told to wait. He could still see nothing but had the sense of a person being close by. Confirmed when he went to stand and was pushed roughly back down.

Finally, this. Dragged again across some rough ground, the first face he could make out, squinting against the light, was a grinning Pearce. If that was not enough to make his heart sink, the second was an elderly Turkish man. Arikan, he recognised from the mugshots at briefings. To his left, a confused looking Taverner. Calloway did his best to pull himself up to his full height.

"What the fuck is this?" he croaked, his throat parched, his knees weak.

"This, Mr Calloway," Pearce said, "is what we in the trade we call an exchange of assets. And you happen to be one of the assets involved."

As Pearce spoke, Arikan had wiped his brow with a handkerchief. Odd, as the weather was not that hot. Calloway found himself suddenly bemused, there was something hot and wet on his face. For a moment he wondered if he had been shot, especially given the flat crack that echoed across the docks. But Taverner had vanished. Calloway glanced down. No, Taverner was there, prone on the slightly damp concrete, head, or what remained of his head, laying in an expanding pool of blood.

Chapter 41

Calloway turned to Pearce, expecting some sort of violent action from the man. There was none, Pearce merely hardened his expression and returned Calloway's questioning stare.

"What?" he growled. "I tried to warn him. Months this has been building up now." He took out a cigarette and lit it, inhaling deeply. "You see, Mr Calloway all this…" he waved the cigarette in the air. "All this…. *progress,* it ain't for me." He shook his head and took another drag. "Office ponces with red braces and filey-faxes? No. This is my manor, we do things the old way. Mr Arikan understands that. He's old school, like me. We grew up on respect and honour. We settle our affairs on an handshake, not with lawyers and contracts. T couldn't see that."

"So you double crossed him," Calloway sneered. "Set him up to be shot like a dog."

"It was the only way." Pearce moved close to Cab, blowing smoke in his face. He struggled to move away, but the two men were holding his arms tight. "Thing is, Calloway, this is all I know. This is my life. It's what I do, it's what I *am.* I enjoy it. Golf, lunch with the mayor, cocktails at eight, fuck all that. This is survival of the fittest, the law of the jungle." He leaned in even closer, lips pulled back. "And I'm the biggest fucking lion here."

He stepped back, throwing the half finished cigarette to the floor. "Anyway, that's the least of your worries. Like I said, you're an asset, and now you belong to Mr Arikan. I'm sure the two of you will have a lovely little chat." He spoke to the men holding Calloway. "Take him over to the building, then come back here with the tarp and clear that mess up."

Before he could protest, Calloway was being dragged back towards the building he had recently emerged from. Two other men were carrying gear into it from the back of a van. Inside, he could see another man was just finishing hooking up a set of lights to a humming generator. Calloway turned his head as the dazzling lights were switched on. In the glare he made out two items atop a trestle table. With a lurch in his stomach he recognised a circular saw and a drill. He was pushed forward, stumbling on rubble and falling to his hands and knees. Someone grabbed his collar and dragged him round, pushing him sharply back to the dusty floor. Half blinded by the lights, Cab raised a hand to shield his eyes as a voice spoke from the gloom.

"Well now, Mr Calloway. I do not believe we have been formally introduced. My name is Nasir Arikan. You destroyed my son."

He could make out the silhouette of the old man now, seated on a folding chair. Calloway fought down his rising panic and tried to speak with as much authority as he could muster.

"That was an accident. A terrible accident and I'm truly sorry for what happened."

There was the merest hint of a mirthless smile. "You certainly shall be. I would very much have liked to take you from here to a place of my own, but transporting a kidnapped policeman across half of London carries risks. Instead, Mr Pearce has kindly allowed me the use of this place and these items." He motioned to the table. "So our time together is limited, but nonetheless will be extremely unpleasant for you."

Calloway could only watch in horror as Pearce's men left and Arikan's two companions appeared at his shoulder. Arikan motioned to one of them. "This is my eldest son, Mehmet. In honour of his brother, I am going to let him work on you for a while. But it will be me who takes your life, Calloway. Mine will be the last face you see as I send you to oblivion."

Cab made to stand but Mehmet stepped forward, kicking him in the chest, sending him back to the floor. He groaned, coughed, then, growing increasingly desperate, flung up a hand.

"Wait, wait. Before you kill me, at least let me know why all this began. Why target the girl? What does Birch's daughter have to do with any of this?"

Arikan motioned his son to stop. "Ah, ever the detective. Well, why not?" he shrugged. "Birch came into our sphere of influence in Cyprus. It seems the man has a penchant for young girls, as many of his kind do. Put simply, he was given the opportunity to assist us in our new business venture. A Member of Parliament can open many doors that would be shut in the face of a mere *foreigner*. Especially one of my background." That briefest of grins again. "They despise us yet, at the same time, are very desirous of the products we offer."

"Drugs. Cocaine." Calloway spat.

"Yes. That, and other things that I already mentioned. We can supply them all, and of the highest quality, with tact and discretion. Thanks to Birch, we are already dealing with a Cabinet Minister."

"And his daughter?"

"Ah, yes. Well Birch grew increasingly unhappy with our arrangement. Even the threat of exposure was no longer enough to keep him in line. Added to that, at a chance meeting in an exclusive London club, he recognised and confronted me. He was most disrespectful, and in public, too. I could not let this go unpunished. You see, Calloway, men like Birch think that they are beyond consequences. They think they are above the law. Not just your type of law, but mine. As Pearce said, the law of the jungle. He needed to be taught a severe lesson."

"Then why not just expose him? You had filmed him, right?"

"Ah, now there is an irony. We should have had evidence, we have used this method before. But something went wrong, in the taking of the photos or in the processing of the film, I don't know. So, you see, we actually had nothing to blackmail Birch with. My hand was forced, you might say. Funny how things can work out, don't you agree?"

"Fucking hilarious. But to kill his daughter?"

"It sends out a message, Mr Calloway. Powerful men may be prepared to sacrifice themselves, but never their children. This is the message, that we have complete control. Not just for the MP but for others we have in similar situations. And, of course, the fact we are prepared to take such a course of action also indicates a certain level of professionalism to our new business partners in Colombia. Such things impress them, I am told."

Calloway was back on his knees by now, his chest hurting, his head throbbing again. "Jesus, just how deep does this go? How many people do you have in your pocket?"

Arikan gestured. "Some. Pearce was right, times are indeed changing. Areas such as this will soon become homes for the rich. As corporations take over these areas, we take over the corporations. Do you know how much money the South American cartels make, Calloway? It's enough to buy people. Not just customs officials, or policemen such as yourself. No, it is enough to buy lawmakers, politicians, even governments. That is the future."

"And Pearce and his old ways?"

Arikan sneered. "Pearce is an oaf and, as we have seen, a traitor We will deal with him in due course, but for now, he is useful. Why risk many lives in a war that you can win by killing just one man?" He rose, smoothing out his expensive coat. "Speaking of which. As I mentioned, our time here is limited. Let us begin." He clicked his fingers and Mehmet and his companion moved forward, dragging Calloway up by his arms and pushing him onto the table. Cab struggled and received a punch in the face for his trouble, half stunning him. One man shoved him down onto the table, pinning his shoulders. Mehmet disappeared from view, there came a short pause, then Calloway heard the nerve-shredding whine of an electric drill.

Chapter 42

The whine grew louder when a voice interrupted. It was Pearce.

"Everything alright, Mr Arikan? I'll give you fifteen minutes or so, then the boys will come in and clean up. You can be off away."

Arikan turned, nodding, looking annoyed at this interruption. But there was to be another. Another voice, from the gloom beyond the halogen lights.

"Arikan, you cunt!"

The man holding Calloway relaxed the hold, looking round. Everyone followed his gaze, Cab twisting on the table. From out of the dark came Tony Webb, gun in outstretched hand. He looked pale and nervous, but determined. And right now, the barrel was pointed squarely at the old man. Mehmet tensed to leap at him, then swore. There was no way he could make the distance in time.

"Well, then," Webb snarled as he shuffled closer. "Sorry to interrupt your little chit-chat here. Oi, don't move!" he called out as Mehmet's companion also thought about intervening. "I've come for you, Arikan. You killed my Mum, now I'll kill you!"

Arikan sat back in the chair, raising his palms. "Young man, I have no idea who you are, let alone your mother. And I have killed no women. At least not for some considerable time."

"You liar!" Webb screamed. "I started working for your men. Dealing drugs. You got done over, you thought it was me. Your men kidnapped me, they were going to torture me. He rescued me." He waved the gun briefly at Pearce, a frozen shadow behind Arikan.

The old man slowly shook his head. "Well, now I know who you are. But the death of your mother was not at my hand. I can give you my word on that, if it means anything."

Webb's brow creased in confusion. "What? But it must have been. Who else? The neighbour said she saw a big man. Your man, Serkan. He done it."

Arikan shook his head again. "Serkan is no longer with is. But neither I, or anyone in my organisation, ordered him to do this. Why would we? No, young man, I suspect someone else had a hand in this."

Webb glanced around the room, perhaps the gravity of the situation was beginning to hit home. His lips worked soundlessly as he digested this information. "But… then.. what…" He glanced over at the now grinning Pearce and understanding dawned. "*You!* It was you! But why? Why the fuck?" His eyes flashed, lips pulled back in snarl.

Pearce stepped forward into the light and laughed. "I told you what would happen if you pissed me off. Besides, I wanted to see what you'd do. To be honest, you've surprised me. I didn't think you had the stones, boy."

"You set me up *again?*"

"All the way, son. I even told Ronnie the Leg to sell you a piece for whatever money you had. If you got through to the old man here, well, all's fair in love and war. That was before we'd made our arrangement, see? And when nothing happened, I thought you'd just bottled it. Anyway, look on the bright side. I saved you money on a cremation."

Webb's hand shook and tears rolled down his cheeks. Calloway was sitting up on the edge of the table now. "Tony. Don't do it," he called. "Get out now. Escape while you can, these guys will kill you. Tony, listen to me!"

But Spider was beyond listening. Whether he meant to pull the trigger or not, Mehmet sprang for him and the gun went off. Pearce, in a well practiced move, already had his own pistol out and aimed. Spider's bullet caught him in the chest, his own flew way off target to hit Arikan in the shoulder. Then Mehmet was on him.

Calloway, ignoring the pain, gave the man next to him a sharp jab in the ribs and a hook to the jaw, sending him spinning into the light stand. As halogen beams flashed around the dark interior, Calloway lurched towards the struggling pair. Another shot sounded and Mehmet fell back, clutching at his stomach, shirt red with blood. Calloway got to Webb, hauled him up by his collar and hissed in his ear. "Run! Get out!"

He closely followed as more voices sounded behind him, Pearce's men, no doubt. Webb's footsteps echoed ahead in the gloomy, derelict building, the lad quickly disappearing from view. Darting through a doorway and along a corridor, Cab saw blessed daylight ahead - a window, glass shattered. With a groan he heaved himself over the sill, ripping his coat to shreds on the remnants of broken glass. Outside, he stayed closed to the building and hurried away, expecting shouts or the crack of bullets behind him at any second. Rounding a corner, he found himself out on the dockside area again and took a minute to draw breath and take stock. A noise above caught his attention. There, up on the adjacent building, he could make out two figures, fighting. Even at this distance he could recognise them both - Laçis and Sergei.

Sergei had pressed his handler yet again to push for more assistance. The man had repeatedly mentioned the increasing impatience of his superiors at lack of resolution, that was nothing new. However, this time that impatience and the handler's repeated requests, had miraculously prompted more resources allocated to the mission. That including extra surveillance from various anonymous, London-based assets. Sergei had rolled his eyes at that. He understood the need for security, operating as they were in a potentially hostile country, but being able to co-ordinate directly with colleagues would have made things much easier - if nothing else it would shorten the chain of communication.

Still, intel had come in, and he had acted upon it. A number of Arikan assets had been identified, even those hidden in layers of shell companies. Surveillance had been mounted on a number of them, one in particular drawing attention following a potential sighting of Laçis leaving the premises. Sergei had zeroed in on the place, a nondescript house in an area called Bounds Green. There was little or no intel about who or how many might be inside the property and direct surveillance was out of the question - Laçis had seen Sergei's face and would ID him in an instant. But early that Sunday morning, Sergei received the call that Laçis was on the move.

He was staying in a B&B just round the corner from the watched house, and was out of the place within minutes. Sergei made good time, the voice of the operative tailing Laçis in his earpiece informing him that the target was heading into East London, then, even more specifically, into Limehouse. After that came a problem. The target had entered a derelict docklands area. Following became a challenge, given the total lack of traffic. The target was last seen heading towards a fenced off area directly on the riverside.

Sergei called the tracker off, then drove down the street of the last sighting himself. Sure enough, a turn off of it led to an entrance, covered by a large, corrugated iron gateway. With a curse, he parked up as close as he dared, and scouted the length of the fence on foot. To his relief, access to the site beyond proved simple enough, a loose piece of fencing providing a way in. But on the other side of that lay a large area of empty dockland, huge, deserted buildings and industrial waste. With a sigh, Sergei checked the shoulder-holstered Walther beneath his green flight jacket and, mentally dividing the area into quarters, set off on the hunt.

As he moved into the first derelict building, he caught sight of a group over on the dock edge. He abruptly stepped back from the vacant window, concealing himself in the gloom. He observed for a moment as the men talked. From this distance he could just make out both Taverner and an older man - presumably Arikan, from the intel he had studied. Then another man was dragged across to them, a man Sergei recognised even before the sack was ripped from his head - Calloway! Sergei swore. There was no way he could make that distance before anything happened to the policeman. Besides, he had no idea if any of the men were armed. And, presumably, Laçis was still at large in the area, he was not with the group. The decision was made for him when the crack of a rifle sent Taverner spinning to the floor. Sergei risked a quick glance out of the window. There, the next building, the rooftop... just over the lip at its edge, the end of a rifle barrel protruded. Laçis!

Sergei turned and sprinted through the building, swerving around bits of old furniture and equipment. He smashed through a fire door half-hanging off its hinges at the end and raced into the next building. Similarly derelict, he made for the concrete stair ahead, taking them two at a time as he eased the Walther out of the holster. Approaching the top floor, he slowed, taking the steps on all fours, then pausing to glance carefully above the top step. A large empty room revealed itself, the only point of interest being the metal rung ladder in the corner leading to an open trapdoor in the roof. Sergei was across the space in seconds, glancing up, squinting, into the sunlight above. He took a breath and began to climb the ladder.

He was almost at the top when a sound brought him to a halt. The scuff of boots and a click. Gun in one hand, he took the next rungs slowly, peering over the trapdoor's edge. There, about ten metres away, knelt Laçis, dismantling his sniper rifle. Sergei paused. A shot from here was too risky. At that distance, firing over the lip of the trapdoor, even he was not likely to hit. Instead, he flowed up and over the trapdoor, crawling on the flat roof surface, pistol always ahead and pointing at Laçis.

Perhaps it was a sound that warned the hit-man, perhaps it was instinct. Either way, Sergei had not got far when Laçis wheeled, half dissembled rifle in hands. He made a calculation in an instant and quickly began snapping the gun back into place. Sergei rose and charged forward, pistol swinging up and cracking off a shot as he came. But Laçis was already moving, the bullet whistling out over the roof's edge. As Sergei closed, he aimed again. Rather than continue assembling the rifle, Laçis flung it instead, spinning end over end, full into Serge's face. He lifted a hand to deflect, but the stock caught him a sharp blow on the wrist. With a cry, Sergei dropped the Walther. Laçis was already moving forward, a knife appearing in his hand from nowhere.

Sergei weaved aside at the first slash and kicked the pistol away. No sense leaving it in reach of Laçis. The hit-man followed up with two quick stabs to the belly. Sergei stepped aside from the first, then, drawing his own knife from his belt as he did so, jinked again, this time bringing his own blade up in a reverse grip to slice into Laçis' attacking arm.

Laçis hissed and immediately tossed the knife into his other hand as blood filled his palm. Both men drew back, each nursing a damaged arm. A dull throb pulsed in Sergei's wrist, the bones crunched as he flexed his fingers, shooting pain up his arm. He exhaled sharply and locked the pain into a small box in his mind, he would worry about it later. For now, he focused his full attention on the man before him. In size and build there was little difference between them. Both had received the same training, both were experts in their field, both were killers… but only one would leave this rooftop alive.

Chapter 43

"A government killer, then?" sneered Laçis. "Come to do his master's bidding?"

Sergei edged closer as he replied. "And you are what? A man who kills for money. For drug dealers and pimps. And I don't attack women and children."

"How naive. You work for a system that does exactly that. As they all do, in the East in the West, they are all the same."

"You chose the West, though."

Laçis shrugged, shuffling a little to his right. "At least here I am free to choose who I take orders from, and free to enjoy the money I earn. What do you have? A cold, one-bedroom flat in a tower block? Do you even own a car?"

"A man is not judged merely on his possessions." Sergei shifted position again, mirroring his opponent's posture.

Laçis gave a short laugh. "So all men say when they have no

access to such possessions. Beside, what would you - " Laçis left the question unfinished, lunging at Sergei with the speed of a viper. Sergei jerked his head back as the blade whistled across his face. Pre-empting the follow up he dropped to the floor, lashing out with his own knife as he did so. His strike open up a shallow cut on Laçis' leg, and Sergei rolled to avoid the downward stab that followed. He kicked out with his legs, trying to sweep Laçis, but the hit-man pulled his leg back and sharply kicked Sergei in the side. He rolled again to absorb the impact, but the move left him open. Laçis was plunging forward again, dropping to one knee as he stabbed. Sergei twisted on the spot, forced to drop his own knife as he grabbed the attacking wrist, keeping the side of the blade flat against his left forearm.

Sergei squeezed his fingers tight and Laçis grimaced, blood dripping from his wound. In response, he reached down and grabbed Sergei's left wrist, drawing a grunt of pain from his enemy. The two remained in a deadlock. Laçis had the advantage of weight bearing down, Sergei the stability of the roof underneath him. A voice called up from below.

"Sergei!" Calloway's shout distracted Laçis. His head turned for a second, it was all that Sergei needed. He kicked away Laçis' supporting knee and, as the man's weight fell upon him, twisted, lifted his hips and threw the man with his other knee. Without pause, he snatched up his knife and rose into a crouch, poised, ready. Laçis had likewise rolled out of the throw, which took him, Sergei noted with horror, directly towards the fallen pistol. With a shout of triumph, Laçis grabbed the gun and was up. He stood facing Sergei, close to the edge of the roof, bleeding right arm extended, the snub nose of the Walther pointed directly at Sergei's chest.

The hit-man gave a low chuckle. "And so it ends. Any last words, government man?"

Sergei scowled. He had the knife in his hand, Laçis was close enough for a throw, but by the time he raised his arm the shot would be fired. Then he smiled himself, remembering a trick the Old Man had taught him. Sergei dropped the knife, point first. It slid down his leg and as it reached his ankle, Sergei kicked out, whipping his foot forward to send the blade point first straight at his opponent. It caught Laçis in the shoulder, sending the shot whining across the rooftop. More, it sent him staggering back, knife hilt protruding from the bloody patch on his jacket. One step, two... and on the third, Laçis' calf hit the low ledge that fringed the roof. For a second he teetered, one arm flailing, the other bringing the Walther round to point at Sergei again. But before he could fire, with a brief cry, the hit-man disappeared into the void.

Calloway winced again at the stabbing pain. Felt like a cracked rib at least. He pushed it aside, taking shallow breaths as he stumbled towards the building. He found one door, but it wouldn't budge. Glancing up at the roof he called out, "Sergei!" hoping, at least to let the Russian know that help was on the way. *Some help*, he thought. Then Cab's blood ran cold as a shot rang out overhead. Before he could respond there was a cry, then a dull thump as a body plunged forty feet to crash onto the concrete just a few yards away from him.

Fearing the worst, he lurched to the body, laying face up, arms outstretched in a widening pool of blood. It was Laçis! With a sigh of relief he quickly examined the body. A knife protruded from the shoulder, a gun was gripped in the hand. A Walther. Calloway glanced up. Sergei's face appeared over the ledge above. He nodded to Calloway, then looked up at the sound of an approaching police siren. He gave a brief salute and was gone.

Cab made a snap decision. He quickly checked the body over, prised the Walther from the dead man's hand, limped over to the dockside and hurled the pistol into the Thames. The pain in his chest was increasing, he was growing increasingly faint, so his next decision was simply to park his backside on a bollard and wait for the cavalry to arrive.

Chapter 44

Calloway placed two coffees from the canteen on Denham's desk and smiled at the large slug of rum his guv poured into them both. Each man drank in silence for a moment, before Denham spoke.

"How are the ribs?"

Calloway placed a hand on his chest, feeling the tape beneath his shirt. "Sore as fuck. Mind you, so is everything else. This is a young man's game."

Denham smiled as he lit a cigarette. "Can't argue with that. So what exactly did happen at the docks?"

"You've read the report, guv."

"I have. Which is why I ask. Our people found a dead hit-man, some blood stains and bullets, a few power tools and not much else. Taverner's mob had you bagged, how did you really get out?"

Calloway took another gulp of the fortified coffee and smacked his lips in appreciation. "Like I wrote, guv. A big row started between the Arikans and Pearce's people, shots were fired, in the confusion I made a break for it. I got outside, found Laçis. Looked like he'd taken a dive off the roof." He shrugged. "That's it."

"You know Laçis had a knife stuck in him?"

"Aye. Can't imagine how that happened."

"And Taverner's body was nowhere to be found, though there was a big puddle of claret on the dockside."

"Aye. Laçis got him, just after they unbagged me."

"And there was more blood in the building, enough to indicate two or three serious wounds, if not deaths. Bullets, too, but again, no bodies."

"I guess whoever was left standing cleared everything away quick. Local uniform turned up, they'd had a call from a jogger who'd heard gunshots."

"Yes. According to their report, as they came in a van and a Merc were seen coming out at high speed. So quick, uniform didn't get the number plates. Once they found what they found at the scene, they called it in. By the time an alert got out the van and car could have been anywhere. And there you were, sat enjoying the view over the Thames."

"Aye, that I was, guv. Not much else I can tell you, really."

Denham shook his head. "Cab, what am I going to do with you? Anyway. Laçis is dead, Taverner is dead. Rumours are that Pearce might be, too. Seems word got out about him stitching up his boss, even Pearce's reputation wouldn't protect him on that. Oh, and Wood Green tell us that something's up with the Arikans. We're not sure exactly what yet, but it looks like the old man is out of the picture, for the moment at least. You think they'll still be out for you?"

"Who knows, guv? Still, I don't suppose all this noise will have gone down with their cartel. Hopefully that will keep the Arikan's attention off of me. I'm just a small fish, after all. And, hopefully, what with my statements and all the other intel coming through, there's enough to build a decent case against them - especially now the full story is coming out. Speaking of which, what about Birch?"

"Officially, he is *helping the authorities with their enquiries.* Unofficially, he's in Special Branch hands now. He may even go to Five."

"And what will happen to him?" Calloway scowled.

"You know how it works. Pensioned off, I imagine."

"And the coke supplies to our glorious leaders?"

"I doubt they'll get interrupted. Cab, I don't like it any more than you do, but that's the world we live in."

Calloway drained his plastic cup. "Aye. Isn't it just. He wasn't wrong about our system here."

"Your Russian friend?"

"Yes, guv. Still, is what he is going back to any better?"

"No. In fact, it may be worse. Anyway, that's all above our pay grade. We're just simple coppers, right, Cab?"

"Right, guv."

They sat in silence for a moment or two before Denham spoke again. "Did you ever see him again?"

Cab merely shrugged and shook his head in reply, before heading back to his own office. Pavitt was in place at Turner's desk. The young DC was making a full recovery, though he wouldn't be back in post for a while yet. Calloway said "Morning," to Pavitt, then sighed as Smith came in with a bundle of folders.

"Nice to see you back, sarge," she smiled. "Here's the files for those TDA cases. No rest for the wicked, eh?"

Calloway gave her a mock scowl and settled back in his chair. His mind cast back to a couple of nights after the incident. He'd been relaxing to Charlie Parker when the doorbell rang. It was Sergei, smiling, carrying a holdall in his non-bandaged hand. Cab had invited him in .

"I can't stay," the Russian had said. "I am leaving tonight. There is private plane."

Calloway raised a palm. "I don't need to know. You got him, then?"

"I did. Though it was close. I presume he was dead when you found him?"

"Aye, that he was. As dead as I've seen anyone. He won't be killing anyone ever again."

Sergei arched an eyebrow. "We have a saying. Some people are still dangerous until their head is ten metres from their body. But in this case, I think you are right." He placed a hand over his heart. "Thank you. For everything."

"Anytime, pal. Besides, you saved me, remember. Here,we should have a toast. There's a bottle in the kitchen cupboard, could you get it for me? My ribs…" he patted his chest and winced.

Sergei put the bag down and went into the kitchen, returning with scotch and tumblers. Cab twisted off the cap and poured them both a generous measure. They clinked glasses.

"To us," proposed Sergei.

"Aye, to us," Calloway nodded. "Good men in bad situations."

They drank, shook hands and, as quickly and quietly as he had arrived, Sergei was gone.

Sergei dashed across the tarmac to the twin-engined Cessna. The attendant greeted him with a quick smile, ushering him on board.

There was only one other passenger, what appeared to be a middle-aged businessman. Neither man spoke, they avoided eye contact. Sergei settled back in his chair as the plane began to taxi down the runway. The nose lifted, and soon the lights of Southend seafront hove into view below. Minutes later, they were out across the North Sea heading to Dusseldorf. From there, it was another flight to Moscow and a debriefing. Sergei wasn't looking forward to that. Despite reporting a successful mission, he knew it would have taken too long, been too expensive, and attracted too much attention. Not that he was that bothered. He had a few items in his holdall that he could give to friends, or perhaps even sell. Jeans were still a valued commodity, not to mention cassettes.

He pulled the bag up onto this lap to take out the sandwiches he'd bought in the airport. A frown creased his face as his hand touched something unfamiliar. He pulled out a plastic bag, wrapped around something. There was a Post-it note on the outside of the bag, it read "For your journey home, CC."

Intrigued, Sergei unwrapped and opened the bag, taking out a somewhat scratched Walkman and a set of new headphones. He unboxed the headphones and plugged them in then, seeing there was a tape in the machine, put them on and pressed play. With a chuckle he put the holdall down, sat back in his seat and closed his eyes, as the opening bars of Slade's *Rock and Roll Preacher* filled his ears.

Epilogue

Spider shook hands with the last couple as they left the City of London cemetery chapel and sighed. Angie appeared at his elbow.

"You alright, love? It was a lovely service."

"Yes. And yes, it was, she would've liked it."

"Well, Gav and I will be outside. When you're ready, we'll take you back home. A few of the family are coming round for sandwiches and that."

"Thanks Ange. Without you and Gav…" She smiled and patted his arm. "I'll be out in a bit," Spider assured her. Then he turned to the one remaining figure, sat at the rearmost pew. Calloway stood and limped over to him.

"Mr Calloway," Spider nodded. "Thanks for coming."

Calloway nodded and coughed. "Aye, well. I felt I should. It was a lovely service. Nice flowers."

"Yes. She had a lot of friends." Spider looked down at the floor, not sure what to say next.

"Tony, listen. What happened, happened. I'm not saying it was right, but if you hadn't turned up… well, I'd be dogmeat. So, thanks."

Spider mumbled a reply. After shooting Pearce, he'd taken Calloway's advice and ran. He got out of the site the same way he got in, through a gap in the fencing, and back to where Gav was waiting for him. The pistol had gone into the Limehouse Cut as they crossed it on Burdett Road, then it was straight back home to shower and burn his clothes. The shock had set in a couple of hours later, the shakes, the heaving up, but Gav had been ready and waiting. He'd also been making enquiries, but it wasn't until the next day that news came through that both Taverner was dead and Pearce missing. Calloway was speaking again, and Spider snapped back to the present.

"Anyway, here's what I'm going to do. As far as I'm concerned, you weren't there. I made no mention of you in my report, so unless Arikan or Pearce's lot speak up - and I don't see why they would - you're in the clear."

"Thank you Mr Calloway. I appreciate it."

"Oh, there's a condition though." Calloway leaned in to stare hard at Spider. "You stop dealing that shit, alright? Any hint that you're bringing cocaine or pills or even so much as an Aspirin into my patch and I'll be on you like a tramp on chips. You'll be in a flowery dell before you know it. Clear?"

"Clear, Mr Calloway. And yeah, I won't be getting involved with all that coke stuff again. You can bank on it."

"Aye, okay, then. Well, take it easy Tony, and stay out of trouble!" Calloway turned and left, leaving Spider on his own in the now silent chapel. He sighed. He hadn't lied to Calloway, there was no way he was getting into all that cocaine stuff again. Good money, but too risky, and he'd paid a heavy price. Besides there was a new scene growing, away from the mod thing, away from the casuals and skinheads. All the football lads were talking about something called Acid House. Big raves held in out of the way places, no old bill, all the security kept in-house. And not so much the East London crowd this time, no, this was all being run by a new firm, some lads out of Essex.

There was a new drug to go with the new scene, too, something called Ecstasy. It was cheap, easy to get into the country and, by all accounts, got everyone loved up - so no aggro going on, either. Word was that even old rival football firms were teaming up, something that would have been unthinkable a year ago.

Yes, Spider thought as he walked out into the sunlight. Forget all this cartel and Class A lark. Ecstasy, raves and the Essex lads, that was the future. What could possibly go wrong?

If you liked this book, please leave a review on Amazon.

Thanks!

www.innsmouthgold.com

Acknowledgements

While I now enjoy the rural life in North Bedfordshire, I was
born and raised in East London. Almost all of the places in this book are
very familiar to me, as well as the actual people and many of the incidents
that characters and events are based on.

At around the age of 16 I got very much into the burgeoning Mod revival
scene, which largely originated in the East End. At one time, there seemed
to be mods everywhere, though you always had to keep an eye out for rival
gangs. What with that, football firms and various political demos and
marches, it was always easy to find trouble!

The East End has long had a reputation for criminal gangs, though by the
time I was active the Krays had had their day. Still, their shadow loomed
large, their absence leaving something of a vacuum that numerous old and
new firms fought to fill.

I had what you might call family experience of both sides of the law. You
see, my maternal Grandad Harry was a detective at Forest Gate police
station through to the early seventies. My paternal Grandad Walter was a
Bow-born boy, who worked for Jack Spot, a pre-Kray gangland boss.
According to my cousin, my parents' wedding do was an interesting affair,
with guests literally glaring at each other from opposite sides of the hall!

So most of the places are real, though I have taken slight liberties here and
there where necessary for the plot. As for the people - well, let's say they
are mostly amalgams rather than direct copies. Still, it was nice to revisit
some old places and some old memories in the writing of this book, I
hope you enjoy it.

Thanks, as always, to Lara for her support and valuable input. Thanks also
to Vitali, Andy, Shelley at Graveheart Designs, and to my Systema
teachers Mikhail and Vladimir for their continued guidance.

THE WOLF WHO WOULD BE KING SAGA

WOLF IN SHADOWS

WOLF IN CHAINS

WOLF IN THE NORTH

WOLF IN THE UNDERWORLD

WOLF UNDER SIEGE

WOLF IN THE WILDS

"Great books! One of the better Conan-not-Conan series. Poyton does a much better job of nailing the Howardian vibe than most who have tried." Deuce Richardson

" Action packed and features some solid characters. If you enjoyed the works of Robert E. Howard I believe you will have a fun time with this novel."

" Rob Poyton writes in a dense style, filled with details of the world he inhabits with fierce warriors, that wander the worlds channeling the spirit of Conan, King Kull, and Solomon Kane."

"Great barbarian sword and sorcery in the tradition of Conan and other classics." - Amazon reviews

A NEW MILITARY SCI FI SERIES!

ASSAULT TEAM 5: NAYLOR'S WAR

Humanity has survived nuclear war and finally reached up and out to the stars. Now, Earth relies on its far flung mining colonies and factories to survive.

Mike Naylor is a member of the Landers, the elite Skyborne unit serving the Terran Alliance. He is on the front line when the first rumblings of discontent begin amongst the Outer Colonies.

Mike is recruited to spearhead a new Spec Ops outfit, Assault Team 5. Naylor quickly forges a team of experts, who prove their worth in a series of special missions. But when AT5 are assigned to the frozen hell of Copernicus 9, their skills and capabilities are tested to the limit. Because not all your enemies are in front of you...

ASSAULT TEAM 5: HUNTED!

Following their return from the Copernicus 9 mission, Naylor and the team are drawn deeper into the political crisis on Earth. Meanwhile, the possibility of an internal leak puts the whole unit on edge.

When AT5 are tasked to find and retrieve a rogue corporate chemist, things quickly go wrong. Stranded on a desert planet, the team find themselves up against not only the Cartel, but also a crack mercenary team... and the hunters become the hunted!

"An extremely enjoyable adventure novel, a bit like The Dirty Dozen in space. Rob Poyton manages to still get the intimate feel of a group of comrades living together as a platoon, and needing very much to rely on one another." - Amazon review

Lightning Source UK Ltd.
Milton Keynes UK
UKHW020711030622
403942UK00009B/723